THE MARQUESS SHE LOVED

JESSIE CLEVER

D1260798

SOMEDAY LADY PUBLISHING, LLC.

ISBN-13: 979-8-9861220-0-7

Edited by Judy Roth

For Peanut

CHAPTER 1

*A*daline Atwood knew the difference between beauty and money.

The difference being that beauty was a luxury and money was a necessity. It was unfortunate that of the two she had been gifted the luxury.

This imbalance was the reason she stood with the wallflowers by the refreshment tables at every ball. She didn't mind really. The thing about wallflowers was they didn't miss a moment of what happened in any ballroom.

After her first awkward year of standing on the periphery, she had grown accustomed to it and almost looked forward to her chats with the spinsters, matrons, and wallflowers that littered the edges of society.

Only sometimes she wished her years of seeing and never being seen hadn't cultivated quite such a skill in detection.

Because for four years she had watched the man she loved fawn over a woman who gave him no more thought than she did the dust on her slippers.

And it hurt.

It hurt Adaline to see it because while she stood and

watched the man she loved be humiliated, she harbored in her a wealth of adoration and respect that she would happily shower upon him if only he turned in her direction.

But he never did. At least, not in the way she had always hoped.

And so she hurt even more for the obvious disdain the woman showed him, disdain he seemed destined to remain oblivious to.

Some nights she made an attempt to ignore him. She would turn to her companions, keeping her back to the ball-room so as to avoid any accidental sighting of him. It hurt less that way.

But tonight she deliberately sought him out at the Fairfield ball. She must because Ashfield Riggs, the newly minted Marquess of Aylesford, had recently traveled to Kent. He had told her that he would need to return to London by this week, and she had searched every ball for the past three days for him for surely he must return soon.

She knew such intimate detail of his travel plans because not only was she madly in love with the man, but she had, as previously mentioned, the absolute worst luck imaginable.

Ashfield Riggs was also her best friend.

That was why she stood on tiptoe to peer over the heads of the gentlemen who had congregated in front of her. She had to know if Ash was there. It was quite possible he had seen her sister in his travels to Kent, and she must know what he had thought of her.

Amelia sent letters, of course, but they were not enough. The written word could so easily hide the true state of one's life, and Adaline had feared the worst for her little sister since she had left their home two months earlier to marry the Ghoul of Greyfair.

She closed her eyes, inwardly chastising herself for thinking of her new brother-in-law in those terms. Amelia had said time and again in her letters that the duke was no ghoul, and yet Adaline couldn't bring herself to believe such.

Because Adaline was drowning in guilt, and as anyone who had the occasion to feel guilty would know, it was terribly difficult to extricate oneself from the mire.

Adaline's guilt had come on like a wind across the moor, sharp and cutting and unexpected. Unexpected quite simply because she had been blind to what was happening around her. It wasn't until her mother was dead and her father had left that she realized what had happened to Amelia. What had happened to her dear little sister right under her nose.

And then Amelia had been sacrificed to the ghoul.

Er, the duke.

The homelife of the Atwood sisters had not been the rosiest. It had not been gloomy either though. Ruth Atwood was an exacting woman, however, and she paid particular attention to her daughters. Namely in how they continued to fail her.

Adaline had learned early on to avoid the woman, and she believed this was the reason for her fast and lasting friendship with Ash. She avoided her home at all costs, preferring to visit with friends, and Ash had been among them. But it was Ash's own struggles at home that had bonded the pair.

It was only later when Ash returned from Eton late one spring, coming to see her first before returning home, that she realized her mistake.

While her childhood friend had left for school, a man had returned in his place. A man with broad shoulders and a deep voice and warm eyes and a quick smile.

She'd fallen in love with him as he'd dismounted in front of her house. She could remember the day clearly. She'd run to the front door at the first sound of hooves on the cobblestones on the square, and so she'd been standing on the stoop when he'd arrived.

She'd clutched at the wrought iron railing, dazed by what she had seen, confused by what was happening. Her childhood friend was gone, and suddenly she felt a surge of feelings so foreign to her they were frightening.

She knew in an instant feelings so scary could only be love.

And only too quickly did she realize he didn't return those feelings.

It was obvious because the first words he'd said in greeting to her that day were to ask if she was acquainted with Lady Valerie Lattimer and could she arrange an introduction for him.

Lady Valerie Lattimer.

Of course Adaline knew her. Everyone of their age knew her. Lady Valerie Lattimer had beauty and money and charisma and connections. It was a combination any debutante would envy. And at the time, Lady Valerie hadn't even been out.

It didn't matter. Any lady nearing the marriage market knew there was no defeating Lady Valerie Lattimer, and every girl had lowered her expectations for a match. For surely all the good ones would gravitate toward Lady Valerie like a hound to a fox.

Adaline only wished Ash would eventually see the truth.

Lady Valerie Lattimer was the worst person Adaline had ever met.

The woman was petty and selfish, cruel and unkind. But her ability to convince a man he was the center of the universe kept the male of the species in the dark.

Including Ash.

Adaline had thought now that she was four and twenty and firmly on the shelf, she would forget about her love for Ash. She could tuck it away like an old, beloved heirloom that one took out from time to time to admire and remember when things were simple.

Because nothing was simple anymore.

Her mother was dead, her father lost at sea, and her sister sacrificed to a ghoul. Sorry, a duke. And it was all Adaline's fault.

She should have been there to protect Amelia from their mother's scorn. She should have seen what was happening instead of assuming her sisters knew to keep out of their mother's line of sight.

But Adaline knew Amelia hadn't. She was quite certain Alice, the youngest Atwood sister, had survived their mother without too many scars because Alice was largely oblivious to the world around her, her books and her experiments occupying her attention. But not Amelia. Poor quiet Amelia, lost somewhere in the middle of her sisters, had taken the brunt of their mother's scorn.

That was why she had so readily sacrificed herself to the Ghoul of Greyfair.

Uh, Duke of Greyfair.

Where was Ash?

She craned her neck around the side of the matrons who had now approached the gentlemen to discuss the quality of the champagne being served.

She wasn't paying attention to how she was leaning until her elbow struck the cut crystal of the punch bowl on the table beside her. She watched, unable to move, as the bowl rocked ominously before a hand shot out, stopping her humiliation in a single motion.

"I'm gone no more than a fortnight, and you start assaulting punch bowls."

"Ash." She hated how his name came out like an oath, but she couldn't help it. "You've returned."

"Of course, I returned. You didn't think I was going to

stay in Kent forever."

He was handsome tonight. He was always handsome with his almost boyish features, his quick smile, and warm eyes. When she looked at him, she couldn't help the feeling of happiness that bubbled up inside of her.

"I've heard Kent is quite lovely."

He laughed. "I would say it's rather empty." He paused as if thinking. "And there are an extraordinary number of cows. I felt rather outnumbered."

"By cows?" She couldn't stop the disbelief from entering her tone.

His expression folded until she almost believed she'd actually wounded him.

"Have you ever seen a cow? Menacing creatures. I shouldn't like to be left alone with one."

She smiled, and it was only then that she realized that was his intent.

She wasn't sure how many exchanges they had had like this. Standing at the edge of society functions. Attuned to only each other and how they didn't *quite* fit in with the rest of the *ton*.

Only now Ash did fit in. He was a marquess. She took an involuntary step back. It was another change, one she hadn't realized until it stood directly in front of her. Her chest squeezed uncomfortably, and she turned away from him on the pretense of adjusting her dance card along the folds of her elbow-length gloves.

"I trust your travels went well."

"It was terribly dull."

She looked sharply at him. "You've always enjoyed a good jaunt. What was so different this time?"

His gaze scanned the crowds, a gesture painfully familiar, and loss radiated through her. He had been standing next to her for mere seconds and already he was looking for someone else. She knew who it was he sought, and she could choose to wallow in her despair, or she could get on with it.

She turned away again, setting her dance card carefully between her side and her elbow so it wouldn't poke her, and resolutely ignored her best friend.

"I've never been forced to undertake a journey for *business*." The last word was heavy with spite, and she couldn't help but turn an assessing eye on him.

"Ash, you must understand the title comes with certain obligations. It is the price you pay to be a member of the peerage."

Finally he looked at her, and she saw a hardness in his eyes she'd never seen before. "Obligations? Obligations I am ready to accept. The mess Uncle Dobson left I am not."

She cringed. "Is it truly so bad?"

"The man was opulent to the highest degree. He enjoyed only the best things and then only in the houses he liked most."

She picked up her hand, instinctually reaching to comfort him, before she remembered where they were and what all had changed between them. She withdrew, tucking her hand against her dance card to keep it from straying once more.

"I take it some of the estates are rather neglected."

He made a noise then of affirmation, but his gaze had wandered away again. "I will need to make an assessment of all of the title's holdings to see just how badly. It appears his neglect may have affected the tenants as well. Not just the houses he failed to maintain."

Adaline felt a new wave of sorrow wash over her. She knew what it was like to have one's fortune overturned through no power of one's own.

"I'm sorry, Ash. Surely there must be some benefit to your new station."

He peered down at her, his face suddenly alight. "There is

7

rather. And I intend to employ it tonight."

Trepidation crawled over her skin, and terror sent her heart galloping.

"What do you mean, Ash?"

But he didn't answer her. He only wiggled his eyebrows as he sometimes did to make her laugh.

"Ash. You don't mean—"

"Lady Adaline." The voice startled her, sending her words back down her throat until she choked.

Ash slapped her heartily on the back, and she didn't miss the satisfied gleam in his eye as she pinned him with a stare before turning to the voice at her shoulder.

"Lady Adaline, I do believe this is my dance."

She blinked at the nice gentleman standing there, trying to recall what on earth he was speaking of. No one asked her for a dance anymore. In fact, she couldn't last remember when she had danced.

"I beg your pardon."

The poor boy looked crestfallen, and she wondered just how young he was. Surely he knew she had no dowry, and if he didn't, his mother would certainly correct him after tonight.

"I believe I secured this dance earlier with you…" His confident voice had deflated, and she felt regret hit her.

She had been so preoccupied with finding Ash she couldn't remember who she had spoken to when she'd first entered the ballroom earlier.

She pasted on a bright smile. "Oh, is it our dance already?" She pressed a hand to her forehead. "How silly of me. Time always seems to get away from me."

The boy brightened at once, and she felt as though she'd just given a bite of ham to a dog. She struggled to remember the young man's name but could only remember that he was either a viscount or a baron.

It didn't matter. The dance couldn't last forever and as soon as his mother informed him she had no dowry he would move on.

He extended his arm and she politely took it, turning back to tell Ash she must speak with him, but he had already gone.

* * *

HE WAITED until Adaline had turned away before slipping off.

The stab of guilt was sharp and sudden, but he expected it. He knew how Adaline felt about Lady Valerie. He also knew she had a protective streak that could sometimes cloud her judgment of others.

Slipping deftly through the other guests, he scanned the spots where he thought Lady Valerie might linger.

He had only returned from Kent the previous day, but he wanted to waste no time in seeing this particular deed finished.

He could feel time creeping past him, and when he'd acquired the title, he'd felt it even more. He was nearly eight and twenty. It was past time he had a wife. Yet he had never ventured to propose. Not because he hadn't wooed his fair share of debutantes.

As the son of a judge, he had been little threat to most ladies just out of the schoolroom, and he found they were rather comfortable with him. It was easy to woo them after that, and he hadn't wanted more from them than some idle distraction.

He had had affairs. Not to the length or depth Ransom, his friend and the Earl of Knighton, aspired to, but enough to keep him amused.

But he'd never let himself grow attached to another. It

was impossible to do so when he was already infatuated with someone else.

That was how he felt about it.

Infatuation.

It was the only word that came close to describing how he felt about Lady Valerie Lattimer, and he didn't wish to build a relationship upon anything less than total infatuation.

He pictured his mother's string of husbands, first his own father and then the parade of stepfathers afterward. Each worse than the last by a disturbing degree until finally he'd left for school and had tried his best not to return.

His mother was on husband number six. He no longer thought of them as stepfathers, and he hadn't for some time. He had heard somewhere that this latest one was a viscount, and his mother spent her days idling in a cottage somewhere in Yorkshire. It sounded pleasant enough, and he felt genuine happiness for her current position.

He just did so from a distance.

He was making his way to the other side of the room when he noticed the cluster of young men by the terrace doors. Where there was a cluster of gentlemen, there was often Lady Valerie Lattimer.

This should have alarmed him, but he chalked it up to her vivacious personality. It wasn't her fault men were attracted to her presence. She couldn't very well help who she was.

Adaline disagreed and claimed Lady Valerie had honed her skills in duping men into believing her charming facade. That was entirely rubbish. If it were true, she would be wed by now as this was Lady Valerie's third season.

Again he felt that stab of guilt. This was Adaline's fourth season, and he knew she was unwed for entirely different reasons.

For a moment he faltered in his progress across the ballroom, a memory from his trip to Kent floating suddenly to the surface of his mind. It was probably the trappings around him that made him recall that moment during the ball he had hosted to introduce himself to the local gentry, and Amelia Atwood, Adaline's younger sister, had embraced her husband.

It had been a strange moment for more reasons than he could fathom. Amelia was married now, and he supposed not an Atwood any longer. She had wed the Duke of Greyfair, a man with more rumors surrounding him than London had fog. But he had been struck in that moment at the ease with which Amelia had taken her husband's arm, and he had wondered at it.

He knew from Adaline that it had been an arranged marriage. The financial troubles of the Biggleswade title were no secret, and Amelia had been married off to the duke for a large sum. But in that moment, standing amongst the guests of the assembly, the way Amelia turned her face up to her husband, laid her hand upon his arm, that had not been the look of an arrangement. That had been a look of love.

It had been rather confusing as only days before Greyfair had tried to murder Ash with his bare hands when the duke mistakenly thought Ash was attempting to seduce his wife.

Seeing how Amelia turned her face up to Greyfair, her expression open and trusting, had severed something inside of him, something he feared would never be quite right again.

But Lady Valerie had been his goal for too long now, and finally he could have her.

Because the son of a judge was worthless, but a marquess was not.

Now was his chance to ask Lady Valerie to be his wife.

It couldn't have been more perfect.

He would have Lady Valerie, and he would show all the world just how worthy he was. His heart thundered in his chest as he resumed his search for her in the crowd. He was closer to the cluster of men by the doors and could peer over them now.

A small dark head bobbed amongst them, and he smiled, unable to stop himself.

He pushed between two of the chaps and ignored their meager protests as he stepped in front of Lady Valerie.

"Lady Valerie," he said with a flourishing bow.

He didn't miss the murmur of disdain surrounding him, but he also understood it was not at the intrusion, but at the fact that the gentlemen had been usurped by a marquess.

"Lord Aylesford!" Lady Valerie's face lit, and he wanted to close his eyes and bask in her warmth. "I had worried you were now a prisoner of Kent."

"Fear not, my lady. The wilds of Kent could not keep me from you." He took her hand and bowed gallantly over it, which earned him a flutter of her eyelashes.

He stilled, cradling her hand longer than was proper and looked up, meeting her gaze and holding it. He watched her eyes turn, grow darker, and he didn't miss how she swallowed.

This was not a facade. Adaline had it all wrong. It would be impossible to think Lady Valerie could fake the heat he saw in her eyes, in the way she held his gaze with such intensity.

This must be real, and finally he would be worthy of her.

She smiled, slowly, seductively, as he straightened and released her hands. "Then I can only assume you appreciate beauty when you see it."

Beauty and wit and so much more.

"I don't suppose you have reserved a place for me on your dance card."

She picked up her hand, the object in question dangling from her wrist. "I wouldn't dream of doing otherwise." She lowered her chin, and he swallowed at the sultry expression directed at him.

He felt his resolve harden, and he forgot entirely of that moment at the ball when he had mistakenly believed in something as fragile as love.

"Gentlemen, if you would excuse me." Lady Valerie stepped between the remaining boys who lingered at her elbow to slip beside Ash, her eyes expectant.

He offered her his arm, and when she touched him, heat coursed through his body. It was as though he'd been cold for too long, so long he hadn't realized how cold he'd become. But with Lady Valerie on his arm, he was alive again, vibrant, expectant.

He kept his focus on the woman on his arm and shifted her easily into the waltz. Had he been thinking, he would have remembered Adaline was somewhere on that dance floor, but he had resolutely pushed his friend and her misgivings aside.

It was just that, misgivings, and he would think nothing more of it. Not tonight. As he spun Lady Valerie into his arms and across the floor, he felt the whole of his life speed up until it was as though it stood beside him. The first time his father had taken a belt to him. The first time his father had made him sleep in the mews because he was unfit for the house. Standing next to his father's open grave and feeling no remorse. The first time he had left home in the middle of the night, having no direction and little money, only knowing he had to get away and knowing the last thing he saw of home were the tears on his mother's face.

None of that mattered now. Not when the golden light of a thousand candles shone down on them, illuminating the woman he would call his wife. Lady Valerie laughed as he twirled her about, her head going back, her thick black hair shining even more beautifully than her smile. She wore a dress of the palest pink that only served to illuminate her perfect skin and fine features.

This was it. This was everything.

He spun her once more, but when the dance would have him lead her back to the right, he swung left, carrying them off the dance floor. She laughed, her eyes going to his.

"Ash," she whispered. "What are you doing? The waltz isn't finished."

Her words trembled with laughter, and her eyes lit with excitement and expectation.

"I had something else in mind," he said close to her ear, so only she could hear, and before she could respond, he turned them, slipping them neatly behind a fern that guarded the arched doorway leading from the ballroom. He cast one last look over his shoulder, but the guests were all entranced with the dancers twirling about the floor. No one was looking in their direction.

Lady Valerie practically vibrated on his arm as he pulled her down the corridor. He had been down this way earlier to see if there were somewhere private he could have this conversation, and he was pleased to learn the small corridor led to a conservatory. He could not have pictured a better place in which to propose marriage to the woman with whom he intended to spend the rest of his life.

He pushed open the door and drew Lady Valerie in behind him. The conservatory was warm and lush, the space around them littered with overhanging ferns and thick with the scent of blossoms.

Lady Valerie stumbled against him, her hand going to her chest.

"Oh, Ash, where are we?" Her tone had turned sour, and if he didn't know her better, he would say she sounded almost disappointed.

"It's the conservatory. Surely you've seen one."

She pulled away from him, using both hands to gently pat her head. "The air in here is going to ruin my hair."

He tugged one hand away to try to lead her farther into the room. There was a spot at the very back between some potted orange trees that was awash in moonlight. Even he thought it romantic, and he just knew Lady Valerie would think so too.

But she pulled her hand away, taking a full step back. Something pinched in his chest, and he shoved it away. It was only scars that plagued him now. It wasn't real danger.

Except Lady Valerie continued to fret with her hair and lingered at the door. This wasn't how he had planned for this to go. Surely Lady Valerie would see the romance and daring in what he was attempting. She should appreciate his efforts instead of shirking his touch.

"Lady Valerie, I wished to speak with you in private."

She dropped her hands only to ball them into fists against her skirt. "And you thought to do so in here?" Her tone was plaintive now, and he felt the first stirrings of unease low in the pit of his stomach. Adaline's face popped into his mind, her expression disappointed, and he blinked as though to rid himself of her image.

"I thought it was romantic," he finally whispered.

Lady Valerie scoffed and actually stomped a foot. "Fine then. Let's get on with it. What is it you wanted to say?"

She peered around them, moving her skirts as if they were too close to the drooping lilies behind her.

He gestured to the far side of the room. "I thought perhaps we could do this over there. In the moonlight."

"I'm so sick of moonlight," Lady Valerie muttered, but she picked up her skirts and marched over to the spot he indicated.

He followed, but the anticipation he had felt only moments ago was slowly turning to stone.

CHAPTER 2

*I*t was already too late when Adaline realized she'd made a mistake.

When she couldn't find Ash after the waltz, she shouldn't have gone searching for him. She knew that the moment she heard Ash's voice, lost in the shadows of the conservatory because if Ash was speaking it meant he wasn't alone. Her heart trembled as her mind connected the whisper of hushed voices with the reality of what must be lurking just beyond the leafy orange trees and voluminous ferns of the Fairfield conservatory.

She didn't need to see it because there was only one person Ash wished to be alone with in the dark, and no matter how she might wish it, it wasn't her.

It was Lady Valerie Lattimer.

She reached out a hand, steadying herself against the cool tiles of the pillar beside her. At the sound of Lady Valerie's voice, a lightheadedness overcame Adaline so swiftly she feared she'd lose her balance.

Ash had found the lady then.

Adaline was several years older than Lady Valerie and had

heard people excuse the woman's tendency for idleness and selfishness as a symptom of her youth, but Adaline suspected it wasn't something Lady Valerie would outgrow because while she feigned superficiality, Adaline saw the shrewdness in the young woman's eyes. She had an idea of what she wanted out of life, and she wouldn't let anyone get in her way. Including Ash.

A protectiveness so strong coursed through her then, and she pushed away from the pillar, moving closer to the pair and ducking behind a fern, its fronds curling opportunistically over the edge of the walled garden box. Her thighs struck the rough stone of the box, and she bit her lip to hold back a gasp. The space was dark, the wall sconces unlit as guests were not supposed to be there, and at once she was both comforted and concerned about the lack of light. While it helped hide her, it also prevented her from seeing her quarry.

She should retrace her steps, slip out the conservatory door, and wait for Ash in a more proper place. She had no business being here at all. If someone found her, what would happen to Alice? Her younger sister finally had a true chance for a season in which to find a husband, and Adaline would ruin it before it had begun.

Guilt pierced her, swiftly and completely, as though it were a spear splitting her body in two. She had already lost one sister. She would not ruin the life of another.

She had spent her youth with her eyes on everything else but her family, and now her other sister was banished to the wilds of Kent, married to a beast of a man, and Adaline was responsible. She shouldn't have strayed to her friends when her mother demanded her attention. She shouldn't have allowed her father to wander into the carelessness that could come from the passion of horses.

The Biggleswade funds were already depleted when her

mother took ill, and the rest hardly required an effort when they were applied to everything her father had tried to find a cure.

She closed her eyes and swallowed her guilt. She had sworn off her frivolity. It was time to return to the ballroom where it was proper. Only Ash's voice came to her then, louder now, more distinct. She froze, willing her heart to slow, to quiet the thump in her ears, so she could hear what he was saying.

It was only Ash who could do this to her, who could make her bend her resolve, who could make her stay when she knew she should flee. But the sound of his voice alone was enough to draw her.

For how long had she been in love with him? How long had she yearned for the smallest of attentions from him?

She wanted to hate herself for it, for this desperation, for the way she allowed herself to fall at his feet when he'd never indicated they were more than friends in the years they had known each other. But then how could she hate herself for having hope?

She leaned against the stone wall, her gloves catching on the craggy stones that were undoubtedly chosen to give the conservatory beds a natural flair but which were most vexing when one was trying to be discreet. She curled herself nicely into the frond of the fern, and now that she had stopped moving she could hear their voices more distinctly. They must be standing in the cluster of potted orange trees at the end of the box against which she hovered.

Lady Valerie laughed, the sound grating after the gentle lull of whispers.

"It's hardly romantic, Ash," she said. "Look what it's doing to my hair."

Adaline stilled, her fingers curling against the stone. She

got the distinct sense she had entered in the middle of the conversation, but her brain seemed to scramble at the word *romantic*. What was romantic? What was Ash doing? What were *they* doing? She wished she could see them.

"It's just that I wished to speak with you in private."

Her heart thudded, and she feared it would stop entirely. *Oh, Ash, no.*

She wanted to surge up, to run to him, to stop him from making this terrible mistake, but he kept going.

"You see, I have a title now. The Marquess of Aylesford."

She pressed a hand to her chest now at the sound of hope in Ash's voice. God, how many times had she told him he didn't need accolades to commend him? Yet here he was. Laying himself before the one person he thought could give him validation.

Adaline knew that because it was the same thing Ash always sought, except the one person who could give it to him was no longer alive.

"Yes, I'm well aware, Ash. You didn't drag me in here to tell me that, did you?"

There was a beat of silence, and Adaline wondered if she had missed something. She leaned forward, finding a space between the ferns. She leaned a little too far and one hand slipped into the wet, spongy earth of the garden bed. She peered down at her hand, the dirt enclosing the white kid of her glove, but she didn't snatch it back. Instead she tested the firmness of the ground and leaned forward, slipping between the ferns and finally, *finally*, she saw them. At least the outlines of them as they were silhouetted by the moonlight coming through the glass panes of the conservatory walls.

Lady Valerie reached up a hand and patted at her hair. "A marquess is a rather large leap from being the mere son of a judge. I will give you that."

At the mention of Ash's father, Adaline widened her eyes as if it would help her see better in the dark and perhaps she could make out Ash's reaction. While Adaline knew Ash had relegated the man to the deepest recesses of his memory, she also knew the man was responsible for much of Ash's cavalier attitude when it came to life, and it was a topic that always drew her interest. But true to form, Ash ignored Lady Valerie's overture.

"Yes, well, now that I'm a marquess I'll be required to see to the title, and its longevity."

"Of course. There's a great deal of responsibility that comes with a title. I'm sure if anyone is prepared to take that on it's you, Ash." Adaline didn't miss the dismissive tone in Lady Valerie's voice now, and she wondered how Ash didn't hear it.

There was a flash of white, and Adaline realized Ash was smiling now. She curled her fingers into the dirt, wishing she could scoop it up into her hands and fling it at the horrible woman. But she remained still, willed her breath to steady and her heart to stop pounding so she could hear.

"I'm glad you feel that way, Lady Valerie, because I should very much wish to have you for my wife."

The words were like a thousand tiny daggers slicing through her all at once, and the air simply released from her lungs in the shock of surprise. She faltered, her hand sinking into the dirt until she came to rest directly upon the stone wall she sat on.

It was the words she had wanted to hear her whole life. The ones she had dreamt about, the ones she had held in her heart, kept most tenderly in a place where only she could see. Now when she'd finally heard them, it was to hear him speak them to someone else.

He'd finally done it. He'd asked Lady Valerie to marry him.

Of course. He was a marquess now. Lady Valerie could actually find him worthy of her attention. Adaline looked away, blinking furiously as tears suddenly filled her eyes. Ash would get everything he'd ever wanted, and she would lose everything she had ever loved.

It was somehow fitting. That this would be her punishment. She'd let her family fall to ruin, and because of her neglect, her sister had been sacrificed. She deserved to have everything taken from her.

But then...Lady Valerie laughed. Adaline swung her head about, knocking into the curling ferns and sending the plants aflutter. She froze, her hands seizing the trembling plants, but when her eyes adjusted, she saw Ash and Lady Valerie hadn't moved.

Lady Valerie's mouth was open, the last of her laugh falling away as she shook her head. "I'm not marrying you."

Ash's shoulders went back. "What do you mean? I'm a marquess now. Such an offer should be—"

"Not enough," Lady Valerie cut in. "I will accept nothing less than a duke. Why do you think it is I'm still on the marriage mart after three seasons?"

Adaline's fingers tightened on the ferns, heedless of the damage she was doing to the poor plant. She didn't know where to look. At Ash's blank expression? At the haughty tilt of Lady Valerie's chin as she prepared her rebuke?

"I would never sink so low as to marry the son of a judge even if you are a marquess now. I am obviously meant to be a duchess, and I would never sully myself with someone of your ilk." She assessed him with a long glance as if he were nothing more than a smudge of soot on her slipper. "Why would you ever think otherwise?"

Adaline knew the answer. She knew it only too well, because Ash was just like Adaline. He had never given up hope that Lady Valerie would come to him one day, realize what a catch he was and how fortunate she would be to call him her husband. Adaline knew because she was possessed of the same kind of devastating hope.

But it was more than that. Lady Valerie's father, the Earl of Weybridge, had been friends with the late judge just as Adaline's father had been. That was why they had all moved in the same circles long before Lady Valerie was officially out. Sometimes one could confuse the length of an acquaintance for the depth of one, and Adaline knew Ash had always hoped that Lady Valerie had seen him as more than a friend after such time.

But Adaline had always seen the truth, and sometimes she felt like she was the only one who did.

Ash's mouth opened and closed, and she heard a rumble as he must have cleared his throat, taken a step away from Lady Valerie. "I do apologize, Lady Valerie, if I misunderstood. I never meant any harm."

Lady Valerie's laugh was like the tines of a fork scraped the wrong way across the china. "Of course, you didn't." She shook her head. "You really should learn though."

Ash's shoulders straightened as his chin went up. "And what is that?"

"Not to put yourself above your place," Lady Valerie spoke quietly and then left, slipping between the potted orange trees as if she were never there.

Adaline held her breath, making herself as still as possible, but Lady Valerie turned, going up the opposite path through the conservatory.

Adaline couldn't move even though she knew she needed to get out of there. She couldn't be caught, not like this. If Ash knew she had witnessed the moment of his worst humiliation, he would...he would—

She couldn't finish the thought. And yet, she sat there,

half sunk in the dirt of the garden box, her hands clasped around the fern she had mutilated in her shock. She watched Ash, but he didn't move. He stood exactly where Lady Valerie had left him, a man among the orange trees. Silently she reached a hand through the ferns as though she could wipe the tension from his brow when a gentle hand landed on her shoulder.

She jumped, her arm flinging itself involuntarily through the fern, but at the sight of Alice's face, the scream stuck in her throat. Moonlight glinted off of Alice's spectacles as she held a single finger to her lips. Without a word, she put her hand under Adaline's arm and lifted her from her precarious perch, pulling her silently in the direction of the door.

How long had Alice been there? How did she know where Adaline had gone? Had she followed her? Alice was always the quiet one, her nose stuck in a book, and Adaline had never thought her one for such clandestine acts.

But when they reached the main corridor, it was as though Adaline awoke. She tugged frantically on Alice's arm.

"No, I must go back. Ash needs me. He—"

She was surprised by the strength in Alice as her little sister pulled her back, wrapping one arm around her waist.

"No." She spoke the single word as if any argument were out of the question. "You can't go back in there, Adaline. You witnessed Ash's greatest embarrassment, and if he were to know…"

Her sister didn't need to finish the sentence. Adaline already understood. As she let her sister lead her away, the last piece of her heart broke completely. But it didn't break for her. It broke for Ash.

* * *

HE DIDN'T RETREAT to his club.

Until a month ago, he wasn't welcomed at most clubs as he wasn't fit for them. Then he'd only been the son of a judge. Respectable and genteel but never good enough.

As Lady Valerie had so helpfully reminded him.

The sound of her departing laugh still grated in his ears as his carriage rolled to a stop in front of The Black Diamond Gambling Den, known by its patrons as simply The Den. Here he was welcomed. Anyone with a moderate amount of coin in his pocket was, and that was something of which Ash had always made sure.

He strode through the door with a brisk nod to the wall of muscle that guarded its entrance and passed through the archway that led to the main gambling floor. He paused for a moment to take in the scene, studying the players at the various tables. It wasn't that he was looking for anyone in particular. It was more of a habit he had acquired over the years.

He liked to know what audience he was playing to. It was so much easier to pretend to be the person they wanted that way.

He bypassed the card tables and followed the periphery of the main room, catching a glimpse of each of the side rooms he passed. Some were used for private games while others were set up for retiring and refreshment, complete with buffets and the scantily clad waitresses who tended them. He went to the very end and slipped inside the curving staircase that led to the upper floor and the balcony that overlooked the main gaming tables.

It was quieter up there as he knew it would be. This floor contained the owner's rooms and a private drawing room for select guests. Once more he nodded to the guard at the entrance and slipped inside. The noise muted immediately, and instead of hearing the cheers of triumph and the cries of defeat, he heard only the rustle of newspapers and the crackle of a fire.

A manservant approached, and Ash ordered his usual before moving deeper into the room. There was only a smattering of gentlemen there that night as it was the height of the season, and most gentlemen of any social standing would be required elsewhere.

Ash found a seat in the section known as the library. It housed one wall of shelves filled from floor to ceiling with books, although Ash was sure no one read them. This part of the room was slightly closed off from the rest as it lay behind two potted ferns. He paused slightly as he dropped into a chair, his hands holding him up as they rested on each arm. He eyed the ferns, feeling his humiliation anew.

He scrubbed his face with one hand, settling back in his chair as a decanter and a glass appeared at his elbow.

He drank an entire glass before pouring another and settling back into the chair, letting his head go back as he closed his eyes.

Not enough.

If she had said anything else—*anything*—he might have been able to convince himself it didn't hurt so much. He might have even said he could bear it, perhaps even understand it. But not that. Not those words.

Because those words already haunted him.

He swallowed more whiskey, savoring the way it burned down his throat and reminded him that he was still alive.

Until someone spoke his name and he choked on it.

"Aylesford! Jesus, what's happened to you?"

Ash sat up, whiskey sloshing in his glass as he tried to clear his throat.

Ransom Shepard, the Earl of Knighton, stood in front of him, his cravat askew and his waistcoat misbuttoned.

"Is that rouge on your jaw?"

Ransom scrubbed his hand against the other side of his face, leaving the telltale crimson slash untouched. "Did I get it?"

Ash nodded. "Sure."

Ransom dropped into the seat beside him, kicking his booted feet up onto the low table that sat between the chairs. "You look like you've had a hell of a night." He gestured to a manservant who scurried off in search of another glass.

"I don't think it was as good as yours appears to have been."

"Is going," Ransom corrected, taking the glass from the manservant and helping himself to the decanter of whiskey. "I'm just popping in for a drink and perhaps a bite to eat. I need to keep my strength up." He gyrated his eyebrows.

"Dare I ask where you're coming from and where you're going to?"

Ransom took a swallow of whiskey. "I've just been to the theater. Look at me. I'm reformed and have accepted culture into my life."

That would explain the cosmetics on his jaw then. "And where are you going?"

"The widow Suttonhall." More eyebrow gyrating.

"Lady Suttonhall?" Ash paused with his own glass almost to his lips.

"The very one." Ransom knocked back the rest of his drink and made to stand. He set his glass down on the table as he slapped Ash's knee playfully. "Hope your luck turns around, mate."

"I proposed to Lady Valerie." Ash hadn't meant to admit it. In fact, it was only after the words were out that he realized the fewer people who knew the moment of his greatest defeat the better.

Ransom froze like a half-finished charade, his arms

reaching as if to turn his body toward the door, but his eyes traveled back to Ash and he sank back into his chair.

"Dear God, tell me you're joking."

The earnestness in Ransom's voice was like a ramming rod directly to his chest. "Of course I'm not joking. I told you I was going to propose, and I approached her as soon as I was able. I've only just returned—"

But Ransom sucked in a breath and cast his head back, running his fingers through his black hair until it stood on end only to fall artfully back to frame his face. Ash could see plainly why Ransom was so desired amongst the *ton*'s widows and unhappy wives, even the debutantes for that matter. The man was as close to a god as Ash had ever seen, and this made his reaction to Ash's news even more damning.

"Ash, Ash, Ash, we talked about this, mate. I told you not to do it." Ransom met his gaze, and in his friend's eyes, Ash saw only despair.

"You knew she would refuse me." He didn't know why this felt like betrayal.

Ransom shook his head. "Of course she was going to refuse you. The whole bloody world knows she's holding out for a duke."

"I didn't know that," Ash whispered.

"You did know it, but you chose not to see it. It's easier to only see the things we want, and you've wanted Lady Valerie since we were lads." Ransom shook his head. "Jesus, mate, I wish you hadn't done it."

"I haven't told you her answer."

Ransom gestured to the whiskey decanter. "Would you be here with this had she said yes?"

He had a point.

"I still don't see why you're on this crusade. Who needs a

wife?" Ransom said this with obvious distress before holding out his hands as if to encompass his own circumstances. "I'm a bloody earl, and you don't see me seeking out a buxom bride to help me carry on its lineage." He waved a hand as if to push the entire idea away from him. "You can have them. The lot of 'em."

"Women?" Ash asked.

"Wives." Ransom spoke the word as if it were foul.

Ash sat forward. "You've known about your title your whole life. I'm only just adjusting to mine. The pressure to carry on the line is tremendous."

Ransom leaned in, elbows to knees, and Ash caught the scent of heavy perfume. He wrinkled his nose and leaned back.

"Exactly, mate. You need to take time and get acquainted with yours. There's no need to hurry off to the altar, now is there?"

Ash opened his mouth but snapped it shut. He knew what he meant to say because it was what he had felt at Ransom's suggestion.

If he married a lady, then he might be good enough.

But it wouldn't happen now. Lady Valerie had refused him. Hell, she'd dismissed him completely. He felt hollow inside, as if her refusal had cored him, but it was a strangely numbing feeling too. It was as though everything he had built his life on had turned out to be nothing more than illusion. How could he have been so blind?

He hadn't been blind though. He'd been hopeful, and that hope had made him see things that weren't there. Like the possibility that Lady Valerie would accept him now that he had a title.

But even the title hadn't been enough. Still, after all that, he wasn't enough.

He realized Ransom was speaking to him and straightened in his chair. "What was that?"

"Was it a public humiliation or did she at least have the decency to put you down in private?"

In his mind he saw the conservatory, its hushed plants muted in the moonlight. It had all seemed so exotic, and for a moment, he had believed his life would be different now. But Lady Valerie had convinced him of his foolishness.

"Her slaying was done privately."

Ransom shook his head, massaging the back of his neck. "Ah, mate, I wish you had waited. I thought you weren't yet back from that godforsaken—where did you go?"

"Kent."

Ransom sucked in a breath. "Kent. God. What's the point? There's nothing outside of London. Nothing worth seeing anyway."

Ash couldn't stop a grin at this. "I'm sure one day something will change your mind. After all, you're now a gentleman who attends the theater."

Ransom raised both his eyebrows as he gestured with one hand as though Ash had a point. Finally his friend gained his feet.

"I'm sorry, mate. I really am. I know the spell Lady Valerie cast over you, and I'm only sorry it had to end like this. I'm just glad the whole world doesn't know of it."

Ash felt his humiliation grow as if it were a tangible thing, and he watched as it inflated and consumed him. He shuddered. His whole life his inadequacy had been his own, but if someone else knew of what happened that night, someone who had the power to cut him further, it would be unthinkable.

He swallowed. "You're right in that regard."

Ransom leaned over and squeezed his shoulder with one hand before giving a jaunty salute. "I'm off, mate. No need to wait up for me." He grabbed the lapels of his jacket and mimed sticking out his belly as though he were a gluttonous man off to a second dinner, and Ash once more couldn't stop the grin that came to his lips.

The quiet scratched at him after Ransom left, but he couldn't make himself get up and leave. What had he to go home to? The Aylesford townhouse still didn't feel like home, but then neither did the place in which he had grown up. Any of them, for that matter. After his father had died, his mother had trundled them from one townhome to another as she married a string of men older and older, each one dying off. But not before they'd had their fun with him.

He could list the names he had been called, the faults his stepfathers had found in him, ones his own father had missed by some miracle. In the end, Ash didn't know what was himself and what was the product of his upbringing.

He had no single tragic event to point to that had brought him to this moment. It was a slow and careful extraction of anything that might have been worthy in him. And that night, Lady Valerie had taken the last of it.

He set down his empty glass, the sound of it ringing in the quiet of the room. The fine crystal caught the light from the sconce, and it shown for just a moment in a spectacular gold. Something in his memory caught, and suddenly he saw Amelia again.

The flash of light reminded him of her gown that night, but when he remembered her, it was to see her leaving the ballroom, the light of the chandeliers sending her golden gown aflame as though it showered sparks, but it wasn't her dress he remembered most. It was the way she watched her husband as he led her from the ballroom.

Something deep and familiar twisted inside of him as Amelia's words came back to him. Something about there being more Atwood sisters on the marriage mart that season.

He stood, resolution rushing through him, driving the last of his humiliation away. The hollowness took over, and soon he felt nothing at all. Nothing but determination.

He didn't need Lady Valerie Lattimer. There was another lady he was certain would marry him.

CHAPTER 3

$\mathcal{T}$he sketchbook lay unopened on the table before her.

It was one of those days in late spring that could almost convince one summer had arrived early, and she had opened the window in the drawing room to let in the breeze. The house was quiet around her, Alice having left early that morning for what her sister liked to call a walk of natural history through the park. Adaline didn't know what this was, but she assumed it involved collecting all manner of natural specimens like bugs and decomposing leaves.

Adaline missed Amelia with a sharpness that nearly took her breath, and she pressed a hand to her ribs to ease the pain.

She had few regrets in her life, but the one that haunted her the most was Amelia.

It wasn't until her sister had quietly accepted her fate as a bought bride that Adaline realized quite how much had been on her sister's shoulders. When their mother took ill, Adaline had spent more and more time outside the house. Her mother's critical nature was difficult to bear when she was well. It was impossible to endure when she'd grown unwell.

But Amelia had stayed.

Why hadn't Adaline realized it?

Why had she allowed her sister to suffer alone in what had been a cold and emptying house?

She peered around her now, her fingers absently tracing the folds of Amelia's letter where it sat on the table next to her unopened sketchbook. The house was no longer cold or dark. The funds Amelia's marriage had secured had brought light back to the Biggleswade house, but it had taken her sister from it.

Amelia's letters were full of stories of the estate where she was now duchess. Of the castle so immense and dark, Adaline feared it would give her terrors, but Amelia spoke so glowingly of it.

A castle on an island?

It seemed lonely to Adaline. She was convinced Amelia wrote such flowery letters to convince her sisters she was well and happy, but Adaline knew better.

She pushed her sketchbook farther away from her and reclined in the chair, allowing her back to touch the scroll-work of the piece.

What did it matter? Her frivolity had cost her a sister, and she would no longer give in to such whims.

Nothing really mattered in fact. Not since that night in the conservatory.

Her whole life she had dreamt of what it would be like. To hear Ash speak those words.

I should very much wish to have you for my wife.

Ash's beloved voice saying the words she had never thought she'd hear.

Only he spoke them to someone else. To Valerie Lattimer of all people.

The pain in her chest blossomed, but she didn't bother pressing a hand to it. She let it come coursing through her.

She deserved it. She deserved any manner of punishment for what she had done. She loved a man who only saw her as a friend, and she had neglected a sister who was now lost to her.

She and Ash had the unfortunate circumstances of being lost together. He the son of a judge, she the daughter of an impoverished earl. Both just on the correct side of respectability but never the first to be welcomed into any circle of consequence. It was this that had formed such a strong bond between them.

At least she had thought it a strong bond, but she realized suddenly he had never told her he planned to propose marriage to Lady Valerie. In fact, she hadn't even seen him since that night. More than a week had passed since that awful scene in the conservatory and yet...nothing. Surely he would have come to tell her about that. Or was Alice correct? Was it too humiliating for him? Or was there something else he was hiding from her?

She sat up, her hands clutching the side of the table.

Was he keeping something from her? Had he seen Amelia? What had he learned? Was she tortured and kept prisoner in that horrid castle? Did her ghoul of a husband force her to write those misleading letters?

She surged to her feet, a sudden need to see Amelia spiking through her. She would go to Kent. She would see her sister for herself.

The door to the drawing room opened as she turned toward it, and she stopped, momentarily confused. So absorbed was she in her sudden realization, she hadn't remembered anything else or anyone for that matter could be moving about in the house.

Uncle Herman stood in front of her, his hand still on the

doorknob as if he didn't quite know how doors worked any longer. He blinked, his bright blue eyes appearing slightly confused.

She took a step forward. "Uncle Herman, are you well?"

He made a blustery noise that agitated his mustaches as he came through the door, closing it softly behind him. She was still getting used to her uncle as she'd only just met the man when he became the Atwood sisters' legal guardian and the new earl upon the death of Adaline's father, and she took a certain amount of joy in watching the curious man bundle about.

"Adaline, I have a matter I must discuss with you, but I must admit, my darling niece, I don't know how to go about it." He pressed his beefy hands together as if trying to work out the problem manually. "You see, it's just that...well, it appears as though..." He shook his head and pursed his lips, making his mustaches dance with his expression. He sucked in a great breath and spoke in a rush. "I've had an offer for your hand in marriage, and I've negotiated what I think is a reasonable marriage contract. I should like to ask your opinion on the matter."

Thankfully she still had one hand on the chair she had recently vacated as Uncle Herman's words slammed into her.

An offer of marriage? For her?

It was preposterous.

She was without dowry. The only reason someone would wish to marry her would be if he were desperate.

For the second time, a realization so awful hit her, she sank back into her chair.

She swallowed. "Oh?" The single word took all her strength to press from her lips. Her heart hammered, and a rustling noise reached her ears. She looked down and saw her hands shaking, the movement striking the folds of her skirts. She clasped them together and willed them to stop.

She pasted on a false smile, hoping to encourage Uncle Herman to be out with it.

He came farther into the room and took the upholstered chair opposite her own, bending forward until his elbows rested on his knees. She could see the white strands of hair that protruded haphazardly from the fluffy, gray crown of hair that remained atop his otherwise bald head, and she focused on the white flecks, willing herself to remain in control.

"I believe the gentleman is an old family friend. Amelia mentioned him in a letter, I think." He licked his lips and seemed to press forward, hunching closer to her.

She sat up straighter, pulling in a breath as though the air itself could shield her heart from what was about to happen.

"He's a marquess actually, which is rather fortunate for you. I think the terms of the contract are all respectable and highly flattering for you, my dear. I'd be proud to accept it. That is if you are in agreement."

No, no, no.

The word stampeded like a prayer through her mind, but instead she said, "A marquess? Well, that would be quite an advantage for the family."

Please don't speak his name.

Uncle Herman leaned back and slapped his generous palms to his thighs as if in triumph and stood. "I knew you would see it like that. Should I tell the gentleman you accept?"

No, no, no.

The words were not for Uncle Herman this time. They were for herself. She wanted to hear him say it. She wanted to hear the words spoken, so she knew exactly the sentence she was accepting. It was as though she wished for a judge to hand down her punishment.

"Who is it that has offered for me, Uncle?"

Uncle Herman laughed, a wobbly, self-deprecating sound, and pressed a hand to his forehead, pushing the tuft of hair there back until it stood straight up. "Oh bother me, I knew I was going to make a mess of this. I've got no experience with daughters and never expected I would, you see. And now I suppose I'm trying too hard. After all that's happened to you, I should wish for you to only have the best, you understand."

She smiled tightly. "I do understand, Uncle Herman. The gentleman's name please?"

Uncle Herman nodded, and then he said it. The words she already knew were coming, and the words that broke whatever was left of her heart.

"His name's Ashfield Riggs. He's the new Marquess of Aylesford."

For the second time in a fortnight, she saw the thing she had wished for most in her life unfold before her but with the slightest difference that changed everything. First it was to hear Ash speak those words to Lady Valerie, and now it was to hear she was to be the consolation prize. And worse, to have heard it from Uncle Herman.

Could Ash not bring himself to ask her? Were his own shattered dreams too much to bear?

She blinked, knowing tears hung suspended in her eyes and willing them not to fall. "Oh Ash," she said his name as though it were nothing more than noticing a daisy in bloom in a bed full of roses. "Ash is, indeed, a very old friend of the family."

Uncle Herman nodded, his bright blue eyes going round and encouraging. "I thought as much. It's a terrific offer, I should say. You should be very proud of yourself, my dear."

She swallowed as pain gripped her throat, as the tears shimmered in her eyes, as she tried so very hard not to disappoint Uncle Herman. He truly believed what he said for why should he believe anything else?

An offer of marriage from a marquess was a boon no matter how Lady Valerie felt about it. And for that marquess to be Ash...

Uncle Herman studied her, and she realized he was waiting for her to speak.

"Yes, it is a terrific offer."

He motioned with his hands. "I say, my dear, you are crying." He dropped into the chair he had so recently vacated, taking her trembling hands into his. His brow furrowed, his bushy eyebrows coming together to almost form a complete line across his forehead. "If you have any misgivings about the chap, I'll march right over there and—"

"No, it's not that at all." She tried to form a smile, but her lips shook. "Ash is a gentleman and comes from a respectable family. I'm just overwhelmed is all."

But she couldn't say it.

She couldn't say the words that would bind her to him forever. She couldn't speak the words she had dreamed of saying for almost her whole life.

Because it wasn't Ash asking the question. Could he not make himself do it? Had he thought it unnecessary after arranging the contracts with her guardian? He had made arrangements with her uncle as though he were purchasing a parcel of property from the man.

Perhaps that was how he saw her.

The tears disappeared from her eyes, and a cold stillness settled over her. Her hands lay unmoving in her lap, and her mind cleared. A feeling of stunning weightlessness came upon her then, and it was as though speech were the easiest thing in the world.

"Yes," she heard herself say. "Yes, I do accept his offer."

Uncle Herman slapped his hands to his thighs once more and stood. "Then I shall go sign the contracts, my dear." He rubbed those same giant hands together. "Your sisters shall be so pleased to hear this. You've made a match with a marquess and a family friend no less. You couldn't ask for anything more, my dear." He marched from the room, his ponderous feet booming in the sudden stillness of her mind.

She *could* ask for more actually. She could ask that her future husband have the decency to ask her for her hand himself. She could ask that he might love her in return.

But she knew that would never be. She had watched him as Lady Valerie had shattered his every expectation, his every wish. But he hadn't even bothered to propose to Adaline himself. She wasn't worth such attention.

And there it was. The very reason she had to accept his offer.

Because she deserved it.

She deserved to be married to the man she loved, the same man who thought of her as nothing more than property.

It was the only punishment fitting enough for what she had done, and she would accept it gladly.

No matter how much it hurt.

* * *

ALICE DID NOT KNOCK when she entered Adaline's room much later that day.

Significantly later, in fact. So much so that it had Adaline looking to the clock on her dressing table.

"Alice. Where on earth have you been?"

Alice didn't hesitate. She pushed her spectacles up her nose as she replied, "At the library, of course. I was studying a text on—"

Adaline crossed her arms. "The library? Really, Alice. Do you expect me to believe that?"

39

Alice's brow furrowed. "It's the truth, so why shouldn't you believe it?"

"It's the middle of the night," Adaline said, her voice quivering with accusation as she threw out a hand in the direction of the clock. "It's gone after midnight. If you expect me to believe the library is open at this hour, you are gravely mistaken."

Alice waved a hand as if this were inconsequential. "Of course the library isn't open at this hour. If you would take a breath, you will recall my words. Did I say the library was open?"

Adaline stilled, her mind flittering back over her sister's rushed greeting. She had, indeed, not indicated that the library was open.

"You gained entry to the library after it was closed?"

Alice released an aggrieved sigh as she dropped to the bench at the foot of Adaline's bed. "I didn't gain entry. I was still in the library after it closed. Mrs. Montgomery had just unearthed a text on the regeneration of—"

Adaline held up a hand. "You had your nose in a book, and this Mrs. Montgomery—a librarian, I presume?" She paused to allow Alice to nod in affirmation. "Was aiding you in your obsession."

Alice crossed her arms over her chest now and raised her chin. "Scientific study is never an obsession. It is a calling."

Adaline shook her head and dropped to the dressing table stool. It needn't matter where her sister had gone off to or what sort of regeneration she was studying. There were other more pressing matters.

"Alice, I must tell you—"

"You agreed to wed Ash. Yes, I've heard."

Adaline stilled. "How did you know that?"

Alice only rolled her eyes as she shook her head. "That

hardly matters. What's more important is why you agreed to it."

Adaline's teeth snapped against one another at the blunt statement. "I beg your pardon?"

Alice leaned forward, her eyes earnest behind her spectacles. "Adaline, I know you love the man, but surely you understand he does not love you. Why on earth would you agree to a lifetime of torment?"

Adaline blinked, the numbness that had overtaken her hours before when she'd sat in the drawing room with Uncle Herman intensified until it was almost a buzzing in her ears. "It's hardly a lifetime of torment, Alice. Don't be so dramatic."

Alice got to her feet only to drop to the floor on her knees directly before Adaline, scooping her hands into her own. "Adaline." She said only her name, squeezing her hands firmly. "I know you've loved Ash forever. We all do. But we also know he is infatuated with Lady Valerie Lattimer. You cannot ignore that."

Adaline tried to pull her hands away. "How..." But she couldn't finish the sentence.

How could Alice know such things? She rarely raised her eyes from whatever book she was consuming. How could she possibly be so familiar with Adaline's long-suffering, inner torture? More, how could she know of Ash's feelings for Lady Valerie? It wasn't as though he'd made his intentions public. He only addressed Lady Valerie in the politest of circumstances and only when propriety allowed such an encounter. Surely his actions would appear as nothing more than a respectable gentleman addressing a lady of some rank.

Once more she wondered how long Alice had been in the conservatory that night.

Alice gave another heavy sigh and leaned back until she

sat on her heels, dropping her hands to her lap. "Oh, Adaline. I do worry about you."

Adaline drew back her shoulders at this. "I do not require your concern."

Alice laughed, the sound more of a bark that shot through the quiet of the late night. "Between you and Amelia, you have always deserved more worry."

At the mention of her sister's name, Adaline's stomach twisted, and she wrapped her hands around the tie of her dressing gown. "You cannot be serious. Amelia is married to the Ghoul of Greyfair."

Alice scrunched up her nose, causing her spectacles to rise at an unusual angle. "Are we still calling him that? Amelia's letters do not suggest he is the ghoul rumors paint him to be."

Adaline opened her mouth but found the words stuck on her tongue. Was Alice correct? Or was she merely fooled by the pretty words Amelia had penned? It was easy to conceal lies in some flowery script. They had no true way of knowing what circumstances Amelia found herself in.

"I suppose you're correct. We should refer to him as the duke now that he is our brother-in-law. It is only respectable." She paused, worried her lower lip before continuing. "But I reserve the right to withhold judgment until I have met the man in person."

Alice looked about them as if considering. "I think that's fair." She pressed her palms to the floor and pushed back, coming to her feet in a single fluid motion. "Now then. I think we should discuss your impending nuptials." Momentarily confused by Alice's sudden show of physical prowess Adaline would not have expected from her studious sister, she was not prepared for Alice's next words. "You should tell him you've changed your mind and beg off."

Adaline surged to her feet, a reaction so strong coursing

through her she was standing before she realized it. "No." The word shot from her lips, startling both of them.

Alice tilted her head in question but thankfully didn't say anything.

Adaline pressed a hand to her forehead and paced to the window concealed in heavy drapes to close out the dark night. She fingered the thick fabric and flicked it back just enough to peer down into the quiet street.

"I must marry him, Alice. I can't explain why."

"I can explain it."

Adaline let go of the drape and turned to face her sister, arranging her expression into one of curiosity. Alice was proving rather more insightful than Adaline had ever given her credit for, and she worried what her sister might say next.

Alice took a step toward her. "You love Ash. Ash has offered to marry you. You have accepted because in doing so you will be the wife of the man you love." She stopped nearly in front of Adaline and met her gaze with a ferocity Adaline hadn't seen in her little sister before. "Have you forgotten that he proposed to someone else not a week ago? And that someone else refused him?"

Adaline swallowed, her fingers going to the folds of her dressing gown, trying to shield how they shook. "I have not forgotten." Although she managed to get the words out, her voice trembled more than she liked.

"Oh, Adaline."

Alice was four years younger than Adaline, and through all their lives, Adaline had always considered her to be too young and too absorbed in her own pursuits to understand the feelings and desires of her sisters. But in her voice just then, Adaline heard the depth of her sister's understanding, and it broke her.

"You don't understand," Adaline whispered, hating again

43

how her voice trembled. She swallowed and tightened the tie of her dressing gown before squaring her shoulders and meeting Alice's gaze directly. "I must marry Ash. Not because I love him or because Lady Valerie refused him. I must marry him for reasons all my own."

Something flitted across Alice's face then before Adaline could decipher what it was, but then her sister turned, spinning away from her to retrace her steps to the door.

"And I suppose these reasons are selfless and well thought out."

The words stung at first until Adaline had a chance to sift through them and realized her sister was driving for a deeper understanding.

"I am not trying to take care of you." She was grateful the words were true. For once in the past several weeks since their entire world had been upended, she was not trying to protect her sisters. Instead she was trying to assuage her own guilt.

She licked her lips and raised her chin, hoping her sister could not see past her mask.

Alice studied her in silence for several seconds before shaking her head. "Adaline. We are, despite perhaps feeling otherwise, all adults now. We are in charge of our own fate. You mustn't think—"

"I know." She spoke the words softly. "That's precisely why I have made this decision. We are all adults now. Mother and Father are gone, and poor Uncle Herman cannot be expected to care for us forever. That wouldn't be fair to him." She shook her head and paced the length of her small bedchamber. "Perhaps if we were still in the schoolroom I would see things differently, but I am four and twenty, Alice. I should have been married ages ago, and now I am nothing more than a financial burden that Uncle Herman should not need to address."

Alice snorted, the reaction so unexpected Adaline pinned her with an astonished look.

"You are hardly a financial burden, Adaline."

"I have no dowry, and without a dowry, no means of attracting a proper husband. I should be grateful Ash has asked me to marry him." She spoke the last words in a rush, feeling her throat closing even as she pushed them out.

Was she grateful to be Ash's second choice? Should she be grateful he had asked her at all? That familiar pain radiated through her, and she shoved the thoughts aside. Her feelings mattered little. Her girlish dreams of love and happily ever after didn't matter now. She was a grown woman who, whether she liked it or not, needed the protection of a husband. That was all this was, even if it hurt.

Alice was silent again, but Adaline knew her sister was carefully cataloging her every word and gesture, and so she kept still, her chin raised, her lips steady. She would not give away even a scrap of evidence of her true feelings.

"Then I suppose I should congratulate you on a fine catch, sister," Alice finally said, but there was no feeling behind her words. "If you should like, I would be happy to help you prepare for the ceremony and the wedding breakfast."

Again that familiar pain traveled through her, spreading over her skin like gooseflesh.

"There is to be no occasion, I'm afraid. Ash would like to wed by special license. He's already applied for it, and he has good reason to think he should have it by this time next week. He'd like to wed quietly as his new title has come with demands he is not only unused to bearing but also seem a great deal more complicated than he had expected. Apparently his uncle was not the best at tending to the title and all it entailed."

She watched her sister's face as the words spilled out of her, wishing her not to ask any further questions. Adaline didn't think she could bear to talk it over once more. It had been enough to discuss the specifics with Uncle Herman earlier that day. The way she had cataloged the events of her impending marriage, the thing she had dreamed about with a fervency only young girls could muster, as if it were nothing more than an inventory of one's linen closets. She couldn't repeat the exercise. Not tonight.

Alice seemed to understand because her lips turned up into a tentative smile. "Then I will simply congratulate you again and bid you good night, sister." She turned to the door, and Adaline wished to say something, but words were lost to her just then. Except Alice turned back, her expression strangely sentimental. "You know I've heard sometimes a husband's feelings toward his wife may change over time, and if a union should not begin in love, it may end in it."

It was an oddly saccharine observation for her normally clinical sister, and it touched Adaline in a way nothing else ever had. She smiled then, truly, for the first time that day.

"That's encouraging to hear. Thank you, Alice."

Her sister nodded and left, closing the door softly behind her, and leaving Adaline all alone with her thoughts.

CHAPTER 4

The day of his wedding dawned with shrouds of gray and sheets of rain.

He found it comforting. It matched his inner turmoil, coiling around him like a cloying quilt.

When he had first thought of seeking Adaline's hand, it had seemed so simple. Adaline was his friend. His very good friend if he were honest. He had known her for years, and it seemed like a natural thing to make her his wife.

He had been mistaken to think his title would garner the attention of Lady Valerie. Stupidly he had thought his lack of a title was what kept her interests elsewhere. As Ransom had said, Ash had been too blind with his own infatuation to see that, and it had cost him.

He still simmered with humiliation from that night more than a fortnight later, and he was determined to never let such a thing happen again. He would be wise to others' feelings. He would be observant and rational and not believe his new title to be the key to opening every door for him. For clearly it wasn't. He was still Ashfield Riggs, the son of a judge and nothing more. Hardly deserving of that really.

It was best that he was marrying Adaline actually. She had known him before he was a marquess and could remind him of his station despite the title. She could probably even remind him should his aspirations grow too large. Adaline had never been good at holding her tongue when it came to telling him her feelings.

He swallowed down his guilt and adjusted the cuffs of his shirt.

What he hadn't anticipated was this. Upon signing the marriage contracts with Adaline's uncle, a wave of guilt so strong swept over him he'd nearly choked.

But why?

It wasn't as though offers were thick on the ground for Adaline. Quite the contrary. She was by all aspects of it a spinster. He was saving her really from a life on the shelf.

He looked away from his reflection in the mirror, disgusted with himself.

Adaline didn't need saving. He knew that. What he was doing to her was nothing short of trapping her. Trapping her in a marriage with *him*.

He should be hanged.

Instead he took leave of his rooms to go downstairs to wait in the green drawing room for his wedding to commence.

He had wanted to get the matter taken care of with the greatest expediency once his humiliation had turned to a cold memory. It had taken what was left of his courage to ask his father's old colleagues for their assistance in procuring the special license. Adaline's uncle seemed to think a wedding in Ash's drawing room was acceptable.

Again he felt that flash of guilt. Adaline deserved a church wedding. Didn't all ladies dream of such? Yet even as he thought it, he couldn't bring himself to change his mind. He didn't want some spectacle, not with his humiliation still simmering coldly through him.

He wanted something quiet and expedient, and then once the matter was closed, he could continue with adjusting to the new title. He still hadn't visited all the estates the title owned, and he was only just beginning to understand what would be required of him in the House of Lords. Ransom had told Ash what little he knew as he was not always the modicum of respectability when it came to his obligations to Parliament.

Still, once the matter of a wife was no longer a concern he could focus on more pertinent matters. Adaline would be perfect in the role. He already knew her well and got along fine with her. She could perform whatever duties were required of a marchioness, and he needn't worry.

If all went exceedingly well, he would gain more respect from the *ton* once he had a wife.

Yes, it was all perfect despite the guilt that coursed through him. He must ignore that. Having a title required one to make certain sacrifices after all, and he was sure Adaline understood that.

So why hadn't he gone to speak to her himself about his offer of marriage?

He reached the drawing room then to find it oddly festooned in bouquets of flowers ranging from roses to lilies to orchids. He hadn't instructed the staff to do any such thing, and the sight of such unnecessary decor had him stalling, the guilt flashing anew.

Perhaps Adaline would enjoy the flowers, and she would think he had done it for her. There was nothing wrong with that.

Never before had he hated himself more than in that moment, standing amongst the bouquets littering his drawing room, waiting for his bride to arrive.

He should have spoken to her. He should have gone to her and explained and listened to her feelings. All he knew was filtered through her uncle. The man had said Adaline was amenable to the terms of the contract.

Amenable?

That was certainly not the kind of feelings he had hoped to one day inspire in his bride, but all of that was irrelevant now. Now that Lady Valerie had reminded him of his place, the same place he had always been in, from the moment he was born.

He strode across the room, unable to keep still as one emotion tumbled over the next inside of him, each clawing to gain the upper hand. He stood in front of the doors that led into the gardens and watched the rain strike the panes with painful staccato.

The air crackled with an energy he hadn't felt earlier, and he wondered if the rain would turn into storms. He looked to the sky, watching the clouds roil much as his insides did, and for the first time that day he felt the shift of anticipation.

He was marrying his best friend. Surely it couldn't all be terrible.

As if sensing his shifting mood he heard the front door open, followed by Higham's deep tones as he greeted the guests.

It would appear his bride had arrived.

He turned to the corridor, eager for the first time in days to see Adaline, but suddenly stopped, arrested mere paces from the threshold.

He *was* eager to see her. He was embarking on a life-changing act, and it suddenly seemed less daunting knowing it was Adaline to whom he would be wed.

Feeling lighter than he had in days, he made his way out into the corridor just as the Atwoods reached the hallway leading to the drawing room.

He bowed to the new Earl of Biggleswade first as the man had hurried ahead of the ladies at the sight of Ash.

"Aylesford. Splendid to see you again." He shook Ash's hand, and he felt the power of the man's grip radiate up his arm.

His eyes strayed to where Adaline stood slightly behind her uncle, Alice fussing over her gown or some other frippery. He couldn't tell from that distance.

"Biggleswade," he said. "Pleasure as always."

Ash meant the words. Herman Atwood had proven a respectable and worthy gentleman. Moving his eyes down the corridor to his bride, he realized with alarming clarity that he hadn't seen Adaline for any length since her world had been upended with the tragic death of her father at sea. They had seen each other in passing that night at the ball, but he had been desperate to find Lady Valerie.

The guilt rushed through him so viciously then he almost choked.

Now he regretted it, seeing her standing there in her quiet dress of soft blue, her face mostly hidden from him as the way she turned to Alice presented her ever-present braid to him, shielding her face from view.

He felt a jerk of familiarity in him. Adaline had always worn her hair in that braid, even when propriety dictated she start pinning it up. Some things never did change, and he was comforted suddenly by her presence. If she held a sketchbook somewhere on her person, it just might undo him.

He found himself smiling again, and it startled him.

"If it's not the ladies Atwood."

Alice turned first, her nose wrinkled in his direction. He'd forgotten how formidable the youngest Atwood sister was if provoked.

"Ash," she said, ignoring any reference to his title. "I understand you've been to Kent. How is our sister then?"

Although out, Alice did not often move in the same social circles, and Ash rarely saw her. That wrinkled nose was more often in a book than not, and he found it almost odd to be conversing with her now.

"I am happy to say she is quite well." He moved his eyes to Adaline as he answered, aware she hadn't spoken, and her expression was rather closed. Remorse perked up inside of him, and he swallowed. "She even talked me into a railroad actually."

This sparked a response from Adaline, her eyes rounding. "Amelia? Our Amelia?"

Ash nodded. "Yes. It seems Aylesford's estate is the only passable land for a spur line. Amelia's husband had been trying to get old Dobson to agree to it when…"

He trailed off. It was well known what had happened to his uncle, and he didn't wish to bring up unpleasant matters in the company of women. His uncle and his heir, Ash's cousin, were killed in a duel with each other over the same mistress. If there were a more fitting way for someone unworthy of a title to suddenly inherit one, he wasn't sure what it was.

He was prevented from further explanation anyway when Ransom popped around the corner, stopping with raised arms as he reached the group.

"I understand there's to be a wedding," he pronounced, his smile wide, his hair particularly rakish falling over his forehead.

He moved forward to make the introductions when the scene was stopped by a single small sound from Alice. Ash was certain everyone heard it. It was something akin to an exclamation of discovery, a curious sound, and one he had certainly never heard Alice make previously.

Ransom slid his gaze to her, his expression suddenly wary. Ash knew there was nothing Ransom feared more than the attentions of a respectable debutante.

But Alice only folded her arms over her chest and regarded the man with a studious gaze. "How interesting," she murmured.

Adaline stepped forward, pulling Alice's arm through her own. "I believe my sister is overcome with the spirit of the day," she said quickly, her smile bright if not carrying a veneer of falseness.

Again shame swam inside of him, and he moved ahead. "Ransom, may I introduce Lady Alice and my bride, Lady Adaline."

Ransom bowed. "It's a pleasure as ever."

The sisters curtsied in response, and Ash continued, "This is Ransom Shepard, the Earl of Knighton. He's agreed to act as my witness today."

"An earl. How lovely," Alice murmured, and Ash didn't miss how Adaline tightened her grip on her sister.

"Knighton," Biggleswade said coming up behind their strange group. "Thank you for coming today."

Ash finished with the introductions, keeping a wary eye on Alice as they moved into the drawing room. He wasn't sure how weddings were conducted in drawing rooms, and he'd had the piano moved into this room in case Adaline should wish for music. But as soon as she entered the room, she stopped, taking in the whole of it with a decidedly cool glance.

"Where is the clergyman? The weather is worsening, and I should wish for Alice and Uncle Herman to return home before it becomes dreadful." She spoke with cool efficiency, startling him.

But then he realized what this was. It was a marriage of convenience, for both of them. It was as much a matter of contracts for her as it was for him, and he could tell she wished to be concluded with the day's business. Her efficiency was like a balm on his raging guilt, and once more the weight seemed to shift along his shoulders.

"I do apologize," came a voice from the doorway, and they turned to see a man shedding a sodden cloak, bundling a thick leatherbound book in his arms. "I was delayed by an overturned cart out in the square. I fear the weather is growing quite abominable."

Ash frowned. "You must be the clergyman then?"

He wasn't sure what happened next because Adaline stepped up, ushering people into places and urging the clergyman forward. Ash reached out and took her hands into his before she could open the man's Bible for him.

It wasn't until he held her hands though that he realized what was happening, and the regret he had carried for days was replaced by the suffocating weight of failure.

He was holding the wrong woman's hands.

He had spent his whole life infatuated with Lady Valerie, had pictured her standing here with him, seeing her dark hair reflected against the white of her gown, drinking in the look of love from her hazel eyes, and knowing she loved him in return. Finally.

But that wasn't what happened, and now everything was wrong. He rushed his vows, speaking as quickly as possible, his heart rabbiting in his chest.

Through all of it Adaline showed no emotion. She spoke her own vows coolly and calmly with a detachment he envied.

That was at least something that brought him comfort. They thought of this marriage in the same way, as nothing more than an advantageous union.

It was a relief when Adaline shooed her uncle and sister from the room, promising to visit them tomorrow when the weather had improved. Ransom nearly ran for the door once Alice's attentions weren't occupied by the ceremony, and soon the house was quiet around them.

He stood in the foyer of his home, standing next to his friend who was now his wife, surrounded by stacks of trunks that he realized contained all of her life. Because she lived here now. With him.

He swallowed and tried to smile but it wouldn't come. "That went rather well." He gestured to the trunks as footmen spilled into the foyer already shifting them about to start moving them up to the marchioness's rooms. "I'll leave you to it then."

He strode away before she could respond, not knowing where he was going, only that he had to get away.

Because just then, standing there in the sudden quiet, he had thought his wife looked rather beautiful.

* * *

When she had thought of her punishment, she had pictured scenes of torture. Thumb screws, the rack, and even being forced to listen to an opera slightly off key.

But as it would happen, her punishment was loneliness.

Ash left early each morning to attend to estate business, sometimes leaving long before she came down to the breakfast room. She supposed he was still settling into the title and had much to learn or uncover about both being a marquess and about the holdings of the title itself.

More than once she had seen him leave the house with the earl who had acted as witness to their marriage, Knighton if she recalled correctly.

But Ash had not once in the past several days spoken to her of any of the matters which called him away every day, and she got the acute sense he was avoiding her.

It hurt. Not because she wanted his attentions in a lovelorn way or that she believed once wed he would magically fall in love with her.

But it was more that Ash had been her friend long before they had wed, and she feared somewhere in the changes that had fallen on them both in the past several months their friendship had suffered. That hurt more than any of the rest of it.

Ash had always brought a smile to her face when the unpredictability of her life at home grew too great. It was as though he knew her distress, could sense it, and would seek her out at whatever social function they were attending. He would have her smiling in minutes with his impressions of what it might be like if gentlemen wore whatever were the latest ladies' fashions and hairstyles or in his commentary about the function's food offerings.

It was light and cavalier, but the point of it was he knew her and she knew him and together they had been able to lift the other's spirits, and that was priceless.

But everything had changed.

Both in the things around her and in her own thoughts and feelings, and she wasn't sure if she would ever feel settled again.

Ash had not come to her on their wedding night, but if she were honest, she hadn't expected him to. In her mind, she could still see him standing there in the conservatory, his body so still, his eyes unblinking as he shattered before her without moving a single muscle. Of course he wouldn't wish to have anything to do with her, not when his pain was still so new.

She had written to Amelia of her marriage, and her sister's return letter was filled with oddities about love and partnership, so unlike her sister Adaline was sure something was dreadfully wrong, and she felt her guilt anew.

She cursed herself again for not being there for Amelia. Adaline knew of her mother's theatrics, of her father's indifference. That was the very reason she had sought comfort elsewhere. For her it had been with Ash. For Alice it was books and experiments. How could she have not seen that Amelia had been left alone to suffer?

She couldn't torment herself with that line of thinking again. She had chosen her punishment. That, hopefully, was enough.

She descended the stairs, the quiet of the house pressing in around her. Aylesford House was staffed with remarkable servants who moved about their daily business with chilling silence as if afraid to disturb the occupants, but Adaline had found both Higham, the butler, and Mrs. Manning, the housekeeper, to be friendly and engaging and startlingly efficient in their duties. Aylesford House was well run, and Adaline had had no trouble slipping into the role of its marchioness.

The only hiccup had been in accepting invitations.

Ash never seemed to be present to confer on which invitations he should wish to accept in his first season as the new marquess. She would be happy to lend her insights, but it didn't matter if her husband was not in attendance to speak of the matter.

She drummed her fingers against the cloth cover of her sketchbook as she slipped into the breakfast room. It was empty as she had expected, and she set down her book next to the place setting she had grown accustomed to using. It needn't have mattered though. She could have taken any place at the table because she always ate alone.

The day had dawned bright and clear, and she was eager to get outside. After the rain had cleared on her wedding day, she had taken a stroll in the Aylesford gardens to discover a lush rose garden tucked into one corner. Samuels, the gardener, had been happy to give her the proper names for some of the blooms, and she had carefully penciled them in under her sketches.

The meditative act of sketching was all that calmed her nerves now, and until she spoke with Ash about what she could do to help in her role as marchioness she had time to spare.

She had just picked up a plate when she heard the click of the front door opening. So startling was the noise in the undisturbed silence of the house that she nearly dropped the plate. She aborted her efforts at breakfast and nearly pranced to the corridor.

She caught Ash trying to slip into his study farther down the hallway without being seen. It was obvious he was being furtive in the way he hunched his shoulders and walked on the sides of his feet as though to keep his footsteps as soft as possible.

"Ash!" She hadn't meant to yell his name quite that loudly, but frustration had her emotions heightened. "Ash, we must speak."

The blasted man kept moving though and disappeared into his study as though he hadn't heard her.

She went after him, surprised to find he hadn't shut the study door behind him. He was at his desk, reaching for a packet of papers when she entered.

"Ash." She spoke his name considerably softer now, but she still saw him flinch.

Her chest tightened at the sight of it, and she straightened her shoulders. It needn't matter that she was not the wife he had wished for. There were still practical matters to attend to.

"Ash, I must have a word with you."

He picked up the packet of papers and held it in both hands. "Adaline. Yes, of course. It's just that I'm needed—" He gestured with the packet of papers as though he were needed anywhere else but there, but she took a step forward and cut him off.

"I must speak with you about the invitations we've received. It would help me to understand how you should like to position yourself this season. I can then use my discretion to accept those invitations that would be most advantageous to your goals."

His lips parted, and he slid a quick glance in her direction before returning his gaze to anywhere else in the room.

"Right, invitations. Of course." His words were sparse as if he plucked them one by one from the air around him. "Whatever you think is best is fine. Now if you'll excuse me."

"Perhaps if you could tell me what sort of associations you would wish to make it will help to narrow down what it is I accept. Is there anything in particular you wish for the Aylesford estates? For the title itself?"

He had tried to hedge around her in the direction of the door, but she sidestepped, blocking his path.

He struck the packet of papers against the opposite hand and shuffled on his feet as he cast his gaze to the ceiling. "I trust you wholly on this front, Adaline. Whatever you think is best is perfectly fine with me." He finally dropped his gaze only to smile weakly and step widely around her. "Now if you'll excuse me, I have a meeting. I only popped in to get these papers I had forgotten."

It was the smile that was the last straw. The agony she saw there was enough to undo what little resolve she still had, and as he stepped around her and made for the door, she couldn't stop the words that left her lips.

"I know, Ash."

His retreating footsteps stopped. She waited, her heart pounding suddenly in her chest, whether at her words or her unexpected decision to say something she couldn't be sure.

"I'm sorry?" Ash's voice was soft, but she didn't miss the hard edge to it, and she suddenly remembered Alice's warning.

She couldn't let Ash know she had witnessed his greatest humiliation. He was a proud man; she knew that. To let on that she would have any inkling about his failed proposal to Lady Valerie would undo him.

That meant she must say something else, something that would be far harder to speak.

She studied her hands as if to buy herself time, even though she knew it was inevitable. If she were to form any kind of working relationship with her husband, she must speak.

This was another part of her punishment she hadn't anticipated. Having to build a new relationship with her best friend, one that protected herself from her own feelings.

She turned, forcing her chin up. "I know, Ash," she said again, and coward that she was, she waited, hoping the silence would make him ask her, that he demand from her what she didn't want to give.

"What do you mean?" His voice had turned steely now, but she had captured his gaze.

He stood framed by the door of his study, and she had a moment to truly see him like she hadn't in weeks. Her heart did something odd then, a strange twisting as if it were uncomfortable to be reminded of how handsome he was, of how easily he smiled, of the expression he made when he laughed.

"I know you love another." The words caught in her throat, tearing at her as though they were small needles, scraping along her delicate flesh, not enough to blissfully kill her, just enough to let her know she was still alive.

He came toward her in two swift steps, and it was the first time she had seen such anger on his face. At least directed at her. He had been angry with his father any number of times and each stepfather after that, but never at her. Another change, something new and frightening with which she would be forced to contend.

"What are you talking about, Adaline?" He was so close now she could see the striations in the brown of his eyes.

"You forget, Ash. You forget that I've known you forever. That I've seen you both happy and sad, elated and despaired. You forget that I know your desires." She paused and licked her lips, her heartbeat building to a painful gallop. "*Who* you desire."

Understanding sparked in his eyes, and the extinguished hope she saw there cut through her like a dagger.

He still loved Lady Valerie. Even after she had refused him.

Her punishment grew, and she let it. She let the pain and rejection of a thousand days wash over her, and she accepted the finality of it.

Even now, after everything, he still loved someone else, and he would never love her. That would be her fate. A cold marriage to the man she would always love. Alice might have been right about love growing in a marriage, but it wasn't to happen to Adaline.

He didn't speak, and she knew she must say the final words. The ones that would make everything clear between them, the ones that would be her only chance at having some kind of understanding with her husband. Even if those same words would be her undoing.

"I know you do not wish me for your wife." Her lips trembled. Her hands trembled. Her very heart trembled, and yet she had to keep going. "I know when you look at me you long for someone else."

CHAPTER 5

*H*is infatuation with Lady Valerie Lattimer had always been a singular thing. His alone in which to suffer.

Standing there in his study in front of his wife he realized he was no longer alone in his suffering. His infatuation had hurt someone he cared about.

For a terrifying moment, he wondered if Adaline had feelings for him upon which he had trod in his infatuation with Lady Valerie. He studied her face, the way her eyes were over-bright, her upper lip slightly unsteady, the color in her cheeks.

Once again he felt that whisper pass over him. The unmistakable feeling of something shifting inside of him as something changed and grew, but it wasn't something tangible. It was as though his perspective were shifting as new light passed over him.

He gave himself a mental shake. There was enough to deal with standing directly in front of him. He didn't need to add the whisper of uneasiness to it.

But then he noticed how steady Adaline's chin was, and the comforting warmth of familiarity washed the rest of it away.

She was only Adaline. His friend. And she was being her usual efficient self.

And more, she was trying to help him.

"Adaline, I've been a fool." He sank, the energy to stand having fled him, and he was only thankful there was a sofa within reach. "I've gone about this in entirely the wrong way."

He held his head in his hands, the packet of papers bent between two fingers. The sofa shifted beside him, startling him into looking up and finding his wife perched next to him.

"I must admit it was rather a shock when Uncle Herman told me of your offer. Ash…" Her tone held neither question nor reprimand but something like curiosity.

He wanted to look at anything else in the room, but he couldn't bring himself to look away from her. The sunlight came through the tall windows at the front of the house at such an angle it left her silhouetted as though she were on a stage and the whole world could see her.

But it was only him, and they were alone. It suddenly occurred to him the intimacy of such a moment, and for one terrible second, he felt the urge to find a suitable chaperone.

Except that wasn't necessary any longer because she was his wife.

"Are you not a sensible choice for my wife?" he deflected.

Her lips closed, thinning to a firm line, her eyes hardening, but she did not speak. She needn't have. He felt her reprimand more effectively than words.

"I thought you the *more* sensible choice," he said.

A shadow passed over her face, and she looked away

briefly. Something hitched unexpectedly inside of him as he watched her face change, her eyes closing only briefly as though gathering some inner courage, and he thought he had hurt her in some way.

Surely Adaline, quiet, sensible, practical Adaline didn't aspire to the romance of novels. She would see reason in his statement surely.

But when she looked back at him, something had gone out of her gaze. "Is that what I am? And what kind of choice would Lady Valerie Lattimer have been?"

Until Adaline had spoken Lady Valerie's name, he thought he could evade the topic. But now he felt the noose of truth close around him, and he gained his feet, striding away from her, dropping the packet of papers back on his desk. "I let those childish notions go a long time ago, Adaline. I'm sure you can understand that."

She stood too but didn't attempt to follow him. "No, I don't because you never explained it to me."

He stopped, turning back to face her. She took a step toward him and stopped.

"You used to tell me things, Ash." Her voice was soft with sadness, but it held no accusation. "You once told me you thought Lady Valerie's voice was more beautiful than bird-song. And yet, I heard of your offer for my hand in marriage from my uncle."

He didn't miss the way her voice hitched on the word *marriage*, and he felt every inch the cad. "I still tell you things, Adaline. It's only..." but he couldn't finish the sentence. The weight of everything that had changed between them suddenly bore down on him until he thought he might suffocate. He shook his head and looked away, unable to look at her any longer. "So much has changed, Adaline."

"Yes, it has." Her voice was sharp, and it drew his attention back. "But that doesn't answer my question, Ash." She strode over to him, stopping close enough that he caught her scent.

Soap.

She always smelled like soap, and it had always comforted him. Adaline didn't reek of perfume the way his mother did, the perfume she thought lured men to her but really only made her smell like a rotting bouquet.

"I know you still love her, Ash." She met his eyes directly, and her tone was level.

There were no theatrics here. Adaline was not a scorned wife because she had known long ago about Lady Valerie. Still, his insides twisted with a feeling of which he couldn't make sense.

"You still love her, yet you married me. Why?" She asked the question plainly, and horribly, he wanted to answer her.

He wanted to tell her everything, but he knew he couldn't.

Because Adaline had always believed in him, and somehow telling her about his humiliation would jeopardize that.

Instead the word *love* rattled around in his head and left a sour taste in his mouth. It wasn't that he didn't believe in love. It was just something he had never understood, and never once had he associated the word with his feelings for Lady Valerie.

It was several seconds before he realized he was caught in Adaline's gaze. It was an odd thing, the quiet way she watched him, and he knew she had always had that way about her, but it was different now. Everything was different now, and he suddenly didn't wish to speak of Lady Valerie any longer.

"Would you believe me if I said it was your sister's idea?" It wasn't the answer to her question, but he hoped it was enough to distract her.

The intense expression vanished from her face as she blinked, absorbing what he'd said.

"Alice?" She shook her head. "Alice would never—"

He stopped her. "Not Alice. Amelia." It wasn't the entire truth, and it stuck in his throat. But it was the only thing he could tell her.

Her eyes flashed as though she'd touched flame. "Amelia? You...you spoke with her? At your assembly?" Something flickered in her eyes, and he wondered why it looked like fear.

"Yes, I did speak with her."

"And she was well?"

It was an odd way to phrase the question, both answer and query in one as though Adaline needed him to answer in the affirmative.

"She was quite well." He searched his wife's face, but her expression didn't calm. "I had mentioned I would be seeking out a wife when I returned to London, and she helpfully pointed out there were other Atwood sisters on the marriage mart this season. It seemed like a logical conclusion."

"Amelia...did she...was she...did she appear happy?"

"Adaline, are you trying to ask me if her husband is the ghoul he is purported to be?"

She bit her lower lip and looked away. He closed the distance between them, putting his hands to her shoulders, and if he hadn't been paying such close attention, he would have missed how she started under his touch. He had probably just startled her, but it was still odd. He had casually touched her any number of times. It wasn't such a rare thing as to cause her alarm.

"Amelia is married to a man she appears to love actually. You mustn't worry for her."

She stepped backed, pulling herself roughly from his grasp. "You jest."

He crossed his arms over his chest and laughed, feeling a lightness now that the conversation had turned away from him. "I would never jest over the state of an Atwood sister." He placed a finger to his chin as though thinking carefully. "Do you know I wouldn't have guessed Amelia for a love match? She seems too dedicated for such things."

Adaline stepped forward and seized his arm, tugging it loose until he looked down to meet her gaze.

"Ash, you must tell me the truth. Was she truly happy?"

"She was radiant." He nearly whispered the words, the stark fear in his wife's face capturing his voice.

There was a beat, and then— "I don't believe you." She whirled away from him. "I can't believe you. She... we...I...I..."

He stepped forward again and this time he pulled her into his arms, tucking her head under his chin. "Atwood, Amelia is all right. She's happy. You mustn't vex yourself like this."

She didn't return his embrace, but neither did she push him away. It was just that she hung there, limp but for his arms around her. He had never held her like this, and he became suddenly aware of the pieces of her. The soft parts of her that pressed into him, the curves that fit beneath his palms.

He realized his mistake too late. Until that moment Adaline had just been his friend, the gangly girl he had watched blossom into a wallflower. But now his hands told him a different story. One of womanhood and desire.

He swallowed, easing her away from him and propped her chin up with a bent finger so he could look into her eyes. "You must believe me. I wouldn't lie to you, Atwood, would I?" The words left his lips before he knew what he would say, and his heart hammered in his chest.

In fairness, he hadn't lied to her. He had only evaded the

67

truth, but studying her face just then, he realized the enormity of what he had done.

Her face melded into memory, and instead of Adaline, he saw Amelia, beaming up at the husband she loved. Adaline would never have such possibility. He had denied her that, robbed her of the chance of a love match for his own selfish reasons.

She was right. When he looked at her, he did long for someone else, and there was nothing that could change that.

Adaline shook her head, shuffling away from him. "No, Ash. You wouldn't."

He watched her as she studied the carpet, her shoulders twitching, until she seemed to gather herself and looked up. She met his gaze directly, and the fear he had thought he'd seen only seconds before was gone, and he was left to wonder if he had imagined it entirely.

"Thank you for letting me know about my sister. You know how I worry over her."

He nodded, suddenly unsure what to do with his hands now that he'd touched her. He'd stood next to her for years without feeling the pulse in the pad of his thumb or the tingling in his fingertips as if they rippled with anticipation. He swallowed and took a step away, pacing back to the sofa.

"So you see why it was that I offered for you so quickly. I'm only sorry I did it in the way I did. It was all too…much." His excuse was pathetic, and he only hoped his cavalier reputation would cover his lack of fortitude.

Adaline picked her way across the carpet, her eyes on her feet, before resuming her seat next to him. He couldn't help but notice the space she left between them this time, and he felt a rush of unexplained annoyance at the sight of it.

"Change can be difficult. It's in the resistance of change though where we suffer. It's always best to get on with things, wouldn't you agree?" She smiled then, that smile that was so familiar, but even he could see it didn't reach her eyes.

"And how do you suppose we get on with it?"

"I'm the daughter of an earl, Ash. I can help you navigate society as a new marquess and position you for success. If only you stop shutting me out."

She spoke as though he were alone in this endeavor and likely he was. As she had just said, she was the daughter of an earl whereas he would always be the son of a judge. Her gaze was earnest though, and he knew she only meant to help him.

"What do you have in mind?"

* * *

"Stop fidgeting. This is the most in demand invitation of the season, and if you're seen fidgeting, we shan't receive another."

She didn't miss Ash's petulant glower even in the dim light of the carriage as it rocked them toward Grosvenor Square.

"I don't see how a mere viscountess would be in demand this season."

"It's not the viscountess who is in demand. It's the viscount. Surely you've been keeping up with the papers."

Ash peered at her, his brow wrinkled in question.

She set down her reticule, abandoning her attempt to remove the knot from its satin strings.

"Ash, you asked me to help you position yourself to be a success in your first season, and you have not even read the papers?"

"I read the *Times* every morning. I still do not know to what you refer."

"I don't mean the *Times*. I mean the scandal sheets."

He turned ever so slightly, brushing his arm against hers, and she hated how even that mere touch had her toes curling in her slippers.

It had been three days since the awkward conversation in the study at Aylesford House. Three days in which she could recall with utter clarity how her best friend lied to her. Her *husband* had lied to her.

She had a strong dislike for that word at the moment, and she focused on the matter at hand to purge her thoughts.

"Viscount Mayberry has been seen in meetings with the Duke of Buccleuch."

"Meetings where?"

"Mostly in social events. They've been seen at the gaming tables together, and at the Gloucester soirée last week they were found sharing cigars on the terrace."

"What does this have to do with the popularity of their invitations?"

"It can only be assumed that the gentlemen are conversing over a business matter."

Ash adjusted again, and she laid a hand on his thigh before she could stop herself. He must stop moving if only to save her sanity, but then her hand was on his thigh. The white kid of her glove shone like a beacon against the stark black of his trousers, and she couldn't pry her eyes from it. Neither could he, apparently, and she felt the flush creep up her neck as she realized he was staring too.

She snatched her hand back, but it was too late.

She had never touched Ash so intimately, but then she'd never been in a carriage alone as they were now.

They had been married for nearly a fortnight, and this was the first time they were in such confined proximity together, *alone*.

She closed her eyes, feeling herself sway between what

she had dreamed of and the crushing reality of where she had ended up.

I thought you the more sensible choice.

It hadn't been the truth. She knew the truth, and yet he had kept it from her. She wasn't the more sensible choice. She was the second choice, and it could be argued his last resort. Every touch from him now was a reminder of this, and she held her love for him more closely as if it could break from only a careless touch from him.

She opened her eyes and continued as though nothing had happened because it didn't matter. To Ash, she had merely touched him, a necessary gesture to stop his fidgeting and nothing more. To her, it had been a wish fulfilled, to feel the muscles of his thigh flex beneath her fingers, to feel the warmth of his body seep through the kid of her glove.

Like how he had held her in the study that day. She cursed herself for not having been clear-headed enough to return his embrace. It was likely to be one of the few stolen intimacies she would share with her husband, because after their conversation that day, she knew precisely what he expected of her in this marriage, and it had nothing to do with intimacies.

"Viscount Mayberry has the largest sheep enterprise in Yorkshire. The Duke of Buccleuch is the largest landowner in Scotland." She waited, the carriage bouncing them together and apart.

"Is it suggested the two are coming together on some sort of scheme?"

She shrugged. "It's all mere speculation, but there's nothing more the *ton* enjoys than speculation."

He looked away and out the window then, and she knew he finally understood. Ash had been the cause of great speculation in the *ton* over the course of his nearly ten years of being out in society, and she knew not much of the speculation had been positive. It was hard to glean as much when one was always considered beneath one as the son of a mere judge.

"So we are attending tonight's ball based on the allure of speculation?" he asked after some moments.

"Yes, precisely."

He picked up a hand, and she swatted it back down.

"I said stop fidgeting. Do you wish to make a good introduction or not?"

"Introduction? This is not my first social event since acquiring the title."

She closed her eyes against the sharp stab of remorse that coursed through her and very slowly opened them again, drawing a measured breath.

"It's your first social event since acquiring a wife." She spoke the words carefully, keeping her tone modulated.

"Oh. Right. I'd forgotten about you." He said it amiably and jostled her shoulder as though they were old friends sharing a joke, but nothing had hurt worse in a very long time.

She forced a smile and prayed for them to arrive at their destination before she simply gave up and exited the carriage to find her fate on the streets of Mayfair.

Thankfully the gods were in her favor that night, and soon the carriage slowed as they pulled into line with the stream of guests making their way to the Mayberry townhouse entrance.

She managed to keep her smile in place as they made their way through the receiving line and even when the Mayberry butler made their introduction. She knew they were the least anticipated guests of the evening, but she couldn't help but feel as though all eyes turned to them as they descended into the Mayberry ballroom.

They'd hardly set foot into the room when heads began

turning in their direction. She held Ash's arm rather too tightly, and he squirmed beneath her touch.

"Stop fidgeting," she muttered through her smile.

"I'm not fidgeting. I'm attempting to work the blood back into my arm as you seem so determined to cut it off."

She relaxed her grip by the slightest degree. "If I wished to cut it off, I would use far more efficient means."

He wasn't able to retort as they were approached by a pair of gentlemen almost immediately.

"Lord Aylesford, is it?" the smaller of the two gentlemen inquired. He gave a small bow. "Lord Beverly here, and this is Townsend."

Ash returned the bow. "Gentlemen, may I present my wife? Lady Adaline."

Adaline curtsied, her heart thumping loudly. She had performed any number of introductions over the years she had been out, but none had weighed so heavily. Ash must appear above all scrutiny, and everything that night must be precise.

"Gentlemen," she returned. She had no idea who the Townsend man was, and whether or not he held a title, so she refrained from any more specific address to avoid a social blunder.

"I say, good lady," Lord Beverly continued. "Might I borrow your husband for a spell? I do like to get to know the new chaps coming to the floor in Parliament."

Adaline slid Ash a glance. This was a development she hadn't expected. She had planned for them to remain together to appear as a united front. It would go so much further to have Ash stand next to the daughter of an earl for the entirety of the night, but it seemed he was to be plucked away.

She smiled, canting her head as if in consideration. "I

suppose I can loan him to you for a time. But do be careful, gentlemen. I should like him back in working order."

Lord Beverly laughed so hard he nearly upset the drink in his hand. "Oh, you've selected a worthy match, I say, Aylesford."

"Only the best, of course."

Townsend nodded along as Lord Beverly continued to laugh.

"Right then, shall we adjourn to the terrace?" Lord Beverly pulled a cigar from the inner pocket of his jacket. "Lady Beverly detests the smell of tobacco, so I ensure I regularly indulge."

Townsend thought this the most humorous of suggestions, and Ash slid her a wary glance as he followed the two gentlemen to the terrace doors on the opposite side of the ballroom.

She was left to stand with a gaggle of matrons by the refreshment table. She recognized them, of course. She'd been standing next to the same group of matrons at every ball for the past four years. She sighed and looked away.

"If it isn't the new Marchioness of Aylesford."

She straightened at the use of her new title and turned about to find the Earl of Knighton approaching. He was dressed impeccably in unrelenting black, and she understood immediately how he had earned his reputation as a rake.

"Knighton," she greeted him with a small curtsy.

"I see the marquess has abandoned you already."

In the few times she had spoken with the earl, she had found his company enjoyable, and it only served to reaffirm her belief in his worthiness of his reputation.

"I'm afraid it's a great deal worse than that. He's been absconded by a Lord Beverly."

Knighton did nothing to hide his grimace. "The man's a

lecher. He routinely strikes down any bill that might address child safety in the workplace."

Adaline had been scanning the crowd to see if there were any other persons of interest in attendance that night, but at this, she turned to face the earl directly. The comment was so unlike what she expected of a rake it garnered further attention.

"You seem rather informed about the goings on in Parliament. I had the impression you may not give such matters quite so much attention."

He raised both eyebrows and grinned. "Lady Aylesford, you wound me. To think I shouldn't keep the welfare of children foremost in my mind."

"I understand you're a rake of the first order, Lord Knighton."

He laughed, the sound quick and light. "I am, Lady Aylesford. And do not for a moment think otherwise."

Humor sparkled in his eyes, and she couldn't help but like the man immensely. No wonder women were in such danger in his company.

"I must say, Lady Aylesford, I was surprised when Ash told me of your impending nuptials."

The lightness of moments before evaporated at the earl's careful tone.

"Oh?" she hedged, unsure of the man's intention.

"Ash faces many challenges thanks in part to his origins, you know."

"I see no issue with my husband's origins, Lord Knighton." She kept her voice firm and watched the man's expression, but he only studied her with obvious curiosity.

He wished to discover something about her, and she wished not to care about his scrutiny, but she gathered the odd sense he was attempting to protect Ash. It had been difficult when Ash had left for school, leaving her behind. He had created a different life for himself then, one in which she was not included, and she wondered suddenly if that was where he had acquired his friendship with the Earl of Knighton.

"I can see that now, Lady Aylesford," he said, his tone soft even as a satisfied smile played at the corner of his lips. "You will forgive me my concern. I'm sure you understand my worry after everything Ash has been through recently."

The room about her, dizzying in its swirling occupants, the buzz of conversation, and the thrum of music seemed to spiral to an abrupt halt as her entire focus narrowed to the earl.

"All that he has been through?" The words passed her lips without thought, escaping on an exhale of air as the earl's words stacked up inside of her until she could read between them.

The Earl of Knighton *knew*.

He knew of her husband's humiliation, and the only possible way he could know was if Ash had told him. But Ash had not told her. In fact, he had lied to her about it.

The blow was crushing, and it took all the skill she had acquired in her four seasons to keep her composure.

Ash had told his school chum of his heartbreak but not her. Just how much was she a second-rate choice for a bride?

Knighton's smile turned brighter. "I suppose someone with your strength doesn't see it as a challenge, Lady Aylesford. I know you will make an excellent marchioness."

An excellent marchioness but not the wife her husband longed for.

She was saved from having to respond when Alice pushed through the crowds.

"Adaline, I must speak with you," her sister said without preamble before her eyes slid to Adaline's companion, and her expression sparked. "Knighton," she said in a tone she had once used when discovering an old text on harnessing power sources.

Adaline seized her sister's elbow. "I do beg your pardon, Knighton. It appears my sister has need of my company."

The earl's smile turned wary at the sight of the younger Atwood sister, but she paid him no heed, tucking Alice's arm beneath her own and propelling them away from the man and the reminder of her latest heartbreak.

CHAPTER 6

*A*sh pressed two fingers to the throbbing that had started at his temples the moment Wilfred Biggins entered his study.

"And how exactly did the gunpowder get into the house?"

It was a question Ash had never thought he would ask, and yet here he was. Sitting in the Marquess of Aylesford's study on a crisp, sunny early summer morning asking the very thing of one of his land stewards.

Wilfred Biggins was a man of average height and build. He wore a suit that although worn was carefully mended, showing a great deal of respect and care for one's appearance. He stood at attention, his hands folded delicately over the felt cap in his hands.

Adaline was right. One really must refrain from fidgeting if one were to convey an air of confidence.

"It is as yet unknown, my lord." Ash raised an eyebrow, and the steward continued. "When the gravity of the situation was uncovered with the light of dawn, I took the first train here. I only apologize that it took me so long. There's no connection in Exeter at Yeovil at the late hour I arrived, and I was forced to wait the night at the station."

Ash sat back, assessing the man before him. "You spent the night at the Yeovil station. The place could hardly be more than a hut."

Biggins did not flinch. "It was adequate, my lord. I wished to be on the first train to London this morning, you see."

Ash glanced at the small timepiece on the corner of his desk. It had only just gone past eleven. It must have been an early train indeed. He tapped his fingers on the desk, letting the news the man had brought wash over him.

"So the house is a total loss then?"

"No, my lord, not in the least. That is why I wished to get here so quickly. Repairs can be made. The explosion occurred in the west wing, you see. Blew it nearly clean off from what I can tell. But the rest of the house is intact, you see. My only concern is looting."

Ash's fingers stilled. "Looting?"

For the first time, Biggins showed a moment's hesitation. "The house is open to the elements, you see, my lord, and I'm afraid it's been left unguarded." The words passed through his lips as though they were stuck on a bit of thick honey.

"Unguarded?" Ash sat up. "The servants have left their posts?"

Biggins released a breath then that might have been a sigh of frustration in a lesser man. "My lord, may I be blunt?"

Ash waved at the man. "Of course. By all means." He leaned one elbow on the arm of his chair and prepared himself for yet another unexpected issue with inheriting a title—as one also inherited the mismanagement performed by the previous titleholder.

Biggins straightened even more than Ash thought possible. "The previous marquess was not an attentive master, my lord. The servants at Grant Hall were left largely to their own devices. If I may be so bold, I would wager the gunpowder that caused the explosion in the hall was brought inside by a gang of nefarious footmen."

"Nefarious footmen?"

"Have you been to Dartmoor, my lord? There is not much to capture the attention of a group of young men ready to make their mark on the world. I'm afraid some fall into dangerous habits."

"Like exploding gunpowder in the ancestral home of a marquess?"

"This incident is the first of its kind that I've been witness to, my lord."

He pressed his fingers to his temples again. "And you assure me no one was hurt?"

Biggins gave a quick shake of his head. "No, my lord. As you are aware, there is a limited staff in employment at the hall at this time, and they were in the servants' quarters at the time of the blast. The servants' quarters are housed in the original structure of the hall, which is now the east wing."

"And yet they fled when they saw the destruction?"

Once again Biggins gave a slight hesitation, one finger drumming against his felt hat. "It wasn't the blast that scared them, my lord. I assure you. Mrs. Hutchinson—that's the housekeeper—she runs Grant Hall with remarkable efficiency. It's only the staff she has to work with are rather inadequate. Not to mention the other challenges."

"What other challenges?"

"It's the ghosts, my lord."

Ash dropped his arm and blinked. "The ghosts?"

Biggins nodded once. "It's the moor, you see. It's haunted. And now the hall is open to the moor directly. The servants didn't feel safe, so...they left."

It sounded all so matter of fact when the man said it.

"So the servants have abandoned their posts, and the hall

is missing a wing that was blown up in an explosion of gunpowder."

"That is the summary of the situation, yes."

Ash placed his hands on the desk and pushed to his feet. "I thank you, Biggins, for coming to get me so swiftly. I shall pack at once and join you in your return trip to Devon."

"Begging your pardon, my lord," the steward said. "But I have a ticket on the next train. If you don't mind, I should like to return to Grant Hall as quickly as possible."

Ash couldn't very well fault the man for his diligence, especially given Grant Hall had apparently no servants as of the moment.

"Very well, Biggins. I shall be directly behind you."

Biggins gave a small bow and turned for the door.

"Biggins," Ash called out, and the man spun about efficiently. "How did the footmen get the gunpowder?"

"It's used in the quarries, my lord. Gunpowder is effective in the tin mines and against the granite. The stuff is manufactured on the moor itself because it's so readily used."

Ash absorbed this. "And how did it come to explode when no one was in the west wing?"

Biggins seemed to consider this a moment before saying, "It was probably stored there and an errant spark from an unattended fire could have set it off. You know how irresponsible young men can be."

Ash raised a hand in thank you, knowing too well the truth of Biggins's words.

He made his way to the breakfast room after seeing his land steward off, hoping to find Adaline. They had only returned to Aylesford House in the small hours of the morning, the Mayberry ball having gone on for an intolerable length of time.

After Lord Beverly and Townsend—he still was not clear who the man was—he had been absconded by a baron, a viscount, and even a duke. The night had spent itself without much notice from him, and it was hours later that Adaline had finally touched his elbow, telling him it was time to depart.

He hadn't spoken much in the carriage home, too tired to put two words together, and then Adaline had quietly drifted off to the marchioness's rooms without a word.

He found the breakfast room empty though, the sideboard cleared of the morning meal entirely. He made to leave when he noticed a flutter of the drapes at the opposite end of the room. The breakfast room opened into the gardens as much of the rooms in this part of the house did, but he had yet to venture into the gardens himself.

He moved toward the doors, pushing aside the drapes to find his wife on the terrace beyond. She sat at a small wrought iron table, a tea service at her elbow as her arm rested atop a closed, cloth-covered book on the table. He recognized the book immediately. He'd seen a dozen like it over the years, but usually it was open, Adaline sketching madly within it. He felt a twinge of misgivings as he saw her now, the book closed at her elbow. How troubled were her thoughts that it could stop her from sketching?

He realized standing there he had never asked her why it was she had accepted his offer of marriage. He had surmised it was for the same reasons as him, the possibility of a marriage of convenience. But the sight of the closed sketchbook had him wondering.

"Adaline." He tried not to startle her, his mind turning as if on its own accord, stepping back from what troubled him to something he hadn't noticed before then.

It struck him suddenly what a lovely image she made. The long, slim fingers of her right hand resting softly against the lavender cloth of the sketchbook under her hand. The way the sunlight flitted over the gold tones of her long braid.

How her eyes drifted over the garden as though absorbing something of the world he could not see.

She turned her head when he called her name, but her eyes retained their unnatural focus, and he wondered if she were perhaps lost in thought.

"I've had a visit from my land steward. He came all the way from Grant Hall in Devon. It seems there's been an accident that requires my attention."

Her eyes sharpened at his words, and she dropped her hand from her book, sitting up in her chair. "What kind of accident? I hope no one was hurt."

He scratched at the back of his neck, not quite sure how to phrase his news. "It appears there was an explosion in the hall. It destroyed the west wing. I am told no one suffered injury."

She stood, coming around the table toward him. "Ash, that's awful. But how did it happen?"

He looked out over the gardens she had so recently been perusing and noticed they were indeed quite lovely. If only he had the time to enjoy them.

"Gunpowder. It's apparently quite common on the moor for mining."

She crossed her arms and nodded. "Then we must make ready to leave. I'm sure you'll wish to set off as soon as possible."

His gaze moved quickly back to her. "Yes, I shall be leaving as quickly as I can. There's no need for you to come."

Her eyes narrowed for but a second, and if she had been anyone else, he might have said she flinched at his words. But that was preposterous. It was reliable Adaline. She never wavered.

"I would be happy to accompany you. I'm sure there are many matters that require addressing at the hall that you will not have time for."

He thought of the staff that had fled and felt the situation slipping from his grasp. He was man enough to admit he had relished at the thought of getting away from London for a few days, from the awkward if agreeable resolution he and Adaline had come to since that day in the study, but he saw the logic of her reasoning.

"I think you may be right, but I wish you to know the conditions will likely be most disagreeable. The steward said the hall is now open to the elements, and the servants have fled."

She canted her head in consideration. "Of course they fled. I wouldn't wish to stay in a house that had just blown up." She emphasized the last two words to mark their oddity.

She was right again. It was rather uncomfortable knowing the house in which one lived had recently suffered an explosion. But he swallowed, knowing he should tell her the whole truth.

"Biggins said the servants fled because they're afraid of the ghosts that haunt the moor."

She blinked. "Ghosts? Are you quite serious?"

"Deadly," he said.

There was a beat of silence before she said, "I shan't be daunted. You know that, Ash." She picked up her skirts and turned back to the house. "I'll have the carriage readied and the trunks brought out."

"I should like to take the train. It will be faster."

She stilled, her entire body freezing into place. It was such an unusual sight he turned to take in the whole sight of it.

"Atwood?" he asked after several seconds when she had not moved.

Finally she turned back to him, her eyes wide with apprehension. "You wish to take the train?"

He nodded. "The steward came by way of Exeter. He left

84

last night and arrived this morning. That's a great deal faster than any carriage could take us, and I wish to assess the situation for myself as soon as is possible."

She swallowed. He could see it from where he was standing, and the gesture was so unlike her it had him stepping forward.

"Adaline, are you well?" He stopped in front of her and placed his hands on her shoulders comfortingly until she looked up and met his gaze.

"I've never been on a train," she nearly whispered.

"Never? They're not so bad as you might think. Drafty at times, but that can't be helped." It was several seconds before he realized Adaline's eyes were blank and the color had escaped her cheeks. "Atwood, are you afraid of trains?"

Her eyes cleared then, and she pierced him with her gaze. "No, I am not," she said sternly. "I am terrified of them."

* * *

"Stop staring."

"I can't. It's a physical impossibility."

If her nerves hadn't caused her to snap the strings of her reticule in two, she would be happy to use them around Ash's neck instead.

"I can assure you it is not."

They stood on the platform, the chaos of the station swirling about them. Porters rushed trunks to and fro. Ladies in billowing skirts rushed past them on the arms of gentlemen. Children scurried here and there, and her heart raced, imagining them slipping from the platform and on to the tracks.

It was at that moment the beast of a locomotive in front of them let out a great whistle, steam hurtling from its menacing innards.

She screamed. She wasn't proud of it, but then she'd never been this close to a locomotive. But what was worse her fear sent her into Ash's arms, cowering against his chest.

She waited for him to berate her or at the least tease her for her insecurity and fears, but instead he made soft shushing noises as his arms closed around her. It was the second time he had held her in the past fortnight, and she hated how good it felt. His embraces meant far more to her than they did for him, and the imbalance was heartbreaking.

But just then she didn't care. She let the thump of his heart drown out the rest of the noise around her.

"Come on," he urged, easing her back far enough to pull her arm through his.

It was a gentlemanly gesture, the way he held her arm pinned against his side. It was almost as though he were doing all he could without actually carrying her onto the train.

They moved along the platform to one of the open doors of a carriage. She balked at the sight of it, her stomach threatening to empty itself, which would be impossible as she hadn't eaten since the day before and then only the few bites of sandwich she'd managed at tea. She shook her head, the power of speech suddenly failing her, but Ash didn't let go of her arm.

"Adaline, I will be beside you the entire time. I promise you."

"That is hardly reassuring. I would hate for you to die with me on this beast."

"Who said anything about dying?"

Her eyes flew to his face, and she was momentarily distracted by how handsome he looked, freshly shaved, starched cravat, and carefully brushed hat. He looked every inch the marquess he was, and it struck then, all that they had been through together. What was one more thing?

She pried her teeth apart. "Do you know how many people are killed in train accidents every year?"

He cast a glance at the carriage beside them. "I haven't any idea, and I should like to know how you do."

She tugged on her arm, but he refused to relinquish it. "It's far more than there should be."

She waited for him to argue, but instead it looked every bit as though he were trying to hold back a laugh.

"You would laugh at me?"

"Of course, I would, but that's not it in the least. It's only I'm pleased to see you are human like the rest of us."

His words stilled her, temporarily capturing her attention. "What do you mean?"

He nodded in the direction of the train. "It's rather unnatural to hurtle through the country on this beast. It's only normal for you to have misgivings. It's only you've never displayed such humanity before. I was beginning to think you were stronger than the rest of us."

She wasn't sure if his words startled her or merely confused her, but it was enough of a distraction that he was able to get her on the train. The first-class carriage was richly appointed in thick red carpets and fine wood paneling, but she wouldn't let the fancy dressings break down her guard.

Ash led her through the narrow corridor to a cabin and ushered her inside, shutting the door firmly behind them. They stood awkwardly for a moment as she refused to relinquish her grip on his arm, but he finally managed to talk her into sitting down.

She selected the seat closest to the door. She couldn't say exactly why as her thoughts bounced between not wishing to be ejected through the window and thinking she may be faster in fleeing through the door should the entire thing suddenly burst into flames. None of this made any sense, and she acknowledged this even in the height of her despair, but it didn't matter. It made her feel better.

Ash went to the window and peered out. "I must say the trains have improved a great deal since the early days. You should have seen it when the carriages were just wooden boxes with benches in them."

She wasn't certain what her expression looked like, but she was fairly certain it was awful judging by the way Ash's eyebrows knitted in concern when he looked back at her.

She clutched the velvet upholstery beneath her, wondering if she might shred the cushion with her very hands. Her husband dropped to the seat beside her then, doffing his hat.

"Do you think I can make it?" he asked, holding the hat in one hand and using it to gesture at the strange mesh shelf above the opposite seats.

It was a shelf for hats, she realized, and touched her own bonnet as though it would need to be pried from her dead body.

"No," she said without feeling.

"You wound me, wife," he muttered and then expertly shot the hat onto the shelf as though he had been doing it his whole life. "Ah, see there. I expect you owe me for your doubt in my abilities."

"Owe you? I hardly think so." She let go of her death grip on the cushion to fold her arms over her chest and glower at him. "Your ability to toss a hat is not worthy of any sort of recognition." She nodded in the direction of the shelf. "Any lad could do that."

"I'd like to see you try it."

"What?"

He pointed at her bonnet. "I wager you can't make the shelf with your own bonnet."

She touched the straw of her hat once more. "I shouldn't think so. I shan't risk ruining my appearance for mere sport."

He pressed his lips together and reclined in his seat, crossing one ankle over the opposite knee. "Very well then."

She had thought the conversation over and reclined in her own seat only to remember where she was. The moment her heart began to pick up pace, she heard him mutter, "Coward."

She eyed him. "Excuse me?"

He turned his head and pronounced, "I called you a coward."

"I am no such thing."

He raised a hand with two fingers as if pointing out the truth in her statement. "You know, I believed that once, but today's developments are proving otherwise."

"Whatever do you mean?"

He dropped his foot to the floor and leaned toward her, bending an elbow on the arm rest between them. "Do you remember the Aubrey house party?"

The change in topic was so abrupt she had to search her memories as if it were a physical chore. "The one our parents made us attend?"

He gave an emphatic nod. "The very one. The family had just returned from the Americas, and the mother had wished for her children to meet others of a similar age, so we were brought along as well."

"Your mother was furious," Adaline whispered with a shake of her head, suddenly picturing the moment as if it had just happened.

"I think she was looking for husband number four then. She likely saw me as a hindrance." She hated his casual reference to his mother's inadequate feelings for her only child, but she didn't comment as he continued. "We were all sent to the nursery to sleep. Do you remember? It was someone's idea of how we should all get to know one another."

She wrinkled her nose. "It was awful. There were too many of us and too many differing ages."

He nodded as he went along. "And do you remember what happened?"

She pursed her lips, the events of the night washing over her. "The adults got exceedingly drunk and began bumbling around the house all night."

"And all the little children were terrified the place was overrun by ghosts, and you had to calm their nerves, assuring them it was only the wind."

She could picture it now. That night spent huddled in the center of so many small children, all frightened and out of sorts, wishing their nannies would come get them. She had been older, probably eight or nine, and had known exactly what was happening downstairs.

"You helped me to tell them stories to distract them." She smiled at the memory, her gaze refocusing on the present only to find he had leaned closer as they'd reminisced, and his lips were so terribly close.

It was funny how she had spent most of her life around this man and only now she was beginning to notice individual parts of him.

She didn't move. She should have. But he didn't move either, and she very much felt his gaze on her, his eyes drifting over her face as if he were seeing it for the first time.

There was another explosion of sound, the shrill whistle sounding from the engine, only now she felt how it reverberated down the length of carriage, vibrating beneath her and around her until she thought the train would swallow her whole. She jumped in her seat, her hands flying to the arm rest to hold on as if it might save her life.

When the moment passed and she was still alive, she found Ash frowning, his eyes questioning.

Regret and annoyance rushed through her in a confusing swirl of emotion. She reached up and yanked the bow of her bonnet loose. She plucked the thing from her head and took aim.

"What am I to win when I make this shot?"

He looked between her and the shelf that now held his own hat. "Oh, are we wagering again? Because I'm not sure you should take the risk."

She lowered her hat to pin him with a glare. "I will have you know my prowess on the archery field is unmatched."

He snorted. "Where your aim is aided by the fineness of the apparatus you use, most likely. I should think relying on your own skill alone shall put you at a disadvantage."

Her jaw fell open, but she couldn't form a retort as she struggled to regain control of her breath. She snapped her mouth shut and took aim again. Tossing the bonnet in her hand she tested its weight and eyed the distance to the shelf. It was hardly a herculean feat, and she knew her husband would never allow her to live it down should she miss.

With a flick of her wrist, she sent the bonnet flying. For one perilous moment she watched it waver, the uneven weight of the hat making it wobble in the air, and then it caught the edge of the shelf. She came up off the cushion of her seat in her elation only to watch the bonnet wobble and fall.

She sank back down, her back straight, her hands loose in her lap. She didn't wish to look at her husband. She didn't wish to see the mockery that was most definitely on his face.

"What is it that I should receive should you not make the toss, Atwood? I'm not sure we ever agreed on it." He spoke the words with a casualness that would suggest they were doing little more than discussing the weather.

She opened her mouth to tell him exactly what he should get when the train suddenly lurched forward. She was quite certain she swallowed her tongue, and her heart was now residing somewhere in her toes. The beast let out another earsplitting whistle, and her stomach turned.

Hands were on her, warm, familiar hands, and she let Ash turn her toward him. His face was calm, his features relaxed, and then he smiled, that familiar warm smile, and for a very small second, she forgot she was headed to what would most certainly be a horrific death.

But then she noticed his eyes, the way they studied her in a curious manner she'd never seen before. It was almost as though he were seeing her for the first time, and she forgot entirely where she was, the panic vanishing as though it were never there.

That was when he kissed her.

CHAPTER 7

*H*e was kissing her.
Adaline.

His best friend.

Why was he kissing her?

Because he had panicked. That was quite obvious.

She had begun to make a high keening noise as the train had rumbled into motion, and he was almost certain she didn't realize she was doing so. But he worried that any moment someone would come to check on them, and he couldn't let her be in such a state.

So he'd kissed her.

He had run through his repertoire of distractions, and none had seemed to work. Not even the silly wager with the hats. He was usually so good at reading the room, at playing to his audience, yet it shouldn't have been a surprise that his tricks hadn't worked on his wife.

She was, quite simply, used to them.

Because this was Adaline. His best friend. The person he had grown up with when he'd had no siblings to fit the bill. She knew all of his tactics, had watched them play out a hundred times over in the past twenty years. It was no wonder they hadn't worked. Not entirely.

He'd nearly had her with the hat thing, but as soon as the train had grumbled into motion, he had lost her again to the vagaries of her own mind.

In all their years he truly hadn't known her to be afraid of anything, and now, seeing her like that, it had crashed open something inside of him. It wasn't a subtle thing. It wasn't silent and unnoticed. It was big, huge, and loud. It rocketed open inside of him as if to make it quite clear it could not be put back.

In knowing Adaline was afraid of something, she became someone different to him.

He no longer saw her as the invincible big sister, avenging those weaker than her even though she was small herself. For what Adaline lacked in stature, she made up for in steely strength. So watching her cower at the mere presence of a train was enough to have the little girl slipping away, and in her place, stood his wife.

His *wife*.

They had been married for more than a fortnight then, and yet he still couldn't think of her as such. Not until now. Only now she couldn't be anything else.

Because it was a woman who filled his hands. It was a woman who burned against his lips.

Gone was his childhood companion so cleanly he wondered how he'd missed it. But it was like anything one sees regularly. One misses the small changes wrought over time until the thing before one is nothing like it was, but one can't tell because it's been there all along.

That was Adaline. She'd simply been there, and to him, she was the same Adaline. Only she wasn't.

Parts of him awoke that he was certain had died that night in the conservatory. Desire gripped him, and it startled him with its intensity. He had only just pressed his lips to hers, and yet the spark was strong and immediate.

His body was responding to hers in a way he couldn't have imagined. But then that was the whole point of desire. It wasn't logical or reasonable. It just was, and when one encountered it, one could not ignore it.

Should not ignore it.

It was then she kissed him back, and even he forgot they were on a train.

She tilted her head the smallest of degrees, and it changed the angle of their lips, bringing her closer to him, and soon his arms were wrapped about her, clinging to her back and pressing her against him.

The arm rest of the seat was wedged between them, keeping her from him. God above if he didn't reach over and tug her onto his lap, his lips never leaving hers. But more, she let him do it, falling against him, until her fingers gained purchase at his shoulders, and then she clung to him, lifting her body against his as she deepened the kiss.

He may have started it, but he was no longer in control of it. The kiss was wild and passionate, unexpected and star-tling. And somehow it felt like the absolute perfect thing to do just then. Or ever for that matter.

He liked the way her lithe body fit against him, how the curves of her hips felt under his palms. He liked the way she so tentatively explored his lips, pressing and nibbling and discovering. It was shocking, her boldness, and he wondered why he had never thought of her this way.

Her hands crept along his shoulders, and he realized she was doing the same thing there, exploring him. The thought sent fire directly to his belly, and he reached up to plunge his fingers through her hair, pulling her more deeply into the kiss.

She moaned, her chest heaving with the sound, and he

suddenly became aware of her breasts. Oh God, Adaline had *breasts*. Before that moment, he couldn't have honestly said whether or not this was true, but now that he was acutely aware of the fact, it stole his breath.

He gasped against her lips, pulling his mouth free to suck in much needed air, but he never let go of her. He couldn't. Not now. He traced his lips along her jaw, her cheekbone, her temple, all while he massaged the base of her skull, letting her thick hair fall between his fingers. Had he been thinking, he would realize he was ruining her braid, but he didn't give a damn just then.

She wiggled in his grasp, and he thought for one terrifying moment she was trying to get away, but it wasn't that. Her wandering hands had reached the front of his shirt, and she was attempting to undo his cravat.

It was like a jolt through his senses, and all at once he remembered where they were.

He pulled away, feeling the strain it took to move his lips from her soft skin, and he stilled her exploring hands with one of his own.

"Adaline, we can't. Not here." The last words slipped free before he realized he meant to say them. So much rested in those two words, and he felt the heaviness of it.

Not here.

But perhaps somewhere else?

Oh God, this was Adaline. What was he talking about? He couldn't…at least not with her…but then…

His mind was foggy with desire, and he couldn't make his thoughts line up in the proper order. He had to put some space between them, draw a breath that was not saturated with her scent.

But he didn't move and neither did she.

She blinked, her gaze unfocused, and he wondered if he'd ever realized her eyes held some many strands of gold. Had he ever noticed the freckles that blanketed her nose were darker the higher they rose on her face? Had he ever seen the faint scar just under her left eyebrow?

Not more than an hour earlier his best friend had stood beside him on the train platform, and now an entirely different woman sat in his lap. An enticing woman, a beautiful woman, a woman he very much desired, and it sent his heart racing.

He couldn't be having these feelings for her. It just wasn't possible. But perhaps it was an accident. His nerves were overwrought after his encounter with Lady Valerie, and he was seeing passion when there was really just desperation.

That was all this was. It was his body's way of coping with devastation and loss. It yearned for the warmth of Adaline's body. That was all.

"I'm—" He nearly swallowed his tongue to stop the words from erupting.

He had nearly said he was sorry. He wasn't thinking clearly; he knew that. But he was aware enough to know that a man did not apologize for thoroughly kissing a woman when said woman clearly had enjoyed it.

The blissful moment of peace he had managed to conjure when he thought this encounter nothing more than the result of stress vanished as a new thought superseded the rest.

Adaline had enjoyed their kiss. More than that, she had seemed to vibrate with a passion he hadn't known existed in her.

This wouldn't do. None of this would do. They were headed for an estate in the middle of Dartmoor. He didn't even know where the nearest neighbor lay, and the staff had all run off. In that moment, he dreaded their arrival. He couldn't be alone with her.

But he was alone with her now.

For one horrible second, his eyes slid to the cabin door and the bolt he had left open when they entered. He could lock the door. No one would know. He could slack his thirst and be done with it. But then his eyes moved back to Adaline's flushed face, her eyes sleepy with desire, and he knew he couldn't do that to her.

She was a virgin, an innocent—she was, wasn't she?

His passion cooled in an instant.

He didn't know anything about his wife.

Because she was no longer Adaline, his childhood friend; she was a woman he'd never taken the time to know.

A different kind of regret washed over him, and a thousand conversations came back to him at once, roaring in his ears like the ebb and flow of the ocean.

Adaline telling him to be careful. Adaline telling him that Lady Valerie was selfish. Adaline telling him to respect himself.

Adaline.

She had been right about everything while he had not been seeing clearly at all.

He eased her from his lap, setting her carefully on the seat beside him. Her fingers moved to the tie of her braid, pulling it loose, threading her hair back into some kind of order, but her gaze was still absent, and he thought she did it from memory.

He had forgotten and set her on the seat closest to the window, and he reached out, hoping to save her before she realized where she was, but too late, her eyes lifted, and like the sun burning off the morning fog, her gaze cleared.

He saw the moment she remembered where they were. Her eyes widened, and her lips parted, but it wasn't that which caught his attention. Her fingers stilled, stopping in the pattern she had likely completed a hundred times over in her life, rendered motionless by the view through the window.

He wasn't sure how long they had been otherwise occupied, but they had left London behind, and the landscape of farmland lay before them like some kind of exquisite painting. Tended fields in tones of green melted into dabs of gold and yellow surrounded by neat stone fences or dotted with herds of sheep and cows. If there were anything more idyllic, he'd never seen it.

But he glanced at it only briefly, his eyes captured by the sight of his wife leaning toward the glass. She raised a single hand and pressed her palm to the window as if by doing so she could absorb the scene beyond.

Her hair lay in a half-finished braid across her shoulder, and her gown was wrinkled from their earlier encounter, and he couldn't bring himself to look away from her.

"Ash," she breathed after several seconds. "I didn't know. I didn't know it would be like this." She glanced back briefly, and he caught the light in her eyes, the expectancy and wonder.

It shook him. There was more to his wife than he could have ever imagined, and he hated the time he had lost infatuated with another. Was he in love with his wife? Certainly not. He couldn't have been. He was only just discovering her. But he suddenly hated how he had let another blind him to her.

In the span of minutes, everything had shifted about him, but it wasn't a shift at all. It had always been there. It was only that now he saw it for what it was.

She shook her head, her hair crackling. "Have you ever seen anything so beautiful?" she whispered.

She had asked the question of her reflection in the window, but he answered anyway, his voice suddenly gravelly and quiet as he watched her.

"No. I've never seen anything more beautiful."

* * *

HE DIDN'T SAY a single word about the kiss.

Not in all of the interminable hours after it happened.

She did the only sensible thing, of course, which was to pretend it hadn't happened.

But it *had* happened.

She'd forgotten entirely about her possible, horrific death in a train accident because really, the fact that Ash had kissed her was far more life changing than death itself.

He had *kissed* her.

In those interminable hours when he pretended to sleep and she pretended to have seen nothing so beautiful as the countryside passing outside their window, she had thought about it at great length and even managed to squirrel down some terrible rabbit holes.

The first being that he kissed her out of pity. This was the most likely scenario.

She couldn't remember clearly those first few seconds when the train had started moving, its great hulking mass lumbering in fits and starts as its giant iron wheels grated along the tracks. Her heart had been hammering, her thoughts like the deck of a ship in a storm, awash in debris and things that shouldn't be there entirely.

And then he'd kissed her.

Had she made a noise to indicate her distress? Had she said something to suggest she might be in emotional turmoil at the thought of the train *moving*?

She probably had and couldn't remember. Her hammering heart and her waffling thoughts had taken out what little sense she had had left to her in that moment.

So when his lips touched hers, it was like a stone cutting

through the glass surface of a lake, shattering the reality that had been to replace it with a new one, one that rippled and undulated from one catastrophic, cataclysmic event to another.

Ash had kissed her.

She had been kissed. Good God. She had been caught up in the semantics of it and had failed to realize the entirety of what had happened.

She may have been the daughter of an earl and beautiful, but no gentlemen had ever taken such liberties with her. Poverty had a way of making one a pariah, and gentlemen stayed carefully away from her.

But her argument that Ash had kissed her out of pity didn't stand up under scrutiny. And she'd had plenty of time to scrutinize it.

For if he had kissed her out of pity, why had he kissed her for so long and so thoroughly?

For he had been thorough.

When he'd pulled her onto his lap, she had felt weightless, as though her soul had left her body in euphoric bliss and so her person could no longer contain weight. Her heart no longer hammered, but instead it had stuttered, itself unsure what was happening just as her brain scrambled to catch up.

But his kiss had been lingering and explorative. He had consumed her, and somewhere in the chaos, her body had taken over, her hands assuming a mind of their own as they caressed and discovered, kneaded and explored.

It was Ash. All of Ash. The man she had known for so long, the man she had loved so painfully. He was finally touching her, kissing her, holding her.

How her heart didn't shatter with the beauty of it she didn't know, but soon her disbelief had been replaced by desire. It had been so startling she had felt it like a hiccup in her throat.

It was one thing to harbor a secret love for the man, but she was no fool about dreams. They tended to be flawless whereas the reality could hold hard edges and unsatisfying truths.

So it was a shock to find kissing Ash was better than anything she had ever dreamed, and her body felt doubly as sure about it.

He had tasted of the orange marmalade he had spread on his toast at breakfast and the bitter tang of coffee. It was such an intimate thing to know, and she held it deep within her as her scrutiny took on greater depth.

Had he kissed her because he was bored?

Had he kissed her as some sort of boon for the wager he'd won?

Had he kissed her because she was there, and they were alone?

This was the least likely candidate as they had been alone numerous times in the fortnight of their marriage, and he hadn't touched her with so much as a passing glance.

So what had overcome him? What had made him do it?

It wasn't...

She couldn't even think it, let alone speak it.

Had he finally *seen* her?

Had his infatuation for Lady Valerie dimmed enough to allow others to enter his vision? Namely her?

She couldn't be sure, and her looping thoughts only served as the most medieval of torture.

When the train lumbered to its final stop, she was grateful. Ash had been pretending to sleep since Exeter, and she could no longer pretend not to notice. She gathered her bonnet and her reticule and took herself to the door, not waiting for Ash to offer his arm. If he touched her now, she would be lost.

The air was cool and damp when she stepped out onto

the platform, and she sucked in great lungfuls of it, relishing the way it stung her cheeks. She swayed slightly and reached out a hand as she felt herself falling, the ground shifting beneath her feet. Ash caught her neatly, his arm going about her waist and drawing her to his chest.

It all happened so swiftly she didn't have time to prepare, and she stood frozen in his embrace.

"It's the motion of the train," he whispered against her temple. "It stays with you long after you disembark."

She heard his words, but they made little sense to her. She was too absorbed in the feel of his jacket beneath her cheek, the scrape of his beard along her forehead, the gentle press of his hands at her back. It was a moment that separated itself from the rest of all the other moments she had lived, and she knew she would remember it this clearly for the rest of her life. The evening air cool and thick around them, the utter stillness of the platform after the train had pulled away.

She blinked, taking in the platform she could see from her position in Ash's arms.

It was empty.

Completely empty.

Their trunk sat on the platform behind them, but the rest of the small station was deserted.

"Ash?" she began hesitantly. "Where is everyone?"

He eased her away, but she kept hold of him, worried she'd feel that odd swaying motion pass through her again. Except her curiosity had gotten the better of her, and she took a step back to look around them.

The platform was simple in design, a barren expanse with a small hut at one end in which, she realized with a jolt, sat a man who quite obviously was dozing, his head thrown back against his chair.

"I'm afraid this is it," Ash said, also looking about them. "Biggins said he would send someone to collect us."

She turned to the side of the platform opposite the tracks and discovered a gentleman on the path a bit from the station, sitting atop a cart.

"Ash." She nodded in the direction of the man and cart.

She could almost hear Ash swallow as he took in the man. "I suppose that counts as sending someone."

They left their trunk and headed down the steps to the man in the cart.

"Good evening, sir," Ash called out as they approached, and the man shook himself awake with a snort.

Was this place so dreadfully dull as to inspire a sleeping sickness?

The man roused himself enough to peer over the edge of the cart at them.

"You must be the fancy gentleman then." He doffed his cap in her direction. "Ma'am," He mouthed more than spoke, his voice raspy with sleep. "I'll be seeing you to the hall then." He turned and picked up the reins, jostling the poor horse awake as well it seemed.

"I beg your pardon," Ash said, gesturing behind them. "Our trunk…"

"Oh, yes, you can bring it as well. Should be plenty of room in the cart," the man muttered, his eyes fastened somewhere between the horse's ears.

Ash turned, and they exchanged a meaningful glance.

"Right," she said, and tossing her reticule in the back of the cart, she picked up her skirts and marched back up the platform steps.

Ash followed more slowly behind her. "Atwood, you can't possible—"

"Grab that end," she said as she made the trunk.

"Adaline, you're a lady—"

She straightened, putting her fists to her hips. "And a very tired one. I should like to find a bed sometime soon." She nodded in the direction of the setting sun, and Ash looked over his shoulder, starting as though realizing for the first time the late hour.

When he turned back, he said nothing and bent to grab his end of the trunk. They wrestled the thing down the steps, and she was grateful they had packed light, the rest of their things coming in the carriage with their maid and valet after them.

When they reached the cart, they hefted the trunk into the back of it, and without a word, she clambered aboard, her legs swinging off the back of it as the trunk took up most of the space, leaving them the very end on which to sit.

She straightened her skirts with exaggerated primness, and she didn't miss how Ash tried to hide his smile. He climbed aboard as well, and the man on the driver's seat shook the cart into motion.

The road was well groomed, but the cart was badly sprung, and they jostled their way from the station onto the main thoroughfare. The setting sun trailed behind the cart as they made their way, and she raised a hand to shield her eyes so she could take in the landscape around them.

"Is this Dartmoor then?"

Ash grunted, his head turning as he too seemed to take in the area. "It would appear so."

Quite honestly there wasn't much to see in the dying light, and she dropped her hand, turning her head away from the sun to rest her eyes.

Her bottom was properly numb, her gloves thoroughly soiled from hanging on when they finally turned off the main road onto a rutted and bumpy drive. A series of sickly trees bent over them, and the last of the dying light shone through them like hellish brimstone.

"Ash," she began. "Did Uncle Dobson frequent Grant Hall with any regularity?"

Her husband snorted. "If the Kent estate is any indication, I'm afraid the man didn't leave London at all."

She turned, her fingers gripping the side of the cart as they bounced through a particularly deep hole in the drive. "Did you ever consider the state the hall might be in? I mean, other than the damage from the explosion."

He too had a fierce grip on the cart and clearly didn't wish to break his concentration as he kept his gaze on the drive at their feet. "I hadn't considered it. Why? What do you think we might be in for?"

She shrugged. "It's only these trees are not particularly healthy, and this drive hasn't seen a rake or broom in some time."

Finally he looked up, his expression blank, but he didn't say anything.

The drive seemed longer than the entire road from the station, and by the time the cart came to a teetering halt, her arms ached from the effort of not falling from the thing into the rutted gravel below them.

She dropped to the ground, shaking the dust from her now ruined skirts even though she knew it would do little good. She made her way around the cart as she did so and nearly collided with Ash where he stood.

"Oh no," she breathed when she finally looked up. To say Grant Hall was a complete and utter ruin was like putting a bow on a donkey. "Oh Ash, I'm so sorry."

The sun had nearly set now, and the last of the orange and purple light lit the front facade of the hall enough to see the state of things. The shattered glass of the windows looked like rotten teeth, the front door yawned open on a single hinge, and the front steps crumbled like chalk. Only then did she turn her head in the direction of the wing that suffered the explosion.

She reached out involuntarily to grip Ash's arm.

"If Biggins hadn't told me thusly, I would have sworn there never was a west wing," he said.

The place where surely the west wing had stood was nothing more than a pile of stone and wood.

"Here it is, gent," the man on the cart said. "Grant Hall."

Ash seemed to shake himself awake from the confusion of seeing the hall in person. "I'll just be a moment," he called up to the driver. "I just want to take a peek inside, and then we'll go down into the village. There must be an inn we can stay at for at least the night."

Adaline nodded, unable to find words. When she had boarded the train that morning, her thoughts had been preoccupied with images of screaming babies torn from their mothers' arms as they lay dying in a heap of twisted metal. She hadn't considered the worst of it would be found once they reached Grant Hall.

"Be careful," she called as Ash's foot went directly through one of the steps leading up to the front door.

He grimaced with obvious exaggeration, and his teeth shone in the fading light. She laughed, unable to stop herself, both at the absurdity of a marquess picking his way through such debris but also at how Ash could still make her laugh even then.

"You'd best be getting the trunk, ma'am. I don't have all night."

She turned at the sound of their driver's raspy voice. "I beg your pardon."

He nodded in the direction of the horizon, and she looked over just as the last of the sun dipped behind the line of trees that bordered the west.

"I won't be out on the moor after dark, ma'am. If you want your trunk, you'd better get it out now."

She gestured toward the hall. "His lordship will return shortly, and then I promise we can be on our—"

"I won't wait another moment," he said and picked up the reins threateningly. "The moor is haunted, it is, and I'll not be caught out on it after the light is gone."

She scrambled forward, her skirts catching on the cart as she hoisted herself up to grab the handle of the trunk. She hadn't even dragged the heavy thing to the end of the cart before it started to move beneath her feet.

"I'll say!" she cried in the general direction of the driver, but then the cart only lurched forward at the same moment she tried to jump to the ground.

She and their trunk fell in a cumbersome heap upon the drive. She heard something rip at the same moment her bonnet flew from her head, but it was hardly a concern after the bite of gravel dug through her bodice and sleeves. She spun over onto her backside in time to see the cart disappear into the darkness along the drive.

"Adaline!" Ash's voice held a decided note of panic, but she didn't bother to turn around to see him approach.

His hands were on her shoulders in seconds. "What's happened? Where's the driver?"

She released a breath. "I'm afraid he too has been scared off by the ghosts."

CHAPTER 8

*a*sh peered down the drive, but the cart and driver were long gone. The shadows cast by the old elm trees bordering the drive lengthened and twisted as the sunlight died away and soon it was all black before him.

He slipped his hand beneath Adaline's arm, urging her to stand. "Come on. We need to get inside."

She pushed herself to her feet, slipping on the gravel. He kept his grip on her, hauling her up until she tipped against his chest. He had spent too much of the day aware of her body, and he regretted once more that he had kissed her.

She had been the sensible one, the one to talk through their arrangement. It was all sorted, and he had gone and turned it into something else.

He held her until she seemed steady on her feet.

"Go inside? Is it safe?" she asked, brushing at her skirts as she stepped away from him.

"Safer than it is out here."

She looked up sharply. "Don't tell me you believe in ghosts now."

His grin was sardonic. "Hardly." He let his gaze travel

around them. "But likely everyone in the area knows Grant Hall has been deserted. I shouldn't like to run into someone with less than respectable intentions tonight."

Her lips thinned, and she turned, taking in the area about them as though for the first time. "Do you think someone would try to vandalize the hall?"

"I think someone would try to steal from it," he said and bent to take up the trunk.

She swatted at his hand. "Allow me."

"I can get it."

"Ashfield."

He stopped at the sudden note of admonishment in her voice. She had scolded him on any number of occasions, but now it felt different.

"I can get it."

She put her hands to her hips. "And I should like my husband to stay in fit condition. Who knows what we'll find in there." She pointed at the crumbling hall.

He pursed his lips but set down the trunk. "You're right." He gestured at the other end. "My lady, may I request your assistance?"

She gave a mocking curtsy. "Of course, my lord."

She picked up the opposite end of the trunk, and together they scrambled their way up the front steps and into the vestibule of Grant Hall.

All the light had faded now, and the little he had seen earlier was hidden in shadow.

"Set the trunk down here." He dropped his side and straightened. "And don't move. Not until I have a light. I don't want you injuring yourself."

"Your concern is too kind, my lord," she said with obvious sarcasm.

Earlier he had seen a lantern on a small table just off the vestibule. He only hoped there was means of lighting it as well. With hands outstretched in front of him, he made his way carefully in the direction of the table. He reached it far sooner than he expected, the toe of one boot connecting with the edge of it. The unmistakable sound of disturbed glass rattled close by, and he groped in the dark, catching the globe of the lantern as it teetered on the base.

He fumbled about the table, but the matches were set close by as though someone had lit the lantern and extinguished it in quick succession, leaving everything directly on the table. He struck a match, and the small light was blinding in the near darkness.

Lantern lit, he raised it into the air and turned about, casting light over the space around them. Adaline stood by the trunk, her hands toying with the folds of her skirt.

"You stayed put."

She met his gaze. "You told me to."

"You never listen to me."

There her lips went again, closing into a scolding pout. He'd seen that look a thousand times or more, but never before had he thought of her lips doing other things to him.

He swallowed and looked away. "It doesn't seem to be that bad really. The condition of the hall," he explained when she looked at him. "I think it's mostly aged is all. Dust and cobwebs and neglect. Nothing that can't be fixed." He gestured behind them. "We should try the east wing first. It should be far enough from the damage to find something habitable."

She only nodded and bent to lift the trunk when he came over to collect his end. They were both silent as they turned down the corridor that most likely led to the east wing. He didn't know if it were out of some kind of subconscious agreement to stay quiet and concentrate or if they were both listening for ghosts.

They had gone only a few yards when he realized why the servants had fled.

"I wouldn't wish to stay here knowing what had happened," he said into the darkness ahead of them.

"I agree," Adaline's reply came from somewhere behind him.

Biggins had been correct. From the state of things around him, the staff at Grant Hall had taken advantage of his lordship's absence. The floors were layered in filth, the furnishings not much better. The large windows they passed were thick with grime, and the moonlight hardly cut through them.

"When was the last time your uncle Dobson visited this place?"

He shook his head. "I haven't the faintest idea. As far as I can tell, he may have never come here."

He didn't miss the sharp intake of breath behind him. "To think the servants had the run of the place. No wonder it is in such a state of disrepair."

They reached a bend in the corridor that presumably led to the main hall of the east wing. He raised the lantern, hoping to cast its light as far as it would reach. He was met with only more moldy carpets and cobwebs.

"Shall we, my lady?"

"What a great adventure, my lord," Adaline muttered from behind him. "I had no idea you had such in mind for our honeymoon."

He turned enough to wink at her through the near dark. "You know me, Atwood. I only wish to give you the best."

She opened her mouth for what he was sure would be a scathing retort when a thunderous crash reverberated through the corridor. Adaline squeaked as though an involuntarily release of air had caught in her throat, but he jumped, swinging the lantern about in the direction of the noise so he couldn't see her resulting expression.

The sound had come from the place they had just traveled through, and he held the lantern aloft, moving it back and forth to scan the corridor behind him. Slowly he set down the trunk, indicating for Adaline to do the same with her side. She did, watching him carefully, and he realized his heart pounded in his chest.

He was their only means of protection. Ashfield Riggs, the lowly son of a judge. He slid around the trunk and pulled Adaline against him, keeping the lantern aloft. She grumbled, and he knew some kind of resistance would come next, but he shot her a look, willing her to be silent.

Her lips snapped shut, and she went still against him.

"It's probably some debris falling in the west wing," he whispered after nothing but silence greeted them for several minutes.

Adaline only nodded.

"Let's move quickly." He gestured back to the trunk, and stepping away from him, she picked up her end without further question.

They made their way down the corridor with greater speed now. He didn't pause to study the doors on either side. He only wished to get to the end of the hall and as far away from the damaged west wing as possible. In the weak light, he hadn't been able to assess the damage, but from what little he'd seen, he knew it wasn't good.

After what seemed ages, they finally reached the end of the corridor, but still he didn't stop. He selected the door on the right and opened it. The squeak of the hinges was not unexpected. The hardware likely hadn't been oiled in ages, and the room beyond wasn't a surprise either.

It had been stripped bare, whatever it had been. A drawing

room was his first guess. There was a single sofa in the center of it, a thin rug on the floor, and a trail of destruction around it. A canvas of some long-dead Aylesford was propped against one wall, its frame gone. Probably snatched and sold by a disloyal servant. The scatterings of a fire lay upon the hearth, crumpled newspaper and some kindling. On the wall opposite were three long windows open to the moonlight.

As soon as Ash set down the trunk, he went to the windows and yanked the moth-eaten drapes closed. He backtracked to the door, shutting it firmly. A brass key stuck out from the lock, and he turned it, sending up a silent prayer the thing was still there in the door.

Only then did he turn to find Adaline standing in the center of the room, her eyes scanning ceiling and floor and walls.

"The honeymoon suite, is it?" she whispered.

"Only the best for you."

She dropped her eyes to him, and he was caught by how beautiful she looked in the lantern light. He was noticing that a lot about her lately, about the way she always seemed to fit perfectly into whatever light fell over her. Why had he never noticed that before?

"Well, we should see to making a bed for the night, shan't we?"

"I'm sorry?" he choked, his heart clearly having jumped into his throat at the mention of a bed.

She put her hands to her hips. "We'll need a proper place to sleep, and that sofa will clearly not do." She nodded in the direction of the hearth. "I take it we shouldn't risk a fire."

He frowned, feeling the calming effects her practical sense had on him. "No, probably not. Someone might see the smoke and come investigate. I shouldn't like to meet any of my new tenants in the dark."

"To say nothing of whether or not the chimney is safe to

use. It would be terrible to accidentally burn down what remains of your birthright."

He smiled sweetly. "You're always thinking of me, Atwood."

"I know." She nodded at the door. "Let's see what's in the room opposite. There must be something we can use for bedding. Should you like to try to find the kitchen for food or drink?"

"You shall do none of it. I'll go see what I can find."

She took an almost threatening step toward him. "You'll do no such thing. We can't separate, Ash. What if something should happen to you?"

"The ghosts will not get me."

"I'm not speaking of ghosts. What if you were to fall in the dark?"

He hated her most when she was being reasonable. "Fine. But we go quickly and get back here. I'll feel safe once we're back behind this locked door."

Adaline shook her head. "Really, Ash. I thought you of all people would know ghosts don't need doors."

He took her arm in his. "No, but intruders do."

She stilled against him. "Ash, do you think we must worry about someone…" Her voice trailed off, but in the resulting quiet, his heart pounded again with the reality of their situation.

He studied his wife's face in the warm glow of the lantern and was struck again by the newness of her. Adaline. He had known her his entire life. Had watched her play at dolls once and trod on toes at her first dancing lesson. And now she stood beside him in the dark of this ruined hall and yet he knew with a suddenness that could only mean it was true that he wouldn't wish to stand there with anyone else.

"No," he said firmly. "You mustn't worry. I'm here." He was surprised by how sure he sounded when the insecurity that had crawled along his skin from time immemorial raged with the futility of his words.

Could he keep her safe?

He had no choice. He must.

But then her face changed, softening and opening, and he felt something shift inside of him.

She laid her small hand against his chest, and it was solid and warm and reassuring. "I know, Ash. I've known all along," she said.

And something about her words unsettled him, but she was already moving, opening the door and stepping out into the dark, and he had no choice but to follow her.

Ash stepped in front of her, raising the lantern high in the air. "Stay behind me."

Between her father's absence and her mother's neglect, Adaline had spent a great deal of her childhood alone. It had made her resourceful and independent, which in turn made her easily chafe when another attempted to provide her aid as an adult. But there was something deliciously heart-warming about Ash stepping in front of her as though he might protect her.

Ash had always been the one to ease her tension in social situations, making her laugh and forget where she was. This was a different side of him, and she suddenly realized they were the adults now. The ones in charge, and it was like watching light shift along the floor as the sun moved through the sky. Ash became someone new to her that night, yet he was still her Ash.

They made their way to the end of the corridor, searching crevices for signs of a servants' staircase.

"Do you know if the kitchen was built in this part of the

house?" She was whispering again, although she couldn't say why.

Ash shrugged, the gesture fuzzy in the darkness. "I haven't the faintest idea. I suppose we can only hope it was."

Her foot collided with something sharp, and she pitched forward, trying to catch her gasp of pain between her lips as she stumbled, her hands reaching blindly into the dark. But Ash's hand was on her arm before she could even suck in a breath, and in a flash, she was tucked against his chest again.

This really needed to stop. She hadn't done more than hold his hand in the proper places of a dance in all of twenty odd years, and now she wondered if she could sketch every detail of his physique from the memory of touch.

"There's something on the floor," she mumbled against his jacket before extracting herself enough to examine the damage to her foot. The appendage throbbed, and she wondered just what she had collided with for it had to have some weight to cause such pain.

Keeping one hand on her, Ash bent, lowering the lantern toward the floor. The light illuminated the moldy threadbare carpet and splintering floors beneath before falling upon the unmistakable lines of a trunk. The iron bands wrapped snuggly about it were flecked with what might have been dried mud, and its lid was hanging open, fabric spilling from its insides like a swollen tongue.

She backed up instinctively.

"Tapestries," Ash whispered, reaching out a hand to pull the fabric into the light. His fingers deftly moved through the fabric, stretching it into the light until she could see the fine weavings and intricate patterns.

She peered about them, willing her eyes to take in the corridor they were in, but there was only a faint light at the end where they had first entered, the one that led to the front door and the hall of large windows at the entrance.

"Was someone trying to steal them?" She recalled the crash they had first heard when they entered, but the sound had come from the other end of the house, she was sure of it.

"I think so," Ash replied, standing and lifting the lantern again but this time to hold it behind them to illuminate the corridor they had so recently passed down. "The question is when the thief attempted to do so. Before or after the explosion."

"You don't think the servants were looting the house before the west wing was destroyed, do you?"

She could make out Ash's sardonic expression in the lamplight. "If they were bringing gunpowder into the house, I have no idea what they might have been capable of."

A shiver passed through her, and the darkness seemed to thicken around them. She wasn't sure if he could sense her sudden unease, but he reached out a hand and took hers into his warm grasp. She looked down to where their hands met, surprise and pleasure racing through her. His grip was sure and strong, and her heart raced at the idea he was holding her hand, comforting her, reassuring her.

She had no way of knowing his intentions, but she let his grip on her hand flood her with unexpected warmth anyway.

He turned back to the opposite end of the corridor and guided her around the trunk. Keeping the lantern somewhere about their waists to illuminate the floor in front of them, they soon found a nearly invisible door that led to a staircase. The treads were worn and warped, and Ash placed the hand he still held firmly on the banister, turning on the first step to walk backwards down the stairs, keeping his gaze on her.

"I'm perfectly capable of walking down the stairs, Ash," she said.

"If you break an ankle, Atwood, I am not carrying you out of here."

She pursed her lips at the use of his childhood name for her, but she couldn't help how it bolstered her courage. Some things might change, but there were others that never would.

Picking her way carefully down the steps, placing her foot on what she thought might be the strongest part of the tread, she nearly collided with her husband at the bottom of the staircase as he had abruptly stopped moving.

"Are we in the larder?" His voice held a note of disbelief, but as she was quite squarely pressed against his chest, she couldn't see to answer him. She poked him, and he started, shuffling away from her. "I say," he muttered objectionably.

She peered around them. "I must agree with you, husband. This appears to be a larder."

They were surrounded on two sides by rudimentary wooden shelves. Though the food stuffs on them was sparse, it was quite clearly what might have been called a larder. There were a few loaves of bread, a wheel of cheese, and a basket of apples.

She reached out a hand to test the softness of the bread, but a noise overhead had her freezing.

"Ash." His name was more breath than actual word, and instead of answering, he placed a hand on her outstretched arm.

Together they tilted their heads back to look at the ceiling above them as though they could see through it. For a moment, she thought she had imagined it, but then the noise came again. They swung their gazes to the right as the noise seemed to be coming from that direction on the floor above them. But that wasn't the worst of it. The worst was that it sounded as though the noise was coming closer.

To them.

"Ash, are those footsteps?" she finally managed.

He didn't respond. Instead he grabbed a loaf of bread and shoved it at her. She hardly had time to grasp it before he was handing her a block of cheese. He stuffed apples into the pockets of his jacket and snatched her hand, pulling her back toward the stairs in what was only a matter of seconds since they first heard the footsteps.

He wasn't nearly as careful taking the steps back up, and he all but dragged her along. Her skirts caught at her legs as she was unable to pull them up, her hands occupied between Ash's grip on her and the bread and cheese.

He only slowed long enough to ease the door at the top open and peer out into the hallway. She held her breath as he slipped his head out into the hallway. It seemed like the sensible thing to do, to make herself as quiet as possible.

But then she was forced to suck in a gulp of air when he lurched forward, dragging her with him. She didn't have time to take in the corridor above. He was running, his stride easy and light, eating up the floor, and she stumbled along behind him, only thankful when he swung her back into the room where they'd left the trunk, the door snapping shut behind them.

She heard the lock click, but her heart continued to pound in her ears.

"There are no such things as ghosts, Ash. We mustn't—"

"It's not ghosts, Atwood. It's looters."

She shut her mouth, her heart racing faster. He was looking about them, his gaze swinging wildly around the room. Did he think the looters were in here? She backed up until her shoulders pressed into the wall behind her, and she held the loaf of bread and block of cheese against her chest like body armor.

But then he placed the lantern on the floor and moved to grasp the sofa. Its wooden legs made an unpleasant keening sound as he dragged it in the direction of the door. She set the bread and cheese on top of the trunk and moved to help him, lifting one end of the sofa before he could object.

Together they swung the piece of furniture around and dropped it in front of the door. Next Ash went for the trunk, and she helped him, lifting it atop the couch. They backed up, eyeing their makeshift blockade.

"It's enough," he said after a few moments. "It won't stop them if they truly wish to get in, but it will give us enough warning."

"Enough warning to do what?"

He shrugged and ran a hand through his hair. "We'll figure that out if it comes to it."

It was hardly reassuring, but then she'd never been threatened by looters before, and she figured Ash hadn't either. Perhaps it was a fair assessment.

She plucked the bread and cheese from the top of the trunk and looked about the floor. There wasn't much left in the room, and she was certain she would not venture back out into the hallway that night to search for something suitable for a bed. They would simply need to make do.

An old drape lay crumpled on the floor, visible now that they had moved the sofa. She went to it, picking up a single corner and dragging it toward the wall. It spread out on the floor behind her. Along the opposite wall were a couple of cushions that appeared as though they had come from a set of chairs that were no longer in the room. She retrieved those as well and set them against the wall.

Cradling the bread and cheese in her elbow, she went back to the trunk. Working the latches loose with one hand, she popped the lid free and rummaged inside. She extracted several freshly laundered handkerchiefs and a shawl.

The handkerchiefs she spread on the unfolded drape, placing their meager supper atop them. She wrapped herself in the shawl before squatting down on the drape.

"Your dinner, my lord," she said, spreading her hands extensively over the picnic she had created.

The entire time she had bustled about the room, Ash had stood facing the door. She could tell he had been listening for the looters. If they had heard the footsteps in the larder, they must have been close, but the house had been silent since they'd returned above stairs. She let the quiet lull her into a false sense of safety.

She knew precisely how dangerous their circumstances were. They were alone, at night, in a stately home that had obviously been looted and was likely still being looted. Even if they should have no desire to stop the thieves, it didn't mean the same thieves understood that and would prevent them from causing harm.

Ash turned now at her announcement of dinner, and a slow smile spread over his face. She started though at the first sight of him. His expression had been stern, almost worried. Perhaps the odd angles of the lantern light had made him appear grimmer than she had imagined, but it was an expression she had never seen on his face before, and it saddened her.

She patted the floor next to her. "Sup with me, my lord."

He dropped to the floor without a word and reached for the bread. It wasn't terribly stale, and the cheese held no mold. The apples were fine as well, and they ate in silence for several seconds.

"I wish we had taken time to find a bottle of something," Ash said minutes later.

He'd hardly eaten anything and mostly crumbled a piece of the bread between his fingers, his eyes straying to the door regularly.

"Should you like to go back? I'm sure we could find their wine cellar."

He laughed, the sound soft and weak. "I think perhaps it would be wiser to forgo drink this evening, my lady."

She tried to smile, but he had already returned his gaze to

the door. She brushed the last of the crumbs from her hands and looked about them.

"I suppose this shall be our bed for the night as well." She drew her shawl more tightly about her. She still wore her traveling gown, but she had no desire to be caught in a nightrail by any intruders.

She pulled the cushion from the wall and plopped it on the floor. Dust rose up, mottled in the weak lamplight, but the cushion must do for her pillow. Ash, however, didn't lie down. He pushed himself back against the wall, crossing his arms over his chest as if to hold in warmth.

"What are you doing?" she asked.

"Keeping watch." His eyes never strayed from the door as he spoke.

She thought for a moment, and then propped the cushion back up against the wall, sliding across the floor until she once more leaned against it. She crossed her arms over her chest as Ash had done.

He eyed her, and it was rather pleasant to have his gaze on something other than the door.

"If you're going to stay up to keep watch, so am I."

"No, you're not."

She turned her head, her hair crackling against the wall behind her. "You would refuse me this, Ash?" She gave her voice as much primness as possible, and he subsided against the wall.

"I didn't know they taught ladies how to keep watch. I thought it was only instructed to the boys."

She shook her head. "Oh no, all the best governesses instruct their wards on methods of subterfuge and stealth."

Ash laughed softly, and she felt the tension in her shoulders ease by the smallest degree.

She looked about them, at the barren room, the crack of moonlight that drifted over the sparse space from the place where the drapes didn't quite meet. The toes of her boots poked out from the end of her skirts, and she pressed her toes together and apart.

"Look at us, Ash. We're sitting in an old country hall in the middle of the night, barricaded against intruders." She turned to look at him. "Did you ever think we'd be in such a state?"

He scrubbed his face with both hands. "That's hardly the most interesting part, Atwood."

She picked up her head to better look at him. "What is it then?"

Finally he met her gaze, and it pained her to see how tired he was. "It's that we're married."

His words cut deeply, and she looked away on the pretense of adjusting her braid along that side of her face.

"Yes, it is rather strange, isn't it?" she whispered, but he had already turned back to the door.

There had been something about his proximity in the last twenty-four hours that had muddled her mind, fogging the truth, and she had forgotten the arrangement they had, daring to wish things were different.

She didn't say anything else, and perhaps it was the food, heavy in her stomach, or the stress of the day, but she found her eyes drifting shut. She forced them open once, but the second time was too much for her.

But she lingered there, with her eyes closed, somewhere between sleep and awake for several more moments, long enough that she thought Ash might have reached for her, drawing her head against his shoulder and tucking her shawl more tightly around her.

But then, she might just have been dreaming.

CHAPTER 9

*I*t was likely the pain in his neck that finally woke him.

He blinked, several seconds passing before he recalled where he was. When recollection dawned, he sat up with a jerk, hissing as the pain in his neck amplified.

"Oh," Adaline whispered from what seemed like a great distance. "Don't move so quickly. You didn't appear to be sleeping in a comfortable position."

With a hand on his neck, massaging the pain away, he forced his eyes open and wished he hadn't. Adaline stood across the room, her hands still on the drapes she had likely just parted. Sunshine poured directly upon her, illuminating her in a way that struck of a domesticity he had never expected to feel.

He had just awoken in the same room as his wife.

They had been married for more than a fortnight, and it had never occurred to him to share her bed. He had been too consumed by his own humiliation, and the end of the infatuation it had marked, and the weight of responsibility that had come with the title. He hadn't considered this. The way

Adaline would look upon first waking, the way the saturated sun of an early morning would make her glow.

He moved the hand from his neck to his chest where a painful knot had begun to grow.

"Are you well?" The words lodged in the sticky dryness of his mouth, and he swallowed hard.

Her smile was almost instantaneous. "Oh, quite well." Her expression dimmed as he tried to sit up. "I'm sorry if the same cannot be said of you. I think you might have fallen asleep while taking watch."

He scrubbed his face with both hands, remembering how she had fallen asleep beside him, her head falling to his shoulder. He hadn't thought about taking her into his arms, about how natural it had felt, how comforting it was to have her warm weight against him in the dark of the night.

He pushed to his feet, surveying their barricade. It hadn't moved in the slightest and for that he was reassured.

"I don't think anyone tried to invade." Adaline's voice was closer now, and he turned to find her standing beside him, her fingers working through her hair, re-braiding the strands at her shoulder.

"How long have you been awake?"

She finished her braid, tying it off with a strip of ribbon. "Only a few minutes before you. I should very much like to leave this room, however. It's been quite some time since I've been able to attend to necessities." She widened her eyes to indicate the urgency of the matter.

At the tense expression on her face, he became aware of his own pressing needs.

"Right," he said and moved to take the trunk down.

She was beside him in a moment, reaching for one end of the trunk. She may have been the daughter of an earl and a respected wallflower of the *ton*, but she was proving far more useful at things other than pouring tea and dancing a quadrille. He wondered why he never expected anything less of her.

When he finally took the knob of the door in his hand and turned it, he felt his need to get out of the room war with a sense of self-preservation.

He turned to Adaline who hovered at his shoulder. "And you haven't heard anything this morning?"

He could hear the footsteps from the night before all too clearly. While the staff and village folk might be frightened of ghosts, it was the corporeal threats with which Ash was concerned.

She shook her head. "It's been quiet."

He drew a breath and opened the door. He wasn't sure what he was expecting, but the silence and sunshine that met them in the corridor beyond was disconcerting. The previous night had been filled with shadows and cobwebs and unseen obstacles. But in the light of the morning, he could see there was nothing more than a neglected hallway to greet them.

The carpet was in fact worn and mildewed, the corners hung with cobwebs, and every available surface sported a layer of dust. But it was not truly as intimidating as it had seemed in the dark.

He stepped out, his feet squishing into the softness of the floor, and he wondered for the first time at the integrity of the floorboards. Surely the estate couldn't have been that neglected.

When Adaline touched his elbow, he started, swinging his head back to look at her, but her gaze was angled away from him, down the corridor toward the servants' stairs they had used the night before.

"Ash," she breathed, his name heavy with conclusion.

He followed the line of her gaze and found the hall empty. "What is it?"

But even as the words left his lips, the pieces of the night before came together with the reality before him. The trunk of tapestries Adaline had collided with the night before was gone. The hallway lay empty and bare before them.

"The trunk," she whispered.

He didn't answer. He only took her hand in his and pulled her in the direction of the front door. A sudden urge to get out of there gripped him, and he rushed them along only to stop, arrested at the sight that greeted them in the vestibule.

The front door was gone entirely.

Adaline made a sound behind him, and her fingers twitched in his hand.

"A ghost didn't do that," she said.

"No, it didn't," he replied and pulled her the rest of the way outside.

The sunshine struck him full in the face, and he was forced to squint, holding up a hand to shield his eyes from the worst of it.

Adaline released his hand to pick up her skirts, already heading for the line of trees opposite the drive. "I'll just be a moment," she called back.

"Don't go far," he called after her, and he felt like a worrying nanny, which was entirely unlike him when he thought of Adaline.

He watched her disappear through the trees before finding a hedgerow to take care of his own business. Wandering back toward the drive, he became aware of a rustling noise behind him, and he turned, his body braced for what he might find. For *whom* he might find.

But instead his eyes met a sight more welcome than he could have imagined. When Adaline burst through the trees along the drive minutes later, he called to her.

"Atwood!" He cupped the flowing water in his hands and held it up like a sacrificial offering. "Grant Hall sports its own brook and waterfall apparently," he said, gesturing to the small waterfall that wound its way through a cornucopia of rocks, twisting east before it met the drive.

He could almost hear her sigh from this distance as she picked up her skirts and ran to him.

"Heaven," she moaned after dunking her hands in the fresh cool water. She proceeded to scoop up the water, splashing it on her face and neck.

It dripped along her neck, droplets falling along the décolletage of her dress. He froze, his own hands in the water.

Desire ripped through him, fast and fierce, until it choked him. He knew now what it felt like to hold her, to run his hands over her every curve. He knew the taste of her, the sounds she made when aroused. In that moment by the brook, the morning sun falling all around her, it all came to a head, and passion strangled him.

He must have made a sound because she looked up, her eyelashes damp with the water she'd splashed on her face, amplifying her already large brown eyes.

He shot to his feet. "I'd like to assess the west wing in the daylight."

"Right, of course," she said plainly as though completely unaffected by all the intimacies of the past twenty-four hours.

He tramped away across the drive and beyond, not trusting himself to look back to see if she followed him.

Something had changed. He wasn't sure when, but he suspected it had been sometime before they had boarded the train yesterday or else why would he have kissed her? Why would that have even been a thought in his mind?

His troubling thoughts were interrupted by the effort it took to cross the front lawn. It was overgrown and riddled with cloying weeds. Had Grant Hall even employed a gardener recently? He doubted it. For if there was a gardener in residence, he was sorely neglecting his duties.

A thicket of young trees sprang up in what he presumed was the middle of the front park, clearly evidence of neglect, and he pushed through them, only to stop suddenly on the other side, arrested by the sight that greeted him.

Adaline pushed through the trees seconds later, falling into him as she sprang free of the clutches of the small trees. She too stopped, her hands braced on his shoulder to hold herself up.

"Oh," she breathed, and he felt the weight of the word like a cannonball to his stomach.

The west wing was completely destroyed.

He had never seen it before, but now it was nothing more than a pile of granite before him.

"Oh Ash, I'm so sorry."

He shook his head at Adaline's apology. "You needn't be. It isn't as though I knew this place."

She released his shoulder and stepped forward, holding out her hands to encompass the damage. "But this is your heritage. Even if you didn't know it, you can still mourn its loss."

The depth of her words washed over him, and he studied her, her face pensive as she took in the destruction.

Change and responsibility swirled all around him as he stood on the lawn of Grant Hall that morning, and yet the only thing that he could think was how long had Adaline been standing next to him and he had never really seen her?

He swallowed, his humiliation growing until he thought it might suffocate him.

He was saved from his own debilitating thoughts by a crash in the trees beside them. He leapt forward even before the sound connected with reason, and he pulled Adaline behind him, readying himself for whatever might appear.

"Biggins?" he muttered seconds later as the land steward tumbled through the trees.

"My lord, I must beg your forgiveness. I only met Howard in the village this morning, and he told me he had left you here last evening. I cannot begin to apologize for—"

Ash held up a hand. "No apologies are necessary, Biggins."

The land steward pulled his felt hat from his head, worrying it between his hands as he had done that day in Ash's study. Could it have only been two days ago?

Ash shook the mental cobwebs from his mind, stepping forward to stand next to the man. He gestured back at the ruins of the west wing. "I should like an explanation for this, Biggins," he said and turned his gaze to the rest of the hall. "And the state of the place in general."

Biggins's lips thinned. "Yes, my lord. I'm afraid it is not an agreeable situation."

"Not at all," Ash said. "And we shall speak of it over some breakfast. Surely there's a place for us to find food and proper lodging in the village?"

Biggins plopped his hat firmly back on his head. "Yes, of course, my lord. I shall take you into the village directly." He pointed at the trees behind him. "I brought my cart and horse. I wasn't sure how much luggage you would have." His eyes drifted in the direction of Adaline.

She was smiling, the sight open and beautiful, and Ash was struck again by the newness of his lifelong friend.

"Biggins, this is my wife, Lady Aylesford."

Biggins made a small bow. "My lady."

Adaline returned the greeting with a curtsy. "I should very much enjoy a cup of tea, Mr. Biggins," she said, her smile stronger, her tone inviting, and it was as though her simple words had the power to put the man at ease.

His fingers uncurled at his side, and a small smile dared

to appear at the corners of his lips. "Most definitely, my lady. If you'll follow me."

The man tramped back through the trees, and Adaline stepped forward and offered him her arm, a playful glint in her eye.

"I shouldn't wish for you to trip in front of the servants," she whispered, a mocking gleam in her eye.

And once more she was the childhood friend he remembered, and he wondered how he could have let himself get carried away. This was only Adaline.

But as she slipped through the trees in the wake of the land steward, he couldn't help but notice how his eyes dipped, taking in her every curve silhouetted by the bright sun, accentuated as she moved lithely through the undergrowth.

He had never noticed that about his childhood friend. He had never noticed that at some point she had become a woman.

He tugged at his crumpled cravat and plunged into the trees behind her.

* * *

WHEN SHE HAD PICTURED her punishment, she had thought it would be a singular thing. Enduring the wedding and then she would be finished. But it wasn't to be like that. She was destined to live plagued by a thousand tiny cuts, each one almost healed before the next one came, keeping her life even as she died a little each time.

Ash's sore neck was her fault. She had woken in his arms, a sensation she never thought she would experience, one that was too much to bear knowing he didn't wish her there, and she had fled, leaving him to fall awkwardly against the wall as she slipped out from his embrace.

She'd scrambled across the floor, her palms slipping on the moth-eaten drapery that had been their bed. When she had put a safe distance between them, she'd drawn her knees to her chest, wrapping her arms about them as if she could physically hold herself together. Her heart thudded so hard it was as if she could feel its beat against her knees.

She wasn't sure how long she sat there, willing her heart to slow, her breath to calm, and most of all her mind to forget. Forget what it felt like to have his arms around her, so tightly, as if he cared.

That wasn't fair. Ash did care. It was only…

She wished he cared in a different way, and she couldn't fault him for her own false expectations.

But now as they drew to a stop in front of The Pigeon and Crow, an establishment in what she assumed was the nearest village to Grant Hall, she couldn't help but wonder if she had been too quick in her judgments because there was a moment that morning by the brook when she had seen something else in Ash's eyes.

Desire.

It had been brief and startling, so startling she'd nearly swallowed her tongue, but she had seen that look on Ash's face a thousand times over. Every time he saw Lady Valerie.

But that morning, the look had been directed at her.

She couldn't let herself think of it, indulge in the fantasy of it. For if she did, she would spend her whole life grasping at a reality that was no more substantial than the wisps of clouds on a summer day. That would be a torture even she couldn't bear.

Mr. Biggins handed the reins to a young boy who had run from The Pigeon and Crow the moment they pulled in front of it, and Ash hopped down, reaching up for her. He let go of her as soon as her feet touched the ground, and she knew it was wise to forgo any further daydreaming. She knew what it was between them for she had heard proof of it that night in the conservatory.

Mr. Biggins was instructing the boy to look after the horses as another pair of young men emerged and took hold of their trunk from the back of the cart.

She had found her bonnet in the drive when they had returned with Mr. Biggins, and she'd donned it for propriety's sake but hadn't bothered to tie it. She needed a bath, a good scrubbing, some proper food, and a strong cup of tea. Then she would have her senses restored, and this nonsense of seeing desire where there was none would pass.

It had to.

"I took the liberty of reserving a room for you, my lord," Biggins said as he led them through the door of the inn.

The red paint of the door was cracked and peeling, the trim hanging loose on one side, but inside, she discovered a pub with gleaming scrubbed tables and a cozy fire that chased away the last of the morning chill.

A tall man stood hunched over the bar, idly turning the pages of a newspaper. He looked up at their entrance.

"Oh, good day, Mr. Biggins. You've brought us guests, I see." The man's face was open and bright where it emerged above layers of beard, and she felt an instant ease to a tension she hadn't realized she'd been carrying.

But it made sense for her to be wary. They were, after all, the new lord and lady at the manor up the hill from the village. She glanced at Ash as he moved forward, hand extended.

"I hope you're neither pigeon nor crow, my good man," he said by way of greeting, and she couldn't help a small smile. Even after the night they had endured, Ash was still his typical, jovial self.

Except the thought didn't sit squarely with her any

longer, and she felt a sharp pain of fear that something else was slipping away from her.

Ash had changed without changing. That was the problem. She had seen a different side to him was all, but it was enough to have her fear more change when already so much had happened.

It was to be expected, of course. She realized that now. As the son of a judge, his responsibilities had been less. He had always kept active in society, but being a marquess was more than just social necessities, and the demands of the title had given an opportunity Ash had never had before.

One in which he could take charge, accept the leadership that had fallen upon him.

And he'd done it. She could see that clearly in the way he had protected her last night. The way he stepped in front of Biggins just now. Leadership came so easily to him, but she doubted if he even noticed it.

They had been young when Ash's father had died, and she had only seen a few of his father's scoldings, but it was enough to recall with stunning clarity the harsh words the man had thrown down at his son's feet. She wondered now if Ash would see this difference for himself and perhaps maybe finally vanquish the last of his father's words from his memory.

It would be a challenge, she knew, for didn't she still see her sister's face the morning of their mother's funeral? The stark look of despair and fear, the look of someone who suddenly didn't know what to make of themselves. Amelia had been lost without the reprimands of their mother guiding her every move, and in the wake her mother had left, Adaline had realized her mistake.

She swallowed it down now. There was nothing more to be done. She needed a hot bath and some food, and then she would see to the rest of it.

135

Ash had made the introductions, and she touched his elbow to gain his attention.

"I should like a hot bath first," she said, keeping her tone low as the barman, a Mr. Hedgeworth she had learned, spoke to Biggins about how the rainfall that spring had forced the creek to overflow its banks by the schoolhouse.

Ash looked behind her, and she turned to find a young woman standing there, her smile soft and beckoning.

"Your ladyship," she said with a small curtsy. "The name's Elsbeth. I'll take you up to your room, ma'am. I can't imagine what you've been through last night," she added with a small shake of her head. "I assure you the folks in these parts are right fine gentlefolk if they are sometimes carried away by local legend."

She was a pretty girl with freckles dotting her pale skin and warm brown eyes. Adaline liked her immediately.

"I believe you speak the truth, Elsbeth." She squeezed Ash's arm. "I'll be back down as soon as I can."

"Take your time," her husband said. "I should like to speak with Biggins about our visitors last night."

She stilled. "Do you think the looting is a recurring problem?"

His features tensed. "If it is, I should like to know the cause of it."

She nodded and turned back to the young woman. Elsbeth took her through a low archway that led into a crooked staircase. The place was scrubbed clean if worn, and a citrus scent lingered in the air. Adaline felt the tension of the past few hours slip away, and for just a moment, everything didn't seem quite so daunting.

Her mind flashed back to the crumpled hall, the west wing entirely obliterated until it was nothing more than a pile of rubble. How much gunpowder would it have taken to cause such destruction? And why was it in the hall in the first place?

Climbing the stairs behind the young woman, she recalled what Ash had said about the possible thieves they had heard the previous night.

"Excuse me, Elsbeth," she said, and the girl stopped on the landing of the next floor, turning a curious gaze to her. "I'm not familiar with Dartmoor, let alone this village. Can you explain to me what it is families do in this area?"

Elsbeth's eyes widened. "Of course, ma'am. I hadn't realized. What with the hall being the marquess's seat I was sure he might have told you of it."

Adaline shook her head, following the woman down the hall to the door nearly at the end of it. She stepped inside and gestured for Adaline to follow. The room was small but surprisingly well appointed with a lush bed covered in linens that still smelled like the sunshine they had likely been dried in. Her entire body groaned at the sight of it, but she couldn't give in to the pleasure of a nap on a soft surface just yet.

"I'm afraid the marquess has only newly acquired the title and is as unfamiliar as I am."

The girl smiled. "Of course, my lady. Well, you've found yourself in Bottlesford, the nearest village to the hall to the west. The only other place you might find folks in is Preston to the east, but it's more of a hamlet I'm afraid. Not many people live there now."

"Oh?" Adaline tried not to sound too enthusiastic about this bit of information, but perhaps it would explain the thieving.

Elsbeth moved to the windows at the back of the room and adjusted the curtains for privacy. Adaline took the time to look about, noting the bath that had been set in the corner, steam softly rising from it. Her heart leapt at the sight.

"Most of the miners have moved on now. The ones that traded in tin that is."

"Tin mining?" Adaline hadn't thought of such out here on the moor. When she had stepped from the train the previous day, she had seen nothing but rolling green for miles. Tin had never entered her mind.

"Oh, yes. Tin mining is how the families of the moor have made their living for generations, but I fear change is coming."

The girl's words rattled Adaline more than she could possibly know.

"Why have the miners left?"

Elsbeth fluffed a stack of towels left on the table by the bath. "The mines are all used up here. There's more of the stuff to be found in the colonies in the east. More and easier to find." She shrugged. "It's just not as profitable to stay here." The young woman's face darkened slightly. "I'm afraid the lack of employment has caused some of the younger men to turn to deceitful practices to feed their families."

"I see," Adaline murmured, rubbing her arms as a sudden chill passed through her body.

She was overwrought, tired, and hungry. Her emotions were getting the best of her. A hot bath and a strong cup of tea would restore her, and she could relay what she had learned from the young girl to Ash.

Elsbeth moved to the door. "If there's anything else you'll need…"

Her voice trailed off as Adaline plucked her bonnet from her head and tossed it on the bed. She looked at it there, so innocent and domestic. Turning about, she straightened her shoulders.

"Do you happen to know the name of the housekeeper or butler up at the hall? It seems the servants have deserted the place, which I can't fault them for. It's in a terrible state. It's only I should like to speak with someone on the staff who might have been in charge."

Elsbeth nodded, her smile brightening. "Yes, of course, I shall send for the housekeeper immediately."

"You know her then?" Adaline felt the weight on her shoulders lift for the first time since they'd stepped onto the empty train platform yesterday.

"Of course," Elsbeth said with a nod. "She's me mum."

CHAPTER 10

*A*sh sipped his tea and watched Biggins slip out the main door into the bustle that had sprung up along the main thoroughfare of the village while they had been talking.

He set down his teacup and stabbed the remaining sausage on his plate with more vigor than it likely called for, but it felt good all the same.

"Is it worse than I imagined then?"

He looked up and wished he hadn't. He nearly swallowed the sausage whole.

Adaline, dressed in a fresh frock that dipped in at the waist, accentuating bits of her he'd never even noticed before —*How had he not noticed?*—stood in front of him.

His eyes strayed to the fine bones of her collar, the sweep of her pale neck to the delicate line of her jaw, and like it were happening again, he pictured her as she'd been that morning at the brook, droplets of water running down that warm expanse of skin, lower, into the lace that fringed the edge of her bodice.

Why had he kissed her on the train? It was as though that

simple act had broken down a dam he hadn't known existed, and now he was drowning in a passion he had unwittingly unleashed.

He nearly choked on the sausage again and finally forced his eyes away.

"Oh dear," Adaline murmured, taking the seat across from him. "Precisely how terrible is it?"

She had no idea.

He took another sip of his tea, hoping he still held the power of speech. "Mr. Biggins informed me the economic situation on the moor is changing. Some young men are finding it difficult to engage in trade here, which lends an appealing light to more unsavory but lucrative activities."

"Such as theft?"

"I'm afraid so." Her hair was still damp from her bath, and he regarded the braid over her shoulder with intrepid wariness. Why was he imagining unraveling it? Running his fingers through the long locks? Pulling her head— "It's apparently become common practice for young men to steal remnants at the gunpowder factories and sell them off to new miners who don't know better."

She stilled, her hand in midmotion over her plate. "Is that why the gunpowder was in the hall?"

"It's what Biggins assumes must have happened. There's no way of proving it."

She dropped her hand. "So what shall you do now?"

"It's not the cause of the explosion that concerns me. It's why these young men have turned to crime to support their families. It seems the Aylesford estate's primary revenue comes from tin mining, but the discovery of tin in some of the colonies have priced out what is mined here, even with the expense of shipping it."

She nodded, reaching for the pot of honey on the table as she sifted through what Hedgeworth had brought him for breakfast. There were piles of scones, still warm from the oven, platters of eggs and sausages, far too much for two people and all of a decidedly remarkable quality for a posting inn.

"Elsbeth said as much."

"Elsbeth?"

"The young woman who showed me our room." She paused as if remembering something and patted her hands about her person as if searching for something.

He watched her hands travel over her torso for just a second and looked quickly away.

"Ah, here." She handed him a key on a piece of twine. "Our room is at the end of the hall on the left. I've asked them to send up a fresh bath." She met his gaze directly, her lips thinning painfully. "I think it would be best if we never speak of the state I was in after last night nor the consequences to the bathwater from my toilette."

He laughed, the sound sudden and unexpected. It died away more quickly as he was overcome by the realness of that moment. Adaline sitting across from him, sniffing pots of marmalade as if deciding which one she'd like best, making light of the terrible situation from the previous night. They had been in danger of being discovered by looters, abandoned at a decrepit, foreign, and likely unsafe estate in the dark of night, and spent that same night sleeping on a hard dirty floor. And yet she joked.

Something shifted, and it was as though a leg of his chair had snapped off. He gripped the table as if it would help right the world about him, but he knew with uncomfortable clarity that things would not go back to how they'd been.

He was glad Adaline was there, and he was even more glad she was his wife.

The thought sliced through him, frightening in its impossibility and scary in what it may mean.

He had never thought to be happy in his marriage, not after the one woman with whom he had been so infatuated had refused him. He had thought that would be the end of any possible happiness for him, and yet here he was. Laughing in the most absurd situation.

"I'm glad you're here," he heard himself say before he realized he was going to speak.

She looked up from her perusal of the platter of scones, her eyes wide, but the look of surprise melted quickly into a smile. "I'm glad as well. I told you we'd make good partners."

Partners.

If they were only partners, he wouldn't be feeling the things he did about her, would he? He clasped his teacup in both hands, hoping he didn't shatter the pottery. She watched him, and he realized she expected an answer from him, but he knew he couldn't speak. Not now. He would say something, something dangerously close to the truth, and everything would be different between them, and he was suddenly scared to lose this.

His best friend.

It twisted in his chest, the sudden realization of what he had to lose if he acted on these unexpected feelings. Adaline had married him in his darkest moment. She hadn't known it, but he had, and he would never forget it.

He was saved from having to say anything when Hedgeworth approached, steaming teapot in hand.

"Your ladyship. A fresh pot of tea." The man had a soft, deep voice and tended to round his consonants, so his voice was almost melodic and soothing.

Adaline lit up at the man's approach. "Mr. Hedgeworth, congratulations! I hear your new son is shaping up to be a fine young lad."

The barman's face turned bright pink. Ash blinked, taking in the sudden change to the tall, burly man's features.

He set down the teapot, avoiding Adaline's eager gaze. "Oh he is, your ladyship. He rolled over just yesterday." He scraped his feet against the scuffed floorboards and fingered the edge of the table nervously. "He's not even six months old, he is." Finally he looked up, a bright smile appearing through his copious beard.

"That's tremendous," Adaline said, and Ash knew she meant it.

She had a way of speaking that allowed one to hear the genuineness in her voice, and he watched as Hedgeworth rocked back on his heels, obviously feeling the veracity of her statement.

"It is at that." He tapped the table one more time. "Should you need anything else, don't be afraid to just holler." He gave a funny, nervous salute and walked away.

Ash blinked at his wife as she picked up the teapot and filled a cup. She gestured. "Would you like a fresh cup?"

"How do you know he has a son and a newborn one at that?"

She set down the teapot. "Elsbeth."

"Elsbeth?"

She frowned. "The young woman who took me to our rooms."

"This Elsbeth seems to be a font of wisdom."

Adaline began filling her plate with eggs and sausages. "I think her skill at collecting information is simply happenstance." She looked up. "A woman who runs an inn? She's in a position to gather all kinds of gossip and rumors."

"Runs an inn?" He looked to the archway where he'd last seen the young woman. "She can't be more than a girl."

"I thought the same, but as it happens, she's older than me. Already has three children." She nodded discreetly in the direction of the bar. "She's married to Mr. Hedgeworth." She said this last bit softly so only he would hear.

"She's married to Hedgeworth?" he hissed, leaning across the table.

"Shh," Adaline reprimanded, looking in the direction of the bar, but Hedgeworth was occupied with an older gentleman who had been sitting there for some time. "Yes, they have a delightful little family, so I hear. This inn has been in Mr. Hedgeworth's family for three generations." She took a bite of eggs, and he saw the moment she realized how good the food was, her eyes widening and her head nodding slightly in delight.

"You went to take a bath, and you've uncovered the entire inner workings of a Dartmoor village."

She looked up. "Something like that. Now we should speak of Grant Hall."

He sat back in his chair. "Yes, I plan to return there as soon as I've finished washing and changing."

Her fork clattered to her plate. "You can't think of going back there. It isn't safe."

"It is perfectly safe. Biggins has gone to find me a horse, so I am better able to travel back and forth from the village, but he's also summoning the local builder. He should have knowledge on whether or not the rest of the house is safe. I should like to begin repairs immediately anyway. I will need to understand the breadth of the job."

"Then I am going with you."

"No, you're not."

She set down her fork more calmly this time. "Yes, I am. We're partners, remember?"

He did not wish to revisit that conversation. "This is not a matter in which you must involve yourself."

She raised a single eyebrow, and he regretted speaking any words at all.

"How familiar are you with inventorying a manor house, my lord?"

"What are you talking about?"

She patted her mouth with the linen napkin by her plate. "Do you recall the frameless portrait we found in that room last night? Surely there must have been a frame on it at one point. Such information will be included in the inventories of the household. As lady of the house, it is my duty to review them and update the manifests."

"You're joking."

Her features tightened, her eyes rounding. "I am not."

He leaned forward again. "You're going to return to that decrepit place to *inventory* a few paintings? It isn't safe."

She sat back, her lips parting in shock, and he knew his mistake almost at once.

"It isn't safe? I just said the same to you, and you dismissed my concerns."

"It isn't safe for you," he clarified and wished he hadn't.

Adaline set aside her napkin so carefully he couldn't help but watch it, knowing she would use such exactness in the reprimand he very obviously deserved.

"It isn't safe for me, but it is safe for you, is that what you're attempting to say, my lord?"

"No." He shot the word out, the muscles at his neck tightening as he tried to extricate himself from this conversation. "What I was saying is—"

"You were saying that we shall return to Grant Hall this afternoon together to begin work on our mutually important duties. Isn't that right?"

He firmed his lips, but he knew this battle was lost. "Yes, that's exactly what I was saying," he muttered.

"Good. Now go take a bath. You look awful."

He tugged on the lapels of his jacket. "Excuse me. I believe I am setting a new style trend. I call it eau du dust."

She smiled, but he could tell she was attempting not to laugh. "I'm afraid it shall never catch on."

He dropped his hands. "Pity."

They sat there, frozen in the moment, and something pressed at his lips, something he wished to say, but he couldn't find the courage to do so.

Before he could say anything at all, the young woman he had seen earlier approached their table.

"Begging your pardon." She smiled in greeting before looking to Adaline. "She's here, ma'am."

Adaline lit up again as she had at Hedgeworth, and Ash wondered what he'd need do to make her look so eager. He choked and tried to cover it by taking a sip of his tea.

"Splendid," Adaline said. "Please bring her here and bring a fresh teacup. I should like to have a nice chat with her."

Mrs. Hedgeworth nodded. "Yes, of course, my lady," she said and slipped away.

"Who are you having a nice chat with?" Ash said, tossing down his napkin and gaining his feet. Every muscle pulled as he stood, and the idea of a hot bath called to him.

"Mrs. Hutchinson. She's the housekeeper at the hall."

"You've already found the housekeeper." It wasn't a question, but he still filled his words with muted surprise.

Adaline nodded. "She's Elsbeth's mother."

"Of course she is," he muttered and went to find his bath.

* * *

SHE WAS FAIRLY certain when she'd found him at breakfast there was a moment when he first saw her that he wished to have her for his second breakfast.

The heat of desire in his eyes was unmistakable. She'd seen that look there before, but it had never been directed at her, and now that it was, it was like a blow directly to her heart.

Because she didn't trust it.

She had been there that night in the conservatory, had seen the absence of life on his face as Lady Valerie had walked away, and now Adaline couldn't bring herself to believe Ash might finally have feelings for her that were far from the quiet tones of friendship.

How she had managed to take her seat and calmly peruse the breakfast offerings, she couldn't be sure.

She had directed the conversation to safer topics as quickly as possible after that, and soon she had lost herself in the comfort of banal things such as house inventories. It still had seemed to take forever for Elsbeth to fetch her mother, although the woman was supposedly staying in the inn now that Grant Hall was seemingly unlivable.

Adaline wasn't sure what she had been expecting, but Mrs. Hutchinson had proven a positive note in an otherwise trying situation. The woman looked as though she was not past fifty, but by Elsbeth's recollections, the housekeeper must be closer to sixty although her unlined skin and dark hair showed hardly any traces of time. It appeared the Hutchinson women aged gracefully.

Mrs. Hutchinson had taken the post at Grant Hall after her husband, a land agent of a neighboring estate, had passed away. She had wished to be closer to her daughter, and the hall had provided an excellent opportunity. The trouble had started soon after that, the housekeeper explained, but they were unable to get into the depth of the situation before Mr. Biggins returned. Mrs. Hutchinson seemed to know the man with a certain familiarity, and Adaline watched them as they greeted each other, her interest piqued.

"Mrs. Hutchinson," Mr. Biggins said with a smart bow. "I trust you are comfortable here at the inn. You appear to be recuperating."

Mrs. Hutchinson's smile was timid, and color appeared in her cheeks, but she didn't speak.

"Recuperating?" Adaline turned concerned eyes on the housekeeper. "You weren't hurt in the blast at the hall, were you?"

The woman waved her hands as if to brush off the concern. "It's nothing as terrible as it sounds. I was in the kitchen when it happened. It was more of a shock than anything."

Adaline could recall the strange larder they had found themselves in. They hadn't ventured farther, but the state of the larder had been suggestive enough as to the state of the rest of the kitchen.

"I had to carry her out of there, your ladyship," Mr. Biggins said, plucking his felt hat from his hands and holding it pensively between them. "It was an awful thing."

Mrs. Hutchinson's hands fluttered before moving to tuck a piece of hair back into her chignon. "It's really nothing—"

Adaline reached across the table and snatched one of Mrs. Hutchinson's wavering hands into her own. "Mrs. Hutchinson, if you should not wish to return to the hall, I will make sure you are handsomely compensated. I shouldn't wish for you—"

Warmth came immediately to the housekeeper's features. "Oh, it's nothing like that at all, your ladyship. I assure you. It was just a bit of a surprise as I'm sure you can imagine."

Adaline's eyes drifted between the housekeeper and the land steward, ideas bouncing about in her head. She could imagine many things really, but she was stopped from speaking of any of them as Ash came bounding down the stairs, his hair still wet from the bath.

She shivered at the sight of him, nearly upending her teacup in her immediate and involuntary response to seeing him fresh and clean and still damp from his toilette. He'd even taken the time to shave, and for a moment, she felt a pang of loss at the stubble that had darkened his jaw, lending him a rakish appearance she hadn't known she'd find delectable.

"Your lordship." Biggins gave a small bow. "I've found you a horse, and the builder says he can meet us there. I'd be happy to accompany you up to the hall as soon as you wish."

Adaline stood. "Mrs. Hutchinson and I shall be coming with you both."

Ash's eyes flashed to hers, and she raised her chin, daring him to object.

He didn't, which was wise. Perhaps he was learning. She made quick work of the introductions between Ash and Mrs. Hutchinson before Biggins led the housekeeper to the door of the inn. She laid a hand on Ash's arm, holding him back just slightly.

She bent her head, hating how the smell of soap on him sent her stomach twisting, and whispered, "I believe Biggins is in love with our housekeeper."

Ash's eyes darted to the door as Biggins held it open for Mrs. Hutchinson. The man smiled, his eyes crinkling in admiration as the woman drew so close to him in order to pass through the door.

"We've not been here more than a couple of hours, and you've already managed to play matchmaker," he whispered, his tone urgent.

She straightened, pursing her lips before saying, "It wasn't me. This happened before we got here."

Ash shook his head and took her hand. "Shall we, my lady?" he said with obvious sarcasm.

She tilted her head back, chin up anyway. "Yes, of course, my lord."

The drive to the hall seemed shorter than when they had made it that morning, and she was startled to find herself enclosed by the fading elms along the driveway to the hall so soon. Ash rode ahead on horseback while she sat on the bench next to Mrs. Hutchinson and Biggins. The two had chatted amiably the entire way, and she was saved from having to make polite conversation when her attention was enraptured by the sight of Ash on horseback before her.

Damn the man. Why had he kissed her?

Seemingly innocuous acts that she had seen him perform for more than twenty years seemed highlighted now, almost pulsing to capture her attention, and while she had become aware of him as a man long ago, she'd never been *so* aware of him as she was now.

She thought of the small room at the inn, dreading having to return to it, having to be shut in with him, this man that was twisting her stomach and squeezing her heart with nothing more than the scent of his soap.

But then the hall came into view, and she forgot all about her torment. What had appeared sinister the night before now appeared only forlorn and sad.

The front steps were crumbling, but it was not as treacherous as she had imagined the previous night. A good mason could set things to right surely. The granite facade shown in the afternoon light, veins of deeper minerals sparking in the sun. But the wooden shutters were faded or peeling paint in jagged breaks, some hanging from one hinge, looking not unlike a smiling jack-o'-lantern with missing teeth. The leaded windows were missing in places, and she wondered if the blast had blown some out that might have been whole the week before.

It was clear, however, in the light of day that the east wing had been spared, and the structure appeared sound if neglected.

Ash helped her down from the cart, and together they approached the front steps, peering up at the hall.

"I think it might have been quite pretty once," Adaline said, taking in the deep mauve hue of the fading paint on the shutters and the way it complimented the mineral veins of the granite.

Ash turned to her but didn't speak. She could feel his gaze on her though, and his silence unnerved her.

Something had happened that morning, she was sure of it. First at the brook when she had splashed water on her face and then again at breakfast. But he never spoke of it, and she thought her mind was getting carried away, seeing things where her heart wished for them to be.

The sound of gravel crunching under the hooves of a horse reached their ears, and they turned to find a man approaching. He stopped on the other side of the cart and dismounted, pulling a worn leather satchel from his saddle.

"Biggins," he called, tilting his head back in greeting just enough that the sun illuminated a weather-worn but friendly face with thick graying eyebrows and bristly beard.

"John, thank you for coming so quickly," Biggins returned.

The land steward introduced them to John Tuttle, the builder, and Ash and Biggins followed the man around to the west wing to assess the damage while Mrs. Hutchinson and Adaline attempted to enter the front door.

Adaline had a mind to help the older woman up the ruined steps, but the housekeeper simply picked up her skirts and like finding a game one had memorized as a child, she skipped up the front steps with ease, turning at the top to smile down at Adaline.

"They've been like this for some time. If you crisscross up the way there, you'll find the route easier."

Adaline discovered the woman was right and reached the top much more quickly than she had the previous night.

The darkness of the interior was cool and somewhat comforting after the heat of the afternoon sun, and they lingered for a moment in the vestibule, gathering their senses in the sudden dimness.

"It wasn't quite this...dusty before the explosion," Mrs. Hutchinson murmured, and Adaline could see the pain in the woman's face at the pinched corners of her eyes. Clearly this woman took pride in her work, and seeing the hall like this was disappointing.

"I can see how beautiful it must have been, Mrs. Hutchinson," Adaline said quickly. "Tis a pity I didn't get to see it before the accident."

Mrs. Hutchinson's features relaxed, and Adaline hoped she had put the woman at ease.

"Shall we begin on this floor then?" The housekeeper turned without waiting for a response. "The receiving rooms are all along here as well as the drawing rooms. There was a sewing room, but I'm afraid most of its contents went missing." She spoke the words delicately, and Adaline admired the woman's tact.

"Have thieves been an issue for some time then?"

The woman slowed, her fingers playing with the fringe of her sleeves. "I'm afraid things were rather neglected under the management of the previous marquess." She flashed a quick glance at Adaline, but Adaline kept her features neutral. She didn't know Ash's uncle Dobson, but she was beginning to understand she wouldn't have liked the man. "I did the best I could, but it was only me here to oversee things, and I..." She let her voice trail off, but Adaline knew the rest of the sentence.

It was the same reality all women faced unfortunately. There was only so much power they held as women, and then it was never enough.

She reached out compulsively and squeezed the woman's arm. The housekeeper started, her eyes flying to where Adaline touched her.

"I thank you for your efforts, Mrs. Hutchinson. I cannot commend you enough for what you've been through. I only hope that you'll give the new marquess a chance and stay on at Grant Hall until he can see things set to rights."

Something flashed over the woman's eyes, and Adaline wondered what it might be. Surprise? Shock? Confusion?

Whatever it was, the woman recovered quickly and smiled softly. "Of course, my lady. I shouldn't think of abandoning the place now." She looked about her wistfully, and Adaline realized what this woman must be seeing. Grant Hall had been her home since her husband died. To see it like this must have been heartbreaking.

"I'm so very glad to hear that, Mrs. Hutchinson," she said, giving the woman's arm one last squeeze before releasing her.

They had reached the end of the east wing by then, and Adaline couldn't help but let her gaze travel to the place on the carpet where she'd collided with the trunk of tapestries in the dark, the trunk that was glaringly absent now.

Mrs. Hutchinson turned and gestured to a staircase they hadn't seen the night before as it was tucked into an alcove that hid it from view of anyone in the corridor. Adaline wondered briefly if that was where the looters might have hidden while she and Ash had ventured down into the kitchen. Her skin prickled with the sensation she was being watched, but she shook the feeling off.

This was her home, and she had every right to be there. She wouldn't let petty thieves take away her feeling of safety.

That was until Mrs. Hutchinson said, "Would you like to see the marquess's bedchamber?"

The question was innocent, but the way desire flared in her body at the thought of Ash, a bedchamber, and most importantly a bed, tumbling through her mind, the question became anything but innocent.

She forced a smile anyway. "Why not? That would be lovely."

Forcing herself to remember Ash did not have the same feelings for her and never had and most importantly remembering not to see things that weren't there, she picked up her skirts and followed the housekeeper up the stairs, determined to remain sensible about this whole thing, no matter how her heart stuttered.

CHAPTER 11

*H*e wasn't sure how much time had passed before he pulled himself from the depths of the basement. He stumbled through the door at the top of the enclosed staircase, sucking in a breath of air that was not saturated with mold and damp.

Mottled sunlight filtered through windows across the hall from where he stood, and he thought he might be in the east wing corridor they had found the previous night.

He'd left Biggins and Tuttle in the basement, unable to stay in the close darkness any longer. The builder was finishing his survey of the foundations of the east wing, but it appeared the structure was in remarkable condition considering the totality of the blast in the west wing. Tuttle said it had to do with the construction of the wings as additions to the original house. The foundations were not linked, and the east wing was structurally spared.

As he peered around at the mildewing carpet and moth-eaten drapes, he wasn't precisely sure he would have used that particular word.

"Ash?"

He started at the sound of his name. Not because he thought it a ghost. He knew perfectly well it was Adaline, and that was what caused him concern.

"What are you doing in here? It isn't safe."

She brushed a loose strand of hair from her forehead, leaving a streak of dust along her forehead. "It is perfectly safe. I overheard you and the builder in the basement when Mrs. Hutchinson and I were fetching some dusting clothes."

His body tensed. "You're working? You shouldn't be doing that."

The flash of protectiveness toward his wife startled him. He'd never felt such a thing for her before. But then he hadn't spent so much time admiring her womanly bits with such ardor before either. He supposed he couldn't trust himself not to develop other feelings for his friend.

This thought stopped him cold, and the line of their conversation fled his mind entirely.

He couldn't possibly develop feelings for Adaline. The stirrings of desire he felt were only the consequence of the isolation they were enduring. It would go away as soon as he returned to London. He was sure of it.

But how? Would he seek out the comfort of a widow when he returned? The idea seemed entirely unappetizing.

It was several seconds before he realized she'd asked him a question.

"Pardon?" he asked, forcing himself to focus.

Her lips thinned as they did when she was annoyed with him, and somehow the gesture was comforting.

"It's growing late. We should return to the inn for the night." She gestured through the windows, and he turned to find the windows showed a portion of the drive. "Mr. Hedgeworth sent one of his stable boys with the cart to collect Mrs. Hutchinson. I was going to go with her and have a supper ordered for us when you return. Should you like another bath as well?"

It took him a moment to sort through everything she had said when his mind instantly rebelled, populating his thoughts with images of Adaline attending her bath. He choked, looked away, forced his mind to behave.

This was getting out of hand. It was only Adaline. His best friend. He just needed to get back to London. Get out of here, this place that forced them too closely together.

And in that moment, he had his answer.

He straightened and looked back at his wife. "I shan't be returning to the inn. I plan to stay here tonight." He indicated the windows and the cart waiting on the drive. "You should return with Mrs. Hutchinson. You·should—"

"The hell I will."

He stopped, his hand still outstretched toward the window. He met Adaline's furious gaze that had grown steadier in her annoyance. With him.

The problem with marrying one's best friend was that she did not hold the demure nature found in most innocent debutantes who found themselves newlywed. Not when she knew all of one's terrible secrets and vulnerable flaws.

"You're not staying here, Adaline." Again that flash of protectiveness.

He heard the words leave his mouth even when he knew they would not be met with favor. Yet he spoke them anyway, unable to stop himself from whatever chivalrous act he thought he was performing. Adaline didn't want chivalry. He knew at least that, but then a colder thought struck him.

He didn't know what Adaline wanted.

He couldn't be sure how he'd never seen it. In the all the years they'd known one another, she had always stood quietly by his side, taking the blows of neglect society offered to those who were born just a little less. Listened while he pined after Lady Valerie, offering her wisdom and caution even though she likely knew he wouldn't listen.

And yet he didn't know any of her wishes. Her desires.

His mind flashed back to that day in his study in Aylesford House. The conversation she had forced him to have. Why was he only realizing now that while she had forced him to admit the truth of their marriage she had never once indicated why she had accepted the offer? He had made his assumptions but still. Marriage was a serious matter, and she had stepped into it without question. But why?

He watched her now, and something hot and electric coiled within him, tightening to a painful point. In the short length of their marriage, he had ruminated over all the things he couldn't have. He had never once considered the things he could have.

Adaline.

He could have her. It was within his rights as her husband. She was beautiful. It was a simple fact. She was kind and funny and good natured. She was all those things that a man could find commendable.

Why then had he dismissed her as nothing more than a friend? Why then had he not done more to discover her motives in this marriage? Because just then, he suddenly feared she had her own very real motives.

He realized he had let the silence go on too long, and she advanced, a finger held at the ready to poke him in the chest. He knew because she had done it with alarming regularity in their friendship.

"Ashfield Riggs, if you think—"

He cast one quick glance at the door he had just slipped through, picturing Biggins and Tuttle at the bottom of the staircase, and his decision was made for him.

He took hold of her hand, startling a shocked gasp from her as he pulled her against him.

"Ash!" she hissed, her eyes widening, but he didn't let go.

He picked her up just enough to shuffle her across the carpet to the other side of the corridor. A line of doors marched down this side of the hallway, and he preferred any of those mildew-infested rooms to having this conversation out here where any number of people could witness it.

He chose the nearest door and pushed it open, ushering his struggling wife inside before snapping the door shut behind them.

Like much of the rest of the house, the room was largely empty, remnants of its former glory visible in the chandelier hanging lopsided from the ceiling, most of its crystals having been stripped from it and the bookshelves lining one wall with intermittent stacks of books discarded along broken shelves. The windows along the far wall gave enough light to see the destruction, but they were covered in such filth it almost felt like twilight in the room.

"You're not staying here alone, Ash. Those thieves could come back—"

"And I shall be ready for them this time." She hadn't stopped to take in the room at all he noticed, her annoyance making her fixate on him.

Her eyebrows shot up. "You'll be ready for them? How do you as a lone man expect to take on a pack of thieves?"

He crossed his arms over his chest. "We don't know it's a whole pack. It could be one thief." He held up a single finger as if to illustrate the flaw in her argument.

It was absolutely the wrong thing to do. Her lips firmed, and the skin under her eyes tightened as he watched the breath come and go through her flared nostrils.

Then she stepped toward him. Just a single step.

And something inside of him broke.

He grabbed her, hauled her against him, and pressed his lips to hers if only to shut her up. But then he forgot everything. Where they were. Why they were arguing. Even who he was.

The taste of her, the feel of her washed the rest of it away.

He was kissing her. *Again.* And suddenly he wondered why he hadn't been doing it all along. Why had he wasted so much time? Why hadn't he seen her?

Because he'd been blinded by something else. *Someone* else.

Regret spiked through him, but it faded just as quickly as it came because just then she began kissing him back.

Her hands found his back, digging into him with a fierceness that sent his heart racing. She pressed herself against him, angling her head to give him better access, and he took it. He drank her in, nibbling the line of her lips, the corners of her mouth, before moving along her jaw, finding that soft spot behind her ear.

Finally, after forcing himself to wait, prolonging the agony, he allowed his lips to trace the path he had watched the water take that moment as she had knelt by the brook. He groaned, tasting the salt of her smooth skin. He found the ridge of her collarbone, the dip at the base of her throat.

His fingers clenched involuntarily as he felt the thump of her heart against his mouth, and he knew he had done that to her. She was just as aroused as he was, enjoying this as much as he was.

She wanted him.

This knowledge sent a shiver through him even as another groan grew deep in his throat, the only way he knew how to express the enormity of what he was feeling just then.

He had had a few affairs over the years. Nothing more than a passing pleasure. Nothing like this.

Simply holding her made his stomach tighten in anticipation. Caressing her sent his heart racing. Kissing her. God, kissing her might end him.

He let his hands explore then even as he let his lips trace the edge of her collarbone. He ran his fingers down her back, finding each knot of her spine until he cupped her buttocks, pulling her against him.

He flinched as she pressed into his erection, the pain almost too much. But then she moved her hips, grinding against him, and he moaned, his fingers digging into her just to hold himself steady.

"Adaline," he breathed against her skin. "Adaline, I can't…"

She raked her fingers through his hair, her nails skating over his skin, sending sharp points of pleasure ricocheting down him until she reached the exposed skin at his neck. She stopped there, one finger lazily tantalizing the bare skin, and his lips froze against her.

He wanted her. All of her.

The thought shook him, the breath knocked from his lungs as though he'd been physically hit. He wrenched away from her, backed up until he struck the wall behind him, sending dust into the air.

There was that protective need again, coursing through him like electricity, and he shot out a hand to stop her as she tried to step closer.

"No, Adaline." His voice was oddly raspy, and he tried to regain some semblance of control. "No, we can't do this. I can't…"

Ruin her.

That was what he had meant to say, but he wouldn't be ruining her because she was his wife. He blinked, and in the odd half-light of the shut-up room, he realized, perhaps for the first time, just exactly what he had done by marrying Adaline.

He recalled the torment that had plagued him at the inn that morning. How he could not cross this line. Not with her because then he might lose everything, and he couldn't bear the thought.

Standing there, his chest still heaving from his raging desire, his fingers still tingling with the feel of her, he couldn't remember of what he had been afraid.

Her lips were parted, swollen from his kiss. Her fingers still reached for him, her hands half raised as though she still held him.

But it was the look in her eyes that finally unlocked him. For in her eyes, he saw confusion and fear. Was it the same thing he feared? He didn't know. But he couldn't stand the thought of knowing he had put it there.

"Adaline, I'm sorry," he said before remembering this was the absolute worst thing he could say.

The fear vanished from her eyes in an instant, her gaze going cold and unyielding. Her lips snapped shut, and her hands dropped, pressing into her skirts as if to right herself.

"I see," she said, her voice perfectly calm. She brushed at her skirts as if brushing away everything that had happened in the last few minutes, and his heart clenched at the sight of her dismissal. She moved to the door, and stupidly he reached for her, but she was already beyond his touch. She only turned long enough to say, "I'll have Mrs. Hutchinson ready a room for you," before she slipped through the door, closing it softly behind her.

* * *

WAS he sorry he had kissed her or was he sorry she wasn't Lady Valerie?

The first time he had kissed her had been easy to dismiss. He was being nice. The kiss was nothing more than pity. A distraction from her obvious distress of having been on the train.

But this kiss.

She touched her fingers to her lips but only briefly, snatching her hand away and settling her palm against the rough page of her sketchbook.

The light from the small fire and the few lamps she had lit were all the light she had as she sat in the marquess's bedchamber. Twilight hung at the windows, the sky a purpling gray. The air felt thick and hot despite the open window, and she wondered if a storm was coming.

Using her finger, she smudged the outline of the face she had sketched onto the page, softening the silhouette and resolutely ignoring the urge to go find Ash.

She didn't like the thought of him traipsing about this place in the dark even if Tuttle had said it was safe. There were any number of traps he could fall into, rotted boards that could give way and debris to cause a stumble. But she resisted, hearing his voice and the horrible words he had spoken only hours earlier.

Adaline, I'm sorry.

He needn't say it. She already knew he was. The lead of her pencil snapped, the tip skittering across the page. She closed her eyes, willing her nerves to settle.

She had been aware of what she was getting into when she accepted Ash's proposal. Marriage to the man she loved who did not love her in return was bound to be fraught with these kinds of upsets, but she was strong enough to endure them. It was, after all, to be her punishment.

She set aside the sketchbook and stood. Mrs. Hutchinson had helped her prop a grate over the fire that would allow her to boil water for tea. There was a pot simmering there now, and using a rag to lift the pot from the fire she poured some of the hot water into the teapot she had prepared earlier.

Instead of accompanying Mrs. Hutchinson back to the

inn, she had sent the woman to the inn to fetch the trunk and some food they could have for supper. The woman had returned almost at once with two men from the blacksmith's shop who not only carried the trunk up to the marquess's bedchamber but also inspected the chimney to ensure it was safe to start a fire for the water.

Mrs. Hutchinson had brought a selection of meat pies, some crusty bread, cheese, and sliced meats along with a decanter of ale. It made for a nice picnic with some chipped if usable China from the kitchen. She'd even managed to find two usable cups even if one was missing its handle.

She chose to use the cup with its handle. It had been a long day, and she had earned the convenience. Besides, she was feeling mildly childish after what had transpired between them earlier.

Instead of returning to her chair, she went to the open window, looking out across the sloping park as the last of the light faded from the sky. As if he had planned it, Ash opened the door then, stepping only one foot inside before stopping, his face pinched in confusion until his eyes set on her. The confusion was quickly replaced with tightly controlled anger.

She raised her teacup. "I see Biggins delivered my message. I assume he's left for the night?"

Rather than face her husband she had chosen the coward's way of having a message delivered to him. As he was standing in the same room with her then, he'd obviously received it.

Ash didn't answer her. He carefully shut the door and turned to face her, flexing his hands open and closed. "You're not supposed to be here."

"Neither are you." She took a sip of her tea.

He opened his lips as if to say something but seemed to

165

change his mind, his eyes moving about the room. "Where is here?"

She gestured with her teacup. "This is the marquess's bedchamber. I think Mrs. Hutchinson did a splendid job of getting it habitable on such short notice."

His eyes traveled back to her, narrowing to small slits. "I didn't ask for this room to be readied."

"No, I did," she said and moved to the table where she had arranged their dinner. "Would you like a meat pie? Or some bread and cheese? Mrs. Hutchinson brought us quite the selection."

"Adaline."

She had never heard such steel in his voice, and she set her teacup down carefully, turning to face him.

"I think instead of quarreling like children about whether or not either of us should be here, I suggest we remember the deal we struck in London. I am to be your partner in this arrangement, and that is all. If you should feel the need to protect the hall, then I shall support you in your endeavor. Feelings have nothing to do with such matters of practicality."

It was as though she'd slapped him with her words, and for a moment, she was unsure of herself. His lips parted, his eyes widened, and he took the smallest of steps back. What had he expected her to say? Was he worried she was trying to coerce something more out of him after he had kissed her that afternoon? Did he expect theatrics from her? Something heavy with guilt and tears?

Such behavior may have been typical of Lady Valerie, but she would never sink to such machinations. She preferred to behave civilly and focus on the practical aspects of a situation.

Besides, Ash didn't love her. There shouldn't be cause for him to worry so about her wellbeing. She was perfectly fine.

Perfectly.

If she said it enough times to herself, she would begin to believe it.

"Feelings?" He spoke the word as though he'd never heard it before.

He took one small step toward her. She watched his boots against the threadbare carpet as though she had never seen him walk before. This entire scene suddenly fit like a gown that was two sizes too small. Everything was confining, and nothing moved as though it should.

Yet she didn't move, and he took another step toward her.

"You think feelings shouldn't be a part of this?" His tone grew softer the closer he got to her, and when he finally stopped in front of her, she found herself leaning forward as if to understand him.

It brought her face close to his, and she too quickly remembered the feel of his lips on her, bruising her, teasing the soft skin behind her ear.

She gritted her teeth. "We are both adults now, Ash. We can behave as such."

She whispered too although she didn't know why, but suddenly her heart was beating too loudly, and the thought of speaking any louder seemed too much to bear.

"Adults?" Again his mouth seemed unused to the word. "You wish to behave like adults?"

She quivered, her body responding to the way his voice dipped, twisting the words to mean something not so innocent.

"Yes," she breathed.

He shook his head, each movement from side to side slow and pronounced, dragging out the moment. "You'd best be careful, Atwood. I just might give you what you want."

She couldn't take her eyes away from his lips. She knew

what they felt like not only when he kissed her but when he pressed them to her body.

"You have no idea what I want." She hadn't meant to say those words. They lingered too close to the painful truth, but when she looked up, she caught the flash of desire in his eyes, and she worried she had said too much.

So this time she pulled his head down to her and kissed him.

She wrapped her arms around his neck, lifting herself against him, pressing her breasts into his chest, and the sensation that spiraled through her body ripped the air from her lungs. His hands were on her, stroking, exploring, until he lifted her, moving her until her back hit the wall behind her. He pinned her there with his body, his hands tracing the curves of her hip, the dip of her waist.

He slipped a leg between hers, his hand moving to the back of her thigh, lifting her leg until she was wrapped around him. She choked on a moan as the most intimate part of him pressed against the most intimate part of her.

Something primal and needy tore through her then, and she raked her fingers through his hair, framing his face with her hands as if to hold him there.

"Ash." His name was nothing more than a plea on her lips, and she moved her hips against him, pressing herself into him, letting him know what she wanted with her body.

He groaned, the sound deep and almost mournful, as he lifted her against him and swung her about, toppling them to the bed. His weight pressed her into the mattress, and she reveled in it, the feel of him along the length of her. She had wondered what it would feel like to know him like this.

She didn't wish to think how many other women knew Ash like this though. She wanted to keep this sacred, this intimate knowledge of him. This one thing that was hers alone.

He ran his hands along the inside of her arms, stretching and lifting until he held her hands pinned above her head. The position left her exposed, vulnerable, and her stomach tightened, desire burning low and focused deep within her.

She arched, lifting her chin to give him excess to her neck. His greedy mouth traced the line of her jaw, teased the spot behind her ear like he had done that afternoon, but he didn't dip lower. She shifted, lifting her breasts this time, pressing them against his solid chest, but he did nothing but laugh softly.

"Eager, aren't we?"

"Ash." She was pleading now, and she hated it, but she needed his mouth on her again.

He kept her hands pinned with one of his own, but with his free hand, he caressed her jaw, the line of her neck, his finger dipping lower. Her eyes shot open to find him watching his finger moving closer and closer to where she ached for him to touch her. The intensity of his focus made the pain low in her stomach throb, and her legs parted involuntarily as if to ease the coiling inside of her.

His finger was so dangerously close now, but at the last moment, he moved, shifting to cup the side of her breast through the bodice of her gown, and she mewled. He laughed again, his hand sliding around the globe of her breast, cupping the underside as though he were exploring her in the most carnal way.

"Do you want me to touch you, Adaline? Is that what you want?"

It wasn't everything she wanted but just then she needed him to touch her.

"Yes," she breathed, lifting herself against him.

He released her hands, and her arms slid down, her hands reaching for him, but he sat up, lifting her with him. She thought he would hold her again, kiss her, but he pressed her against him, reaching around to her back. She felt the loosening of her bodice almost immediately, and heat flooded her cheeks.

He was doing it. He was undressing her. He would... touch her. Her fingers shook against him, her grip frantic now as she realized what was happening.

Ash. Her Ash was...

He laid her back against the bed, his eyes never straying from hers.

"Are you sure, Adaline?" The way he spoke her name, it was heavy, almost sacred, as though he weren't sure if he were worthy of speaking it.

She touched his face, her hand cupping his cheek.

"Please, Ash."

He didn't speak, but she watched the way his eyes changed, the color growing darker, and then as if at the last moment, he looked away, to where his hand lingered over her collar.

When he finally touched her, her eyes slid closed as though she were unable to bear the reality of what was happening with her eyes open. He touched her with only his fingertips, and she was surprised by how calloused they were, rough against her smooth skin.

The coil deep within her jerked, tightening at the sensation, and her hips lifted.

"Ash, I..."

His fingertips stilled, and when she opened her eyes to see what was wrong, he wasn't looking at her. He was gazing down the length of her, his eyes wide, as if he were taking her in for the first time.

She didn't move; she didn't dare breathe. It was as though they hung on a precipice, and he was deciding whether or not to change who they had been all along. She felt the weight of it, but her heart yearned for it to change because she couldn't bear this punishment. Being married to the man she loved who didn't love her in return. Mere weeks, and she was ready to give up.

But then finally his hand moved, sliding down her chest, pushing aside the edge of her bodice. The gown slipped from her shoulder, and her eyes shuddered closed once more.

Then he touched her, cupping her breast, stroking her nipple, and lightning shot through her. She came up off the mattress, but he was there, cradling her, kissing her, his lips hot and comforting all at once.

He shifted, slipping one knee between her legs, urging her open as his hand moved. She whimpered at its loss at her breast, but she realized he was lifting her skirts, his fingers scrambling along her thigh.

She gripped his shoulders, moaned against his lips.

He touched her. There. Her hips shot up, her body convulsing at the simple touch. The coil inside of her sparked, and she threw her head back, breaking the kiss.

"Oh my God, Ash. That...I want that..." She didn't know what it was she was asking for but for the first time, all of her felt alive at once. There were no parts of her that she held back. She opened herself to him, all of her for all of him.

His fingers were so gentle against her, one slipping between her folds as the other explored her nub. The coil tightened, sharpened. Something was happening. Her body seemed to come to a single point where it was only she and Ash and nothing else, and nothing had been closer to bliss.

But then he was gone.

He made a noise of such pain it couldn't possibly be human as he wrenched himself from the bed, stumbling to the door. He disappeared through it, shutting it swiftly behind him while she lay there, throbbing, unfinished.

And worst of all, wondering if she'd just irrevocably broken what had never been given a chance.

CHAPTER 12

*H*e didn't stop until he reached the drive.

He fell more than walked down the crumbling front steps and crashed to his knees on the gravel drive, the stones cutting him through the fabric of his trousers. He welcomed the pain, letting it distract him from the torment shuddering through him still. He pushed his hands through his hair, sucked in a breath, willing his nerves to steady.

He leaned his head back, stared up into the inky sky, counted each and every star he could see until his heart stopped racing, his hands stopped shaking.

Adaline.

Adaline.

Adaline.

He got to his feet, leaned against the last remaining balustrade of the front steps. He tried to piece together some string of coherent thought, but his mind was a muddled mess. He'd almost made love to Adaline. His best friend. The one person in his life who had always been a constant, the one he had always relied on.

What was he thinking?

It could have changed everything. It could have damaged the one relationship he had always known would be there for him. And for what? To slack this unruly lust that seemed to have built inside of him? He had only to return to London. He knew that and yet…

He also knew he was lying to himself. The idea of another woman appealed to him as much as scraping his own eyelids from his face.

Adaline.

Adaline.

Adaline.

Her name repeated over and over again in his head like an incantation. He'd tasted her. So much of her. He'd felt the way she fit so perfectly in his arms, the way she clung to him as though he were the only other person in the world.

But it wasn't the physical aspect that had him pausing, his boots crunching on the gravel drive. It was the other things.

The way just looking at her made his heart pick up its pace. The way her scent had his entire body clenching. How he longed to wake up next to her.

He turned about, crunched his way back across the drive, forcing his boots over the gravel, ruining the leather but he didn't care.

How had this happened? How had he come to long for such things?

He had to know what this was. He had to understand it. He prodded the humiliation of Lady Valerie's rejection, but he wasn't surprised to find the sting of it had faded. Was this attraction to Adaline a response to that rejection? He doubted it. The entire idea didn't sit well with him because not once had he thought of his humiliation since boarding that train with her. Was it only the day before?

He raked his hands through his hair again, spun about, and began to pace back across the drive.

He had to get his emotions under control. It wouldn't do to let things happen here that might not happen anywhere else. He paused suddenly, his boots settling into the gravel as he pictured it. Adaline, in his bed in London, that damn braid gone, her hair spread across her pillow as she slept beside him, as he—

He gripped the balustrade with one hand like a drowning man would grab hold of a rock.

Something had changed. Something was different, and yet he couldn't move. The mere thought of Adaline being something more than his friend frightened him. She was all he had, and if he damaged their relationship...

A noise in the dark startled him. It was the rustle of leaves perhaps or the wind in the grass. Nothing that sounded out of place, but it was enough to remind him of where he was. He looked up at the house, but he couldn't see the marquess's bedchamber from here. The front of the hall remained dark and shuttered.

He was to be ready for any looters that might appear that night, and here he was, ruminating in the dark like an unschooled dandy. Shoving his hands through his hair one final time, he sucked in a breath of night air.

The hall was quiet around him as he made his way back to the marquess's bedchamber. He climbed the central staircase, one hand tight on the banister even though Tuttle had declared the stairs safe. Even in the dark, he imagined how grand the hall might have looked once, and the staircase would have been its centerpiece.

He paused at the top, looking back over the banister at the vestibule below even though it was largely invisible in the dark. Biggins's words came back to him, about the failing mines and the competition from colonial tin. It left an ache inside of him to think his great hall was suffering the effects of change just as he had.

It was strange to have such sentiment. As the son of a judge, there wasn't much in the way of property that could tug at his heartstrings, and it felt oddly full to have such worries.

His mind was cluttered with the thoughts of tin mines and estate work, and that was why he didn't notice immediately that the door to the marquess's bedchamber was open. He recalled clearly having shut it behind him. Later he would scold himself for his hesitation, the few precious seconds he stood there staring at the open door.

But when voices reached him—strained, harsh voices—his body reacted without him. He plunged into the room, his hands already up, his body rigid for a fight. He hadn't even registered the man standing there before he had tackled him to the floor where he pinned him with his own body weight.

Had he been thinking clearly, Ash would have noticed how easily he had brought the man down and how little resistance the thief gave. But it wasn't until Ash ripped off the thick scarf the man was using to cover his face that reality sunk in.

"Jesus," Ash muttered.

Somewhere over his shoulder he became aware of Adaline, hovering, one arm reaching toward him as if to pull him away or perhaps in some mistaken attempt to protect him. Whatever it was, at the sight of the man's face she breathed a soft *oh* of exclamation.

"You're a child," Ash said, and only then did the lad begin to fight back, thrashing beneath him.

"I ain't no child. You've got a—"

Ash rocked back on his heels, pulling the young man to his feet as he stood. The lad was clearly so surprised by being on his feet once more it halted his speech. Ash took a step back, carefully placing himself between the boy and Adaline. The lad might appear as though he could hurt nothing greater than a wee pest, but Ash knew not to place weight on one's looks.

Briefly he glanced behind him, not wishing to be distracted by Adaline, but he found her standing squarely, her shoulders straight. She had a blanket wrapped around her, and beneath it, he could see her bodice was still loose. He hated himself then. For leaving her and for leaving her like that. So exposed. So vulnerable. What the hell was the matter with him?

He pushed down his self-hatred and turned back to the boy.

"What are you doing here?"

The young man was attempting to extricate himself from the long scarf he had carefully wound around his neck and face as if to conceal his identity. Sweat beaded along his brow and his upper lip as the night was warm and the added layers must have caused the poor boy to be sweltering.

Ash turned and poured a cup of the tea he had seen earlier on the table with the food stuffs Mrs. Hutchinson had brought. He offered it to the lad who eyed the cup skeptically before taking it, drinking it down in a single gulp. When he finished, he eyed Ash warily.

"They said the marquess was some old degenerate with a stomach the size of a barrel of ale."

Ash bit the inside of his cheek to keep from smiling at the lad's unerring description of the late marquess. "That would be the previous marquess. My uncle."

The lad blanched, his lips trembling. "I'm right sorry, sir. I am. It's—"

Ash held up a hand to stop the boy's rushed apology. "The barrel of ale is an accurate description. The degenerate part I had not heard before, but I wouldn't be surprised."

The lad looked sheepishly into his empty teacup. "I'd heard things is all. From my cousin and such. She and her friends used to work here at the hall. They said the marquess was grabby."

Again he heard Adaline suck in a breath behind him, and Ash couldn't fault her as it was clearly his turn to blanch. He knew his uncle had not been the epitome of respectability, but this was the first he had heard the man might have taken liberties with the staff.

He crossed his arms over his chest. "I can assure you I do not condone such behavior." He hoped his words were assurance enough to get the boy speaking, but he only watched them warily.

"Are you hungry?"

Ash peered over his shoulder at Adaline as she tied the corners of her blanket, turning it into a kind of garment that kept her covered but freed her arms. She moved to the table and took up a meat pie wrapped in a linen napkin. Returning to their odd conference, she handed the food to the boy.

Again he watched them warily before his hand shot out and snatched the pie as though it might be taken away again.

"Sit." Ash gestured to the chair behind the boy, and the boy sat, already settling into the pie, his cheeks full of the pastry in seconds.

He took the boy's cup and refilled it before setting it on the small table by the lad's chair. He sat on the closed lid of their trunk, leaning elbows on his knees.

"All right then. What are you doing here?"

The boy chewed a few more ponderous bites before gesturing with the remnants of the pie. "I've come to find something I can sell." He spoke the words quickly, harshly, his eyes darting back and forth between Ash and Adaline. "I'm not proud of it, I ain't. But my ma's starving. And I got brothers and sisters I need to look out for."

"Have you thought about securing employment?"

The boy's face screwed up in disgust. "Ain't no work to be found nows the mines are shutting down."

Although Ash knew of the dire state of the mines it didn't stop him from cringing inwardly at the boy's words. It was one thing to hear of it anecdotally. It was another to see its disastrous effects on the people whose livelihoods were now in his care as marquess.

"Does your family live on Aylesford land?"

Again his eyes darted back and forth. "They do." The words were softer now, almost as though he were hiding something.

"Where?" Ash prodded.

The boy's eyes halted for a second, and then before Ash knew it, the boy was on his feet. "I don't need to explain myself—"

Ash used a single hand to push the lad back into the chair.

"Your father leased the land from Aylesford, but he's run off or is dead. Which is it?"

The boy's eyes dropped. "He's run off."

"How long ago?"

The boy shrugged. "I don't know. A year, maybe?"

Ash's stomach clenched. "I see."

The boy looked up, his eyes frantic. "You're not going to toss us out, are ye? Me ma is weak. She's starving, and she can't—"

Ash held up a hand. "I have no intention of evicting your family. I would ask a favor of you though."

The boy's features tensed, but he didn't speak.

"I will need you to return here in the morning. At sunup or as near to it as you can. I assume you have chores to complete in the morning?"

The boy gave a slow nod.

"Good. I have work to be done and no one to do it. Are you willing?"

The boy's eyes widened the slightest bit before he caught himself, firming his lips as though the offer were tough to consider.

"I suppose I can." He looked about himself as though figuring out what to say next or perhaps how to say it. "But I ain't being your slave forever. I ain't take nothing from here. I only heard about it from the other lads, but my ma—"

Ash held up a hand. "You won't be a slave. I shall pay you for your work. These other lads. Would they be willing to work as well?"

The boy seemed to have forgotten about hiding his feelings because his lips parted in disbelief at the thought of a job, his eyebrows nearly rising into his hairline.

"Oh, aye. I bet they'll jump at the chance." His gaze slid to Adaline, and he straightened, tugging on the threadbare lapel of his wool jacket. "We're a respectable folk here. No matter what is said."

"I believe you," Ash said, getting to his feet. "I'll show you out now. I don't want you falling down a stairwell and breaking your neck. This mother of yours seems formidable."

A look of confusion passed over the boy's face, and Ash wondered if he knew what the word *formidable* meant.

He must have decided it was a favorable assessment because he smiled and nodded. "Oh aye, she is."

"Here," Adaline said, moving back to the table and tucking the remainder of the food into a basket that sat underneath it. She handed the full basket to the boy. "Take this to your family. I'll be sure there's lunch for you and your friends when you come to work tomorrow."

The boy didn't reach for the basket straight away, his gaze locked on Adaline.

"I didn't mean to frighten you, ma'am," the boy nearly stammered. "Honest, I didn't."

She smiled and gestured for him to take the basket. "I know."

Ash touched the boy's shoulder as the lad seemed suddenly unable to look away from Adaline. Ash could only understand too well.

He led the boy back through the hall and down the front stairs. It was only when they reached the drive that he thought to ask. "What's your name, son?"

"Grady, sir. Grady Givens." He paused, blinking. "Or is it my lord?" He scraped a foot against the gravel. "I'm sorry, sir. I wasn't raised to know what to say, sir."

Ash smiled encouragingly. "It's my lord, but you needn't apologize. I wasn't raised to expect such a title anyway."

The boy's eyes widened. "You weren't, sir? I mean...my lord."

Ash shook his head. "I only came by way of the title by happenstance."

The boy's face seemed to transform then, the last of the wariness falling away as though Ash had become another person by his admission, someone the boy was more likely to trust.

He didn't know why, but Ash felt a warmth spread through him as the change overcame Grady's face.

"I thought so, my lord. You ain't like the other gentlemen I've met."

Ash frowned. "How's that?"

"You're kind, my lord." He held up the basket. "And ye've got a right fine lady wife if I may say so."

"You may," Ash said.

He wished the boy good night and waited at the front of the hall as the lad sauntered off into the night as if he weren't at all afraid he might stumble upon ghosts on the moor.

* * *

ADALINE SAT in the chair the young man had just vacated, her mind swirling with too many emotions to sort through them one by one. Her chest hurt, and she put her hand to it, her fingers colliding with the knot she'd made in the blanket that hung on her shoulders.

She made to undo the knot and remembered her bodice was loose underneath. Her cheeks grew hot as she realized how smart it had been to have wrapped herself in the blanket from the bed before she stood up from where Ash had ravished her. Well, almost ravished her.

Her heart thudded, and she shoved the memory down. She had to change. Now. While Ash was escorting the boy to the front of the hall. She couldn't do up the buttons on the back of the gown herself, and she was too humiliated to ask Ash to do it. There was a simple day gown in the trunk, and she went to it, lifting the lid to rummage through its contents.

Her maid and Ash's valet should catch up with them by tomorrow, and the idea sent a wash of relief through her. Perhaps with more people about she wouldn't allow herself to succumb to her emotions again.

It was bad enough she'd let it happen tonight. Shame burned through her, and she made quick work of her gown, shedding it for the simpler one. She didn't wish to don a nightrail. Not here. Another thief could come prowling through the house, and she didn't wish to be found in such an undressed state.

But worse, she didn't want Ash to see her in her nightrail and dressing gown. She wouldn't embarrass him further by appearing so underdressed in his presence.

She had painted feelings where there were none, and now she might have ruined her dearest friendship. How could she have been so stupid? Hadn't she learned? Hadn't Amelia been enough?

She bit back an involuntary sob as it caught in her throat. A great, bone-jarring sadness roared up inside of her, and she shoved it down, hard. She couldn't let herself come undone. Not yet. Tears were for later when no one was watching. She wouldn't subject Ash to such distress. She'd already done enough.

The day gown tightened with a tie just beneath her breasts, and she pulled the bow taut just as footsteps drifted down the corridor. For a terrible moment, she wondered if it was another looter, but the cadence was familiar, and her shoulders relaxed.

She snatched up her sketchbook from where she had discarded it earlier, holding it against her chest as though it were further protection. From what? Her eternal embarrassment? From her uncontrollable wantonness?

Ash paused inside the door, his hand lingering on the knob as he took her in. Something passed over his features—surprise perhaps?—but it was gone so quickly she couldn't be sure. But more, she was done trying to interpret his expressions. Such custom had only brought her pain.

Her lips parted, but she realized she didn't know what to say. The sadness roared inside of her again, but it was more directed this time. She had never been at a loss for words around Ash, and this more than anything undid her. She twirled around, snatching at the pencils she'd left on the table, but her hands were shaking, and she did nothing more than scatter them about its surface.

When Ash's hands closed over hers, she jumped, sending the pencils to the floor. He bent and retrieved them, placing them carefully in her palm and closing her fingers around them.

"Adaline—"

"Were you telling him the truth?" she cut him off, her voice unnaturally high. She had to keep this conversation productive, or she would lose what little control she still had over her emotions.

His eyes moved over her face, and she kept her chin steady, not wanting him to see how close she was to crumbling.

It had been enough, her humiliation earlier, but she still shook with the very real fear that had gripped her when the young man had stepped into the room. She had thought it was Ash returning and had turned back to the door, an apology on her lips, but it hadn't been him. It had all happened so fast. She couldn't remember now the pieces of it. The man's face, covered in something dark she now knew was a scarf, but then she'd only seen someone trying to hide his identity from her, which could never mean something good.

Fear had sent her reeling backwards against the bed, her hands scrambling to find anything to use as a weapon. She couldn't remember if she had spoken. She must have because the man had answered her. He had said he meant no harm. Not that she had believed him.

But then Ash had appeared, plunging through the door-way. They had collapsed to the floor as she had regained her senses, but by then, the whole thing was over.

It was several moments before her brain had caught up to what was happening simply because she couldn't believe it was Ash who had come through the door. She had never seen him...well, act. Not like that. Not with such focus and strength. He hadn't even hesitated. It was as though his instincts had taken over where the carefully constructed person he presented to the world fell away.

It had been...stunning. To see that side of him. The one that acted instead of reacted to the role society had given him.

She pushed that thought aside now too. It could only cause more harm if she were to think about it too much.

Because if she let herself think on it, she might begin to believe she had caused that side of him to emerge. That he was acting that way because of some need to protect her.

Which was entirely unfounded, and she would think of it no further. No matter how she wished to believe it were true.

"The truth about what?" She noticed how careful he was to put space between them after he handed her the pencils.

"About having work for them? For that boy and his mates?"

"Grady Givens," Ash said, his eyes closing and opening slowly.

She saw the exhaustion then pinching the corners of his eyes and pooling in the tension of his neck. Guilt washed over her, and she stepped back as though more space would ease his distress.

"The boy's name is Grady Givens, and yes, I meant it." He nodded in the direction of the other wing. "Tuttle needs a crew to begin sorting through the rubble. He says we may be able to salvage some of the granite and begin to rebuild with that."

"You plan to rebuild Grant Hall?" It wasn't her place to question it, but she was surprised because most of what she had seen of the place was moldered and rotten. It seemed almost a fool's wish to try to save the building.

Ash paused as he'd been about to turn away from her, one foot pointed across the room. "You think I shouldn't?"

She smiled, softly, hoping he might forget her intrusion. "It's not my place," she said quietly.

He didn't respond, and she had nothing more to say and silence hung between them like an albatross. Her eyes drifted to the bed only to flutter away as she remembered the touch of his callused fingers on her collar, on her chest, on her—

"Well, good night then," she said, the words tripping automatically from her lips before she realized the nature of their situation.

She snuck a glance at the bed again, tried to ignore the way her heart pounded in her chest. They were stuck here, together, alone, and she had made the worst mistake.

"I can leave if you wish to—" He gestured toward her person, and she too easily filled in the blanks, but she couldn't let the conversation move to such matters of intimacy.

"It's been strange to watch you as a marquess." The words came out before she realized she meant to say them, and then they hung in the air, weightier than any silence before them.

His eyes narrowed, and her heart tripped, worried that she might have made things worse.

"I mean, I'm used to you being so cavalier about things." No, that was entirely far worse. "What I mean to say—" She licked her lips, curled and uncurled her fingers around her sketchbook. This flightiness was not like her. One transgression should not weaken her composure like this. She met Ash's gaze. "When I needed it most, you made me laugh, and the way you approach things with such a carefree touch is one of the things I like most about you. But since you've acquired the title, I've gotten to see a different side of you. One that I like just as much."

He raised an eyebrow. "What side is that?"

"A responsible side." She laughed softly, her fingers relaxing along her sketchbook. "It sounds painfully grown up, I know, but it suits you, Ash." The words died away then, and she wanted nothing more than to study him, to watch what she said wash over him.

"Responsible? My father is rolling over in his grave just to hear you say that."

She smiled. "Don't make fun, Ash. I'm serious." She

gestured to the door. "What you did tonight, both in protecting me and in saving that young man, it came naturally to you. I could tell." She shook her head, more out of wonderment than disbelief. "I can't imagine what you might do if you applied yourself." She shrugged, adjusting the sketchbook in her grasp. "You have this estate and so many others in which to do it. I would look forward to seeing what you could do."

Something flickered over his face then, and she looked away, too tired and too wounded to try to guess at his emotions anymore that night. But when she did turn, she realized again the impossibility of her circumstances.

"You may have the bed," he said then, ignoring all that she had laid out before him. But then it wasn't unexpected. Ash was good at ignoring the heavier things.

She turned back, forcing a smile to her lips. "I have the marchioness's rooms actually. They're just through here." She pointed to the connecting door as the lie slipped easily over her lips.

There had only been time to air out and tidy the marquess's rooms. The marchioness's bedchamber lay cold and shut up, but it was a warm night, and she doubted sleep would come anyway. She would be fine in whatever accommodations it could provide.

His gaze narrowed again. "I don't like the idea of you sleeping in another room."

Her traitorous heart leapt, and she scolded it. "I will be fine, Ash. You mustn't worry."

She bent and retrieved her shawl from the trunk and slowly made her way to the door. "Good night," she said over her shoulder and slipped through the door without waiting for his response. She closed it softly, her hand lingering on the knob as she took in the bolt. It was nearly at eye-level as if it were mocking her. For a second, she thought about throwing it, about hearing the satisfying click as it separated her from her husband. From her best friend.

But then she let her hand slip from the doorknob, and she took in the room about her. It was much as it had been when Mrs. Hutchinson had shown it to her earlier. What little furniture was left was covered in dust cloths that had gone yellow at the hems. The corners were decorated with cobwebs, the floor with dirt and grim and even a few wayward leaves.

She went to the windows and pried loose one of the panes, popping it open with a terrible sucking sound. The night air was thick, but it carried the refreshing scent of blossoms and earth. In the distance thunder rumbled, and she started at the sound before her mind connected the noise with the storm she had thought might come, and she relaxed into it.

Tugging at one of the dust cloths, she discovered a chair and pulled it closer to the window. The bed contained only the remnants of a mattress, and the bits that were left would not support a grown woman. The chair was generous if musty, and she settled into it, wrapping her shawl tightly around her, and settling her sketchbook on her lap.

She waited until the storm came upon them, and only then did she let the rumble of rain and thunder drown out the sound of her tears.

CHAPTER 13

$\mathcal{I}$t was easier to move the hulking pieces of granite that had formerly made up the west wing of Grant Hall than it was to be in the same room as his wife.

It wasn't the memory of his kiss that haunted him or the feel of her writhing beneath him. It was her blind faith in him, her unwavering confidence in his abilities. It was that she saw the potential he held that he couldn't even see for himself.

It was hard to believe weeks had passed since that night he'd almost destroyed the one good thing in his life. Standing at the edge of the first granite operation on Aylesford land, it was difficult to imagine everything that had transpired so quickly.

It was Adaline's doing, of course.

She had planted the seed with her surprise by his desire to rebuild Grant Hall. She had been right, of course. Just as he was coming to understand she was right about everything.

The morning after that fateful night Grady Givens had arrived with a pack of other young men in much the same state, gangly and directionless, wandering in that time between childhood and adulthood where many got lost. Ash had relied on John Tuttle to show the men how to carefully excavate the site. How to examine the ruins for danger and how to extract the ruined granite blocks one at a time so they could be repurposed.

He wasn't sure when it had occurred to him, but Ash had realized the granite used to build Grant Hall had to have come from somewhere and judging by the size of the granite blocks it wasn't very far. Biggins had located the source within days, and Ash had been right. The source lay not three miles from the hall itself. Evidence of past mining was clear in the scars on the land, but it appeared as though the previous marquess had stopped the mining efforts there once the hall was built. It only meant there was much more granite to be found.

Ash had set to work fitting the quarry immediately. Stores of gunpowder were moved from the few remaining Aylesford tin mines to the granite site. Equipment was either refitted, sold, or newly purchased when they couldn't make do with what they had. Meanwhile Grady Givens and his men moved the granite blocks from the hall to the quarry where they would be repurposed as mill stones for grinding grain.

In four weeks' time, the site had been cleared, and it was as though Grant Hall never had a west wing. John Tuttle and his men had started the repairs to the remainder of the hall immediately, and each night when Ash returned to the house, he noted the gradual change sweeping over it even as he dragged himself upstairs to a cold plate of supper, a hot bath, and bed.

He wasn't so tired that he didn't notice the closed connecting door every night, the one that separated him from his wife.

The demands of the new granite operation called for early mornings and late evenings, but he wasn't foolish enough to deny he didn't embrace such long working hours in order to avoid the house and Adaline. It was just for now, he told himself. Just while he worked through all that Adaline had said to him.

That she could imagine what he might accomplish if he applied himself.

He hadn't believed her, the thought so contradictory to the line of degradation he had been fed since childhood, but then she had been right. He knew that somehow, instinctually. When he'd been granted the title, he could have fettered away the funds that came with it. Continued the lavish lifestyle his uncle Dobson had enjoyed and hoped the money held out.

But that hadn't been his instinct. Instead he had set to discovering what the estate entailed and how the money flowed through it, what his responsibilities were and who the people were for which he must care. Adaline had been right about that much.

As he stood watching Grady Givens carefully measure the gunpowder that would be used to blast the granite loose, Ash knew that even more was possible.

Here in front of him was the thief that had terrorized Grant Hall in those early days, and Ash had given him a job. A means of earning an honest dollar to care for his family. But it was more than that even for Grady. The young man showed an enthusiasm for the work Ash could not have predicted.

That first morning when Grady and his friends had stumbled onto the park at Grant Hall, they had appeared for all the world as if they were simply taking a task to earn a coin. Who would have believed Grady would take such an interest in mining? That he would be skilled and compassionate about it?

The lad had given his advice when opportunity arose. He was, after all, raised in the culture of mining, and he had seen the tin miners at work since he was boy. It was no wonder he carried so much knowledge within him, and Ash would have been foolish not to listen.

Ash was only lucky he had managed to convince a few of the experienced tin miners to join the venture instead of leaving Dartmoor for the lure of colonial tin. One such miner, a Ronald Tibbs, guided Grady on the proper measuring of the gunpowder. Ash watched with some trepidation. Granite was far different than tin, and the tin miners he had hired were still trying to work out the right ratio of gunpowder to stone in order to effect the blast that was enough to separate slabs of the rock without overdoing it.

Ash had seen firsthand what happened when too much gunpowder was used.

The sound of stones crunching alerted him to Biggins's arrival, and Ash turned to greet the land steward.

Biggins touched the brim of his felt cap. "The shipment of drills is here, my lord. I thought you'd wish to inspect them."

Ash nodded and turned, heading up the hill to where they had set up a makeshift equipment barn out of an old miner's lean-to. While the stone salvaged from Grant Hall had been used for mill stones, Ash hoped the granite from the quarry could be sold as building material. But it would mean the stone would need to be cut with greater precision and efficiency. Granite was not a valuable stone, but it was a reliable building material. He had to keep his costs low though if he were to turn any kind of profit and keep the venture viable and an avenue of employment for the young men of the estate and neighboring villages.

"I apologize for the delay in getting them here, my lord.

The courier delivered them to the hall, you see. He didn't realize someone had started quarrying up here on the ridge."

Ash's stomach tightened at the mention of the hall. Even the thought of it made his mind wander, wondering what Adaline was doing. The few times their paths crossed she had been her usual self. She always had a smile for him, her tone soft and hopeful as she relayed the progress they were making on the inventory of the house and the improvements Tuttle's men had made. It seemed the hall could be salvaged, and Adaline was fitting neatly into her role as mistress of the place.

His heart squeezed thinking of it, and he picked up one of the drills, examining the bit for precision.

"I'm sure he was surprised to see the place under construction," Ash said, unable to think of anything less innocuous to say.

Biggins tugged at his cap. "It really is a sight. It's been left to ruin for so long, I assume anyone is surprised by the development. Mrs. Hutchinson says it's right livable again."

Ash slid a glance in Biggins's direction. The man mentioned Mrs. Hutchinson's name casually five or twenty times in a given day, and Ash couldn't help but wonder if Adaline were right about a possible romance stirring between the two. The thought only served to stir up a longing he was badly trying to suppress, and he set down the drill.

"These will work I should think. Have we had any luck finding a miner skilled in granite?" It had been Ash's hope to find a tradesman who was experienced in cutting granite with some kind of precision. If the Aylesford quarry were to compete for building bids, it had to provide the best quality stone on the market.

"Not as yet, but I have a lead on a gentleman who works

in a quarry on the other side of Preston. I'm to meet with him this afternoon."

Ash nodded and moved to examine the next crate of drills. "When do you think we can begin advertising the granite? I should like to take advantage of the summer building season."

A small explosion behind them had them turning in the direction of the quarry toward the bottom of the slight depression along the ridge. Tibbs gestured wildly to the men gathered around him, and Ash thought another test had been unsuccessful. He returned to examining the drills, knowing Tibbs would eventually figure it out.

"If all goes according to plan, we should be underway shortly." Biggins watched the operation below them.

"Excellent," Ash said, distracted by the drill in his hand.

"My lord, may I be forward?"

Ash looked beyond the drill where Biggins stood, his felt cap in his hands now. "Of course," Ash said, carefully replacing the drill in its crate.

"Mrs. Hutchinson says the marchioness is inventorying the house as if she plans to restock it. I was wondering, my lord, what your intentions were with the estate. I know Grant Hall is one of many in the Aylesford title."

Ash didn't have the courage to admit he hadn't really spoken to his wife since he'd attempted to ravish her four weeks previously. But it sounded like Adaline to work out a plan and then speak to him about it once she'd formed a tentative idea of what needed to be done. It was what partners would do, and he realized, standing there on the hillside, he was being a terrible partner. No matter the personal feelings he had stirred up and the way he had left things, running away because he had been too scared to change the one constant in his life didn't mean his wife should shoulder the burden of getting an estate the size of Grant Hall back on its feet.

He would return to the hall earlier that evening than was his custom and seek her out. She was right. They were partners in this no matter how foolish he felt, and he had to start acting like one.

Ash gestured over his shoulder to the quarry. "I think it will depend on what happens with the granite. If we can make Grant Hall a viable income stream, I will need to spend more time here overseeing the operation. I should like your help with that, but I'll need to understand your other duties on the estate. I shouldn't wish to overburden you."

Ash didn't know how old Biggins was, but he gauged the man to be nearing sixty. Perhaps the man wished to retire at some point. Maybe in a cottage in the village with Mrs. Hutchinson as his wife. God, he was starting to sound like Adaline.

Biggins's face opened immediately. "I should like that very much, my lord. I would be happy to discuss—"

Ash never heard the end of the sentence because just then an explosion rent the air. Everything happened all at once. The sound of the eruption, the tearing of stone, the crumbling of rock, it all collided together in one roar of indistinguishable sounds.

But the noise wasn't what captured him. It was watching what happened around him as the force of the blast traveled up the hill to them.

The crates holding the drills lifted in the air as if they weighed nothing at all. Biggins's eyes shut, but slowly as if Ash were watching time slow to infinitesimal steps. And then just like the crates, Biggins floated into the air, carried away from Ash as though swept up in a strong guest of wind.

The same must have happened to him, but he couldn't

have said because the blackness came all too quickly as the silence replaced everything.

But just before the dark could consume him, he had one desperate thought.

Adaline.

* * *

THE MARCHIONESS'S bedchamber was quite lovely now.

Adaline sat in the same chair, her sketchbook propped against her upturned knees. She could still remember that night. Although she had sat here, broken and exhausted, the storm had comforted her. Not once had she felt frightened of the room about her, at the shadows that lurked in the corners nor the crunch of dead leaves underfoot.

It was as though this room had been waiting for her.

She and Mrs. Hutchinson had started in on the repair of the room the very next day, and now, nearly a month later, Adaline was pleased with the results. The mattress had been replaced, and new linens had been ordered and had arrived the previous week. The bed was now a resplendent thing with a thick duvet in lilac and periwinkle. The room sported an armoire and a dressing table and a small desk pushed under the window. The furniture had been plucked from other rooms in the house and none of it matched, but it was all lovely, old pieces that spoke to her, and that meant more than anything in terms of decor.

It was the time of day past the prime of activity and before the nightly routines commenced when she normally responded to any letters received in the post. She favored the small desk under the window in her room because the light was favorable, but today there were no letters that pressed her for a response, so she had retreated to her chair, her body aching from the constant toil of setting the hall to rights.

She was surprised to have found the chair in such good condition the next day, and she supposed she had the dust cloth to thank for that. Still she'd had it aired and beaten, and now it smelled like spring air and sunshine. She nestled into it, propping her feet more firmly against the windowsill, and she stared out the sparkling clean windows at the row of trees now budded, their branches thickening every day with new leaves.

Dropping her gaze to the page in front of her, she smudged at the lines of Mr. Tuttle's face, capturing the heaviness of his brow and the thickness of his beard. She'd rendered likenesses of all the people she had encountered so far at Grant Hall, and she liked to think her sketchbook told a kind of story.

Alice had written from London that Uncle Herman was fretting in his position as earl. Now that the title had been saved with an influx of funds from the Duke of Greyfair, a feat only made possible by her sister Amelia's sacrifice in marrying the man, Uncle Herman found he had very little to do after the worst of it was cared for. The man had retreated to his studies, according to Alice, and Adaline wondered what those were. They had known very little of their uncle before he had come to be their guardian, and she felt a pang of loss at not having known him.

She was certain though that Alice was taking great interest in the man's studies. Perhaps she might even share her own voltaic pile experiments with the burly man.

She let out a sigh at the thought. At least one of the Atwood sisters was happy.

A stab of guilt prodded her at the thought. She had no business searching for happiness. That was made clear after the momentary lapse of judgment she had experienced upon first arriving at Grant Hall. The weeks had shown her that it was only the forced proximity that had caused her to forget herself. She'd spent very little effort in avoiding—er, that was, she had not been called upon to drudge up much willpower to keep her emotions in check since that night.

Things had been going along smoothly for the past four weeks, and she was convinced it was evidence to support her perception of her marriage. A partnership worked best for both of them. Ash seemed fulfilled in his efforts with the estate and especially the new granite quarry. Grant Hall was experiencing a masterful resurrection, and she was pleased with the progress she and Mrs. Hutchinson had made.

They had nearly finished sorting through the rooms. Mr. Tuttle said his men would have most of the major repairs completed by week's end, and they even had a meager staff now. Poor Mrs. Hutchinson had been quite stretched in those early days upon returning to the hall. She assisted Adaline in her efforts in righting things, but there was still the matter of daily chores and procuring food for all of them.

The Hedgeworths had been most helpful on this front, sending food up to the hall for several days when they first arrived. When the kitchen was deemed usable, Mrs. Hutchinson set out to find a cook. Apparently the hall had been without one for some time, the few servants on staff fending for themselves in that regard. Grant Hall now boasted a cook, a scullery maid, and two footmen. It was like living in luxury.

There was always a fire laid now, and the cobwebs were regularly swept from corners. Surfaces were dusted, and the scent of lemons lingered in the air. It almost felt like home.

Adaline dropped her feet to the floor at this thought, her sketchbook sliding along her knees, so she was forced to grab it with both hands.

It was true she had come to think of Grant Hall as home, but it worried her that she had not spoken to Ash about his intentions with the hall. This estate was only one of many in the Aylesford title, and she knew he had been visiting the Kent estate only the week before they were married.

She shook her head and stood, depositing her sketchbook on the desk. She needed to speak with Ash, that much was certain. She was childish in behaving the way she had been. Noting his usual schedule and ensuring she wasn't around when he came and went. Attending meals only occasionally and taking a tray in her room most evenings.

It was easier than facing him, and for that, she was a coward.

This was her punishment, and yet she hid from it. But when she had chosen this marriage as such, she hadn't yet kissed Ash, hadn't felt his hands on her, hadn't known the way her body would respond to his.

Hadn't known how proud she would be of him as he took control of his life and turned it into something more.

Hadn't known she would fall further in love with him when she witnessed his compassion and care for the people under his watch.

It was so much harder now to think of their union as a partnership when she felt so much more for her husband.

She toyed with the letter from Alice still sitting on her desk and knew enough was enough. She would speak to him that evening when he returned from the quarry. Every night she greeted him. It was the one concession she made to her determination to avoid him. There was something about watching him come home, about seeing the traces of his day on him, noting how each day it was different that made everything come into sharper focus.

She had everything she had ever wanted, and yet she had none of it at all.

She was married to the man she loved, the man she had spent years yearning for, and every day she got to be this close to him. To sleep in the room beside his, to share meals with him, to watch as time marched its way over and through him.

And yet she might as well have been a complete stranger to him.

She closed her eyes against the splitting pain that tore through her when she thought it, the gulf that had opened between them since that night. When she lay awake in bed at night, she tormented herself by wondering if their friendship had been broken that day as well. She hoped not. It would be the only thing left to her, and she hoped over time things would be mended.

She had only to keep her feelings for him secret.

Resolved she left her bedchamber to find Mrs. Hutchinson. They must finish the inventory so she could present it to Ash and determine his feelings on maintaining the hall and whether or not she should work to make it fit for frequent habitation.

Ash had already decided not to rebuild the west wing, and she wondered if that were an indication of how he felt about the estate. But then she knew of his efforts to provide work for the residents of the estate and neighboring villages and knew she couldn't make assumptions based on such.

The funds and materials that would have been used to restore the hall to its former footprint had been used to start the quarry. It was a selfless and smart decision, and again she was surprised by Ash's initiative. It only hurt to think what he might have already accomplished had he not been repeatedly told of his uselessness so early in his life.

She found Mrs. Hutchinson in the laundry in the basement off the kitchen. She was instructing Martha, the new scullery maid, on the use of the mangle that had just arrived. Clean linen hung from the clotheslines that crisscrossed one end of the room. The air was thick with the pungent scent of lye, and tubs sat on the floor, filled to the brim with dark water and swirls of fabric.

They had cleared out the linen closets earlier in the week, and Mrs. Hutchinson had said she would have the items worth saving cleaned and mended, and Adaline wondered if the tubs contained what they had been able to salvage.

Mrs. Hutchinson looked up then, folding her hands calmly in front of her. "My ladyship, I thought you had retired to your room," she said, apprehension in her gaze.

Adaline smiled to assure the woman all was well. "I was hoping I could review what we have so far for the inventory. I thought we might—"

The ground beneath her feet trembled, cutting off her words, and she flung her hands out as the room seemed to shift about her, but she only found the flimsy, undulating folds of wet cloth suspended in the air about her.

Mrs. Hutchinson reached for her as Martha screamed, her feet slipping out from beneath her as she tried to grab hold of the mangle beside her. None of it made a difference as all three women fell to the floor with the force of the shaking.

Adaline blinked as pain radiated along her back, but soon a soft keening sound penetrated the haze of her discomfort. Mrs. Hutchinson. Oh God, where was the woman? She had already survived one disaster. Adaline rolled over, her hands slipping on the damp tiles of the floor as she scrambled to gain purchase. She crawled across the floor to where the housekeeper lay and gently picked up the woman's head and cradled it in her lap.

"Mrs. Hutchinson," Adaline whispered, smoothing her hand against the woman's forehead.

The room had stilled almost as soon as it had shaken, and Martha dug herself out from beneath the mangle that had fallen when she'd tried to use it to hold herself up.

Mrs. Hutchinson's eyes blinked open, and Adaline watched as realization dawned in the woman's eyes.

"Mrs. Hutchinson." Adaline brushed the woman's hair from her face. "Mrs. Hutchinson, everything is all right. It was only a tremor."

Adaline didn't know what she was saying. The entire hall had rocked around them but only briefly. Surely it couldn't be so bad as it had been when the west wing had exploded.

Mrs. Hutchinson sat up abruptly as though she hadn't just been knocked to the floor, and once again Adaline got the sense the woman was more than she seemed. It was only then that they both became aware of poor Martha, her back resting against the wall, her breathing labored.

Mrs. Hutchinson took the poor girl's hand, murmuring soothing words as she tried to calm her.

Adaline pushed to her feet, stumbling into the kitchen to find the footmen screeching down the servants' staircase.

The first one reached out a hand toward her. "Ma'am, are you all right?"

The young man couldn't have been more than Grady Givens's age, and yet his concern was genuine.

"I'm all right." She gestured behind her. "Please help Mrs. Hutchinson. Poor Martha had quite a tumble."

The footmen started moving even before she'd finished the sentence.

Shaking her head as if to clear it, she climbed the stairs to the ground floor, her thoughts riddled with what Mr. Tuttle's men may have done to cause such a reverberation.

But when she reached the vestibule where his men were supposed to be repairing the plaster, the room was empty. She heard voices filtering through the open front door, and she went to investigate.

The entire work crew was huddled in the drive at the

front of the house, their gazes pinned to the horizon to the west.

She found Mr. Tuttle at the front of them. The crew was eerily quiet as if whatever they saw on the horizon had captured all of their focus.

"Mr. Tuttle," she said and touched the man's arm when he didn't respond. He turned a worried gaze on her. "I should like an explanation for the shaking of the hall. I had thought all was well with the foundation."

Mr. Tuttle's heavy brow wrinkled, and he shook his head. "It isn't the house, my lady." He pointed up the ridge in the direction of the granite quarry. "It's the new mine. Something awful's happened. I'm sure of it."

A buzzing flooded her ears then, and it was as though she had stepped out of herself. It was the only way she could absorb what she had just been told, because Ash was at the mine, and if something awful had happened there—

She gripped Mr. Tuttle's arms. "Help." The word flew through her lips, her thoughts still scattered. "We must send help. We must *go*." She wasn't making sense. Her legs vibrated with the need to run, which was ridiculous. She knew the mine was miles away and yet her body wanted to go, *needed* to go.

But then Mr. Tuttle's warm hands were on hers, easing her back. "My men are already collecting our horses. You need to send someone to the village for the doctor. Ready the house to take in the injured. Hot water, fresh towels, bandages. Can you do that, ma'am?"

No. No, she needed to find Ash. She needed to know he was safe.

She shook her head. "Ash," she breathed, the only word she was able to get out as she pushed against Mr. Tuttle's grip, her body surging in the direction of the mine.

But Mr. Tuttle was stronger than she, and she moved not at all. "Your ladyship, you must stay here. Ash will need you."

She blinked at the sound of her husband's name on someone else's lips, and she thought the builder had known to speak his employer's given name. It shook her from the crazed response that had overtaken her body, and soon logic swept through her.

"Yes," she said, her voice firm, her chin going up. "Yes, I can do that."

She raced back into the house without another word even as she prepared herself for the worst.

CHAPTER 14

$\mathcal{H}$e came awake slowly, piece by piece, as if his brain were reaching out, checking each limb to see if it were still functional. He wiggled his toes in his boots, flexed his fingers only to find them carving through sand.

He was on the ground, a rock digging into the small of his back. An incessant ringing filled his ears, but through it he heard the muffled shouts of voices as if he were underwater, and the voices were stopped by the water surrounding him.

Finally he tried opening his eyes, but they wouldn't obey. It was as though he'd asked his brain to do something out of order, and it had refused. Something heavy was on him. He didn't know how he hadn't noticed at first, but now he became aware of it weighing him down.

His arms moved, lifting his hands, even though his eyes still wouldn't open. Carefully he reached forward toward his waist where the weight sat. He prodded the air, gently as if he expected to encounter something he didn't wish to feel. But all his fingers touched were the rough planks of what must have been boards. He thought of the crates of drills and wondered if the explosion had reached them, shattering the crates and spraying debris.

His eyes shot open then, the image of drill bits flying through the air sending a fresh wave of panic through him so intense he couldn't have kept his eyes closed no matter how his brain willed it.

He sat up, too quickly, and fell backwards again, the ringing in his ears intensifying until it reached a crescendo and then—

It was gone. The ringing had stopped. In its place came the chaos around him, the shouts for help, the scrabble of feet along gravel, horses and carts.

He sat up again, more slowly this time, blood rushing through him. He looked down. Boards lay strewn about him, over his legs and waist and farther flung. His hands moved then of their own accord, rubbing up and down his arms and legs, feeling his neck, face, and head. Nothing. No blood. He winced when his fingers swept over a knot at the back of his head that must have happened when he hit the ground.

He had to get up. Shoving at the boards still covering him, he tried to gain his feet only to fall back again. It was as though his muscles had forgotten how to move, how to expand and contract to pick himself up. He shook his head. He might not be bleeding, and the ringing might have stopped, but he'd still been blown off his feet by the repercussion of the blast.

The blast.

He looked up. From his perch higher on the hill, he could see the confusion below now. Panic roared through him again. If someone were hurt on his watch...

He couldn't finish the thought. This time when he shoved to his feet, he didn't allow his muscles to stop him. He surged upright, stumbling until he got his feet underneath him. He was two wavering steps down the hill when he stopped.

Biggins.

Biggins had been standing next to him. He swung around, his eyes scanning, but the man was nowhere to be seen. That wasn't possible. He'd been right there. Right next to Ash.

"Biggins!" The name stuck in his throat, and he coughed. Pain radiated through him, and he clutched at his stomach, doubling over.

Was he worse off than he thought? Was something wrong that he couldn't see?

Now when the panic roared up it was a silent thing, cold and deadly, and it coursed through him as an icy chill.

Adaline.

Her name ricocheted in his head, demanding space even as so much else vied for preference. But it was her name that played over and over again like a chorus.

Adaline. Adaline. Adaline.

What had he done? He had wasted so much time. So much time spent worrying if he would ruin their friendship, worrying that it was only circumstance that had stirred his feelings for her, but standing there on the hill wondering if he were about to die, the truth presented itself as though it had been there all along.

He hadn't dared hope for anything more with Adaline because he was worried he wouldn't be enough for her either.

The terribleness of the realization circumvented the pain, and it was like his brain became overwhelmed by it, shoving the rest away so it could grapple with this one heavy truth.

Ash had missed it. Had missed her, and now he was going to die without ever knowing...

He stood up, blinked, and forced his body to move. He wasn't going to die. Not yet. Not now. He had to get back to Adaline. He had to tell her what an idiot he'd been. He had to—

The crates of drills had scattered across the hillside, and the old lean-to they had been using for storage had collapsed in on itself. It was in the pile of rubble that he spotted the pair of boots.

"Biggins!" The name came out more clearly then, and he scrambled up the hill, throwing broken boards to the side as he made progress.

By the time he reached the steward, he became aware of a small noise coming from the rubble. It was a voice. Biggins was responding to him. Thank God. He pulled the last of the boards away, drills scattering.

The steward sat up, his hand pressed to his head. "I'm all right," he said immediately, his eyes wide with assurance only to dim when he must have seen the look on Ash's face. "I'm all right, aren't I, my lord?"

"You've looked better," Ash muttered.

Biggins had not fared as well as Ash had, and the man's face was crisscrossed in shallow cuts. The wound the man had pressed his hand against still oozed, and thick red blood squeezed its way out, sliding down his temple and cheek.

"We need to get you to a doctor." Ash moved and helped the man to his feet.

The steward was lanky and tall, and he draped over Ash as they made their way down the hill.

Ash scanned the chaos for Tibbs, only to find him barking orders as though he were on a battlefield. Ash approached, easing Biggins down on a boulder that had come to rest at the foot of the hill.

"Tibbs," Ash said. "What's happened?"

The man turned, and Ash took in the single scratch along his cheek. He seemed remarkably untouched considering he was much closer to the blast than Ash and Biggins had been.

"Too much gunpowder, my lord. Bound to happen. The

men aren't used to working with granite, you see. My calculations were off."

Ash rubbed at his neck, pain shooting along his shoulders. "They were quite a bit off, I would say."

Tibbs shook his head. "We'll get it right next time, my lord."

"Next time?" Ash couldn't hide the incredulousness from his voice. "Will there be a next time?" He couldn't stop the severe doubts that had been lingering deep in his mind since he realized what had happened from surfacing now. But just then Grady Givens popped up beside Tibbs, his face split with a wide smile.

"Of course, my lord. We're simply refining our technique. We'll get it right." The boy was unhurt as well except for a layer of dust that clung to his face, making his eyebrows look like caterpillars.

"You're unhurt." The idea seemed preposterous.

Givens's smile never faltered. "Of course, my lord. Tibbs always has us take cover when we're working with the explosives. Accidents can happen, you see."

Ash blinked, trying to absorb these words and looked around. Men were picking their way through the rubble but other than a few scratches, they all appeared well.

"I'm a might sorry, my lord. I didn't realize the blast would reach all the way up the hill. Otherwise I would have warned you and Mr. Biggins to take care."

Ash shook his head. It could have been a great deal worse, but clearly Tibbs had everything in hand.

"I'd like to try again, my lord. We'll get the hang of this granite thing for sure." Givens appeared as though he'd been given access to the Crown Jewels, and suddenly Ash couldn't tell the boy no.

Other sounds reached him then. Horses. Shouts. He turned about, peering up the hill in the direction of Grant

Hall in time to see his builder and his men crest the ridge. Of course the explosion had brought them from the hall, and Ash realized Adaline must have heard it too. He had to get back to her.

The need to return to her, to take her into his arms, to reassure her he was all right pulsed through him like hunger, tearing at his insides. He signaled to Tuttle who dismounted and clamored down the hill.

"My lord, what's happened?" the man said, his mustaches twitching.

"All is well, Tuttle, but I have need of a horse." Ash quickly explained what had happened with the blast, and together he and Tuttle got Biggins onto one of the carts the builders had brought.

Tibbs assured Ash he would make certain the other men weren't injured before cleaning up and securing the site for the day. Ash was already on Tuttle's horse before the man finished. Tuttle hopped up on the cart beside Biggins, but Ash had already spurred his horse into motion, headed for Grant Hall.

The panic inside of him had hardened into resolution now that he was in motion, and he felt it as a calming presence settling over him. In the short miles to the hall, he played over the explosion in his head again and again. Picking it apart and thinking how much worse it could have been.

He could have lost everything without taking the chance to see what it could have really been.

How stupid had he been? How foolish. Everything seemed so clear now, and he couldn't get there fast enough.

He leapt from the horse as soon as it reached the circle drive in front of the hall, tossing the reins to allow the horse to saunter onto the grass. But he was already taking the front stairs two at a time. It was late afternoon now, almost evening, and the sun was low enough that only the tops of the hall were lit, leaving the rest in the shadows cast by the trees that surrounded it.

He was nearly to the front door when he was struck by the sense of home that had crept up on him, the sense of rightness that he should be traveling through this door, that he should be looking for—

"Adaline!" He roared her name as he burst through the door, heedless of what he might find.

Did she think him dead? Injured? Maimed?

"Ash!"

His name came from the corridor to his right, and he was moving, his muscles driving him forward without thought.

Adaline stumbled into the hall ahead of him, her arms full of towels, her eyes wide, her hair falling from its braid. He didn't stop. He plucked the towels from her shaking hands even as she tried to speak.

"Ash. What's happened. We heard the blast. What. What." She spoke in a dazed neutral tone. Her words were not questions but rather a litany as though she were pressing all her thoughts into words.

He set the towels aside and finally—*finally*—he grabbed her, dragged her into his arms and set his mouth on hers.

Sensation tore through him. The taste of her, the feel of her—now both so familiar. So *right.*

How had he missed that? How could he have been so stupid to let his insecurities prevent this? Why had he been blind to what felt so natural now?

Her arms came around him then, hesitant, unsure. He didn't know if it were from the shock of the blast, of hearing it and not knowing what had happened, at seeing him there, unhurt, or because he was kissing her. But it didn't matter. She was in his arms, and he could feel her heartbeat, feel her breath, know that she was alive, and she was his.

Reluctantly he tore himself away, put his hands to her shoulders, and eased her back, so he could see her face. Her eyes were open, searching, her lips parted as if she had meant to speak, but then he realized she was speaking. She was whispering as if talking to herself.

"I was so afraid you were dead. That you were dead, and I never got to tell you how I love you. How I've always loved you."

Her words ran through him like water. Always loved him? What was she talking about? Perhaps it was the shock of everything. It had muddled her thoughts. But love? She loved him?

The urgency that had begun low and pulsing inside of him on the hill beside the quarry roared anew, and he no longer wished to be standing there where anyone could see them.

"Where is Mrs. Hutchinson? Biggins is hurt. He'll need tending. Have you sent for a doctor?" He was doing as she had done. Voicing every thought that pranced through his head, but she only nodded.

"In here." He peered behind her to where she pointed even as her eyes remained unfocused.

It was one of the drawing rooms on this floor, but it had been stacked with furniture, mismatched things thrown together.

"We had to move the guest rooms' furniture so the builders could repair the floors. There are beds in here. Biggins can rest here until the doctor arrives."

Mrs. Hutchinson appeared through the rabble of furniture, her hands cupping a ewer as she moved toward one of the tables in the room.

"My lord," she breathed when she saw him. "Are you well?"

He nodded. "Fine, yes. Thank you." His mind rattled as

though it had come undone in his head. He needed to get somewhere quiet. With Adaline. He had to tell her…well, everything. "The builders are on their way with Biggins. He has a small head wound." Belatedly he remembered Adaline's notion that something more stirred between the house-keeper and the land steward, and he raised a hand in assurance. "He's fine. The wound will simply need tending."

The housekeeper put the ewer down, wiping her hands on her apron efficiently. "I shall see to him."

"Thank you." He didn't say anything more. He took Adaline's arm and steered her toward the end of the corridor and the staircase that lead up to the family's rooms. But even that wasn't enough. By the time he reached the bottom of the stairs, his body chafed at the slowness, at the delay. So he simply picked her up in his arms and carried her the rest of the way to his bed.

* * *

He was alive.

Ash was alive, and she had told him she loved him. Oh God, she had told him everything. She hadn't meant to say it. She'd *never* meant to say it. It was her secret and hers alone. It was safer that way.

But he was alive, and he was kissing her, and he was—

He kicked open the door to the marquess's room, and in a flash, she remembered that first night. When he had first touched her. When he had first made her tremble.

Fear shot through her, displacing the desire that had started to hum low in her belly. What if he stopped again? What if something else drove him away this time?

She tried to ignore the misgivings contaminating her thoughts, but there was nothing more frightening than the possibility of rejection. Especially now. After everything.

Could she bear it again? If he were to leave her wanting? If he remembered who she was? That she wasn't the one he wanted.

But somehow it seemed as though he did. She studied his face as he set her on her feet, as he turned to bolt the door. She had never seen such concentration on his features, such focus. It was as though he were assaulted by the same torrent of emotions as she.

"Ash." There were so many questions filling her mouth, and yet nothing came forward.

She couldn't bring herself to question this. Not if it were to be her only chance at having the man she had loved her whole life.

As if sensing her unspoken questions, he stepped forward, raised his hand to her cheek, cupping her face so delicately she wasn't even certain he touched her.

"When I thought I was going to die I could only think of you, Adaline. Everything else just went away, and there was only you, and—" He choked and looked away as if trying to find his voice again.

"Oh Ash," she breathed, touching his face now as if through her fingers she could finally know whether or not it was real, this seriousness that had overtaken him, a seriousness so unlike him that it couldn't possibly be true, and it certainly couldn't have been her fault.

Not her. She was nothing to him. Only and forever his friend. But not now. Not here. Something had happened. Something had rocked him. The explosion. But he wasn't harmed. Was it enough though? Had it frightened him enough to rethink all that he had done?

When he finally looked back at her, his eyes had grown dark and questioning as if he were looking inward instead of outward. It hurt. To see him like that. To see him looking back on decisions he had made and only finding regret.

Did he regret marrying her? Or did he regret not making love to her?

She couldn't let herself explore either question. Not now when her own desire simmered within her. So instead she slipped her hand around to his neck and pulled his head down to hers.

She kissed him with everything she had, pressing her body against him as she rose up on her tiptoes, slipped both arms around him, anchoring herself to him.

His big hands held her, sliding along her sides and up until they cupped her shoulders, pulling her taut against him. He angled his head, deepening the kiss, running his lips over hers, nibbling and sucking, and stoking the flames within her. He moved, sliding his lips along her jaw to that place behind her ear she had learned was so sensitive, but still he didn't stop.

Holding her, he eased her back, tilting her so his lips could gain access to her neck. He nuzzled and kissed and nibbled, and she squirmed, her desire sparking until she thought she might suffocate.

"Ash, please." There were too many clothes. Too much between them, too much stopping her from feeling all of him.

She didn't wait for him. She took what she wanted. Sliding her hands down his chest, she pushed at the front of his jacket, undid the buttons of his waistcoat, and shoved, pushing all of it from his shoulders, and he let her, backing away long enough to let everything drop to the floor.

She was wearing her day gown, and he took that moment to tug at the tie just under her breasts. The bodice loosened, and she wiggled her shoulders, tugging her arms free and letting the dress join his jacket and waistcoat.

Now when he came back to her, she could feel his heat through his thin shirt, through her chemise. Her corset was still in the way though, and she itched to have it off. She wanted to feel him, and there were still too many barriers between them.

"Ash, I want—"

But he was already moving, turning her, keeping one hand pressed to her stomach even as the other made quick work of the ties of her corset. The garment was soon on the floor, and still standing behind her, he pushed at the straps of her chemise, first one and then the other as if he were unwrapping a particularly special present and he wished to prolong the inevitable. The undergarment fell, sliding along her naked body until she stood there in only her stockings and slippers.

She felt no compulsion to cover herself. Not with him. She wanted him to see her. She wanted him to see all of her.

"Ash?" Though she was bold enough to have him look, there were still too many times he had rejected her, knowingly and unknowingly, and vulnerability had her questioning his silence.

He hadn't moved. He still stood behind her, and she straightened her shoulders, wondering what it was he saw as he studied her from behind.

"Oh God, Adaline," he finally said, his voice constrained.

She made to turn, but he stopped her with a finger on her shoulder.

"Wait," he said, the word low and hoarse.

Keeping that finger pressed against her, he traced a line down her spine, lower and lower, until he reached her buttocks. Only then did he press a hand against her, cupping her bottom before sliding around to the front, pulling her against him as he splayed his hand low against her belly.

She felt him then, hard against her backside, and it sent a thrilling shock through her. It was clear evidence of his desire. He wanted her, and she would have him now.

She moved her hips experimentally, rubbing against him. It earned her a moan against the back of her neck, and she shivered.

"Adaline, I've wanted this for so long." The hand he used to hold her to him moved, caressing the soft swell of her belly, lingered at the underside of her breast before skimming higher.

She wanted him to touch her like he had that day, his hand on her breast, but he refused her that, tracing a careful path around her aching nipples before reaching her shoulder.

"Ash." She was throbbing now, and it was difficult to find words. But she had to tell him. She had to tell him what she wanted.

But it didn't seem to matter because he spun her toward the bed, pushing her down and back against the pillows. She thought he would remove her stockings then, but he didn't. Instead he stepped back, tugging his cravat loose and pulling his shirt over his head in one swift motion. She sucked in a breath, the fire inside of her pulsing at the sight of his bare chest with its fine dusting of hair.

She had always loved looking at him, but this was something different. This was elusive and carnal and rare, and yet somehow, she was seeing it. She was seeing him. Her eyes dipped; she couldn't help it. But he didn't remove his trousers.

Instead he knelt at the side of the bed and picked up her legs, one at a time, and again she thought he would remove her stockings. But he didn't. Instead he pressed his mouth to the inside of one thigh, and she jerked. His mouth was hot against her skin, and seeing him do that, watching him put his mouth to her as though she were some rare and precious thing had her body clenching.

"Ash?" Her voice held question and wonder, and she didn't know what she was feeling any longer.

But he moved, his mouth sliding along her skin, moving closer and closer, until—

Her hips came up off the mattress, her hand going to his head. He was too close. Too dangerously close to that part of her he had touched before. Her most intimate part. The one that throbbed for him now. That wanted him to touch her again so badly.

"Ash, you can't—"

But he did. His touch was gentle at first, so gentle she wasn't sure what he was doing, but then he parted her folds and without hesitation put his hot mouth against her sensitive nub. She collapsed against the mattress, her muscles turning to water as all of her focus traveled to the place where he touched her, where he lapped at her with his tongue.

The fire inside of her grew to an almost painful point. Something was happening. Something twisted inside of her, yearning and straining for release, but he was relentless and unforgiving, his mouth working against her. She raked her nails along his scalp, her body winding toward something that was just out of reach, and then—

He stopped. Again. Pulling away from her when she knew something was just out of reach. She saw her hand where his head had been, and her fingers still reached for him. But he was gone.

No, not gone. Relief and something else, something like curiosity, coursed through her. He was shedding his trousers. Frantically shedding his trousers. She had never seen him so undone, and her body yearned toward his.

He was on top of her in seconds, covering her body with his, and pleasure so pure washed through her. She had never felt anything so exquisite, so complete.

"I can't wait any longer," he mumbled against her lips. "I promise next time it will be better. But right now I need you.

I need you to know that I'm yours, and I don't know how else to make sure you understand that."

His words rocked through her like his touch never could, and for a moment she felt herself hanging between the past and the present. It was like she had split in two and was in that moment seeing herself as she had been and now was. Lonely in her love for a man who called her his friend. But now she was his wife, and he wanted her, and the reality didn't seem possible to that lonely woman standing in the periphery.

But it was real, and he was kissing her again, his hands skimming along her body as though worshipping it. The mat of hair on his chest rubbed against her taut nipples. His hips pressed her into the mattress, and she felt the tip of him against her. Her legs fell apart on their own, making room for him, and it was as though her body knew what to do. Like it had been waiting for him all along.

But she had been waiting for him.

He pushed into her, slowly, gently, and somehow her body stretched around him. He sat up, leaning on one elbow as his hand slipped down to cup her breast. She thought he might touch her as she had wanted, but instead he drew her nipple into his mouth, and a gasp of surprise tripped from her lips. This was far better than when he had touched her. It seemed impossible and yet it wasn't. Just like everything else.

He moved inside of her, slowly at first, as if seeing if she were ready for him. He groaned, shifting against her, and he tore his mouth from her body, roaring up to press his lips against hers.

"God, Adaline, this feels too good."

She wanted to agree, but hearing him say her name like that, his voice rough with passion, it was too much, and she thought he would hear the tears of joy in her voice if she spoke.

So instead she ran her fingers up his back, opened her legs, and drew him closer. He went deeper inside of her, and she stretched around him. The hum low in her belly changed then. It grew sharper, her internal muscles working as if in response.

"Jesus," he groaned against her lips, and she realized he liked that. He liked what her body did to him.

He withdrew entirely before slamming back into her, and the sensation was so great it dispersed any coherent thought from her mind. Suddenly it was just them, their bodies, together, and no rational thought could survive where taste and touch and sound prevailed.

He picked up the rhythm, moving steadily within her, and yet somehow always managing to keep her desire just so. Never stoking the flames within her but not letting them die. It was pure torture, and she clutched at him, willing him to do something about it.

"Ash, please," she moaned when he continued to torture her, and finally he seemed to give in because he moved, harder, faster, and she coiled, her desire turning, pinching, drawing itself to a point.

He slammed into her then, rocking her into the mattress, his chest scraping against her aroused nipples. It was all too much, too much all at once, and she became aware of all of her pieces, scattering in the desire he stoked within her.

It was then that he touched her, his finger caressing the sensitive nub he had sucked into his mouth earlier, and the desire that had scattered only seconds before came to a single point and suddenly she came undone.

The cry of pure pleasure erupted from her throat, and she came up off the mattress, her arms wrapping around him as if he were the only thing that could keep her tethered to the earth. She shivered and pulsed, her body echoing with her spent desire, but he was moving faster now within her, his hand still but pressing against that nub that throbbed in an echo of her orgasm, and unbelievably she felt her passion grow again, tightening, changing, morphing, until—

This time when she came, he came with her, pounding into her as together they fell apart.

* * *

SHE WASN'T sure what time it was when she woke, but the gray light at the windows suggested dawn was nearing.

She lay very still, reaching out with her sense as if to better understand this new world she had awoken in. The first thing she became aware of was Ash's quiet breathing beside her, the heat of his body pressed against her side. She moved carefully, rolling onto her side so she could see him.

At some point in the night, he had fallen asleep, deeply, sprawled on his back, and she knew the events of the day had finally caught up with him and no amount of desire was enough to keep sleep at bay. Although he had tried mightily to stop it, making love to her several times, stopping only long enough to scavenge food and drink from the kitchen.

He breathed evenly now, his face relaxed in sleep, and she watched him, willing the shadows to stay away. It was easy when he was awake, when he was pressing his lips to her body, lighting fires within her she had never known were possible. But when he was quiet in sleep, the doubts wandered back in, plaguing her.

Slowly she rolled onto her back, propping her arm behind her head as she studied the ceiling, sorting through her thoughts one by one.

Between their bouts of lovemaking he had told her what had happened at the quarry, about the explosion and the injuries to the men. She could sense how truly grateful he was that no one was more seriously hurt, and she understood not for the first time the weight of responsibility he carried. Sifting through what he had told her, she tried to find something to assuage her misgivings.

Why had he suddenly done what he had spent weeks avoiding?

Was it enough that he had feared for his life? That he thought he might die without having known her in every way?

The thought sent delicious heat curling through her, but still her uneasiness didn't waver.

She hated that she was even doubting the sincerity of his actions. This was everything she had ever wanted. Turning her head just a bit, she caught his profile, his lips slightly parted in sleep, and she cursed herself for being ridiculous. She shouldn't question this. She should embrace it.

Except...she couldn't.

It wasn't enough. She knew Ash too well, and she knew whatever had kept him from her was too great to be solved in an afternoon. She shut her eyes, hoping to stop her racing thoughts with sheer force of will when suddenly the weight of his arm fell over her. Her eyes shot open again, and she found him leaning over her, a devilish grin on his lips.

"You're awake," she whispered, reaching up a hand to stroke the shadow of beard along his jaw as though to check that he was real.

"The sound of your stirring thoughts woke me."

Her hand froze. "What do you mean?"

His laugh was soft, and he bent to capture her mouth in a slow, tender kiss. He lay down, pulling her into his arms so he faced her. The intimacy was far greater than they had done yet, and she wanted to squirm under the scrutiny, but she forced herself to relax, to enjoy it.

Because she didn't know how long it would last.

He sucked in a breath and stroked a finger along her brow. "What was that thought right there?"

She blinked, realizing her thoughts must have shown on her face. She couldn't tell him. Not now. Not ever.

"If you must know, I'm just...worried," she said, hoping it wouldn't be lying if she kept her words general.

He stroked his finger along the line of her cheek and down to her jaw. "The worried part I understood. What about exactly?"

She nestled closer against him, her heart thudding loudly in her chest. "You could have been killed."

It wasn't the thought that plagued her then, but it was one of merit.

"But I wasn't." His hand moved to her back, pulling her closer, although if she did get any closer, they would end up making love again, and suddenly she wished to know.

"Ash," she began before she changed her mind. "Why now? You've been avoiding me for almost a month."

"Because I could have been killed," he said easily.

She tried to squirm away from him. "Don't make fun."

He tightened his hold on her, pulling her against his chest so she was forced to tilt her head back to see him. "I'm not making fun, Atwood. When I thought I could have died, I realized what an idiot I'd been. I had allowed my own insecurities to keep me from this." His lips parted as though he couldn't believe what had almost happened. "For so long I've been told I wasn't enough, and for a long time, I believed it. But you helped me to say they were wrong." He frowned, his brow wrinkling. "Only I'm not sure I can forgive myself for not seeing the truth."

A wisp of unease curled in her chest. She understood what he was saying, knew the lies he had been told to keep him small, but an afternoon did not undo a lifetime of abuse, and more than anything, she didn't know if she could trust him with her heart because she had seen him that night in the conservatory.

She put her hand against his bare chest as though to ground him through her touch. "There's nothing to forgive yourself for," she said. "You weren't responsible for what others did to you. You should be proud of yourself for having the strength to keep going, to become the man you are today." She paused to make sure he was listening. "Just as I'm proud of you."

His brow furrowed again, and she wondered what she had said.

"I'm glad you're here," he said, and she remembered what he had said that first night they had been at Grant Hall.

She braced herself, ready for him to hurt her when he didn't know there was a wound that could cause her pain, but instead his brow remained wrinkled as though he were lost in his own thoughts.

"Through everything that has happened, you've been my one constant. I was so scared of losing you if—" He stopped, his eyes searching her face. For one heart-stopping moment she thought he was finally going to tell her about that night in the conservatory, but then he said, "I wasn't enough for you."

She had heard the same refrain beaten into him by his father and his stepfathers, the fact that he hadn't been the son they wanted. She couldn't imagine what kind of man they had sought because to her Ash was everything a human should aspire to be.

She laid her hand against his cheek. "You know you've always been enough for me."

He wrapped his hand around the one she pressed to his cheek. "I know." His voice was tight with some old pain, and tears came to her eyes. "I just wasn't listening." His face broke into a tremulous smile then, and she shifted, pressing her lips to his as if to take his pain into her, all of it. As if she could finally free him from his torment with her love.

He wrapped his arms around her, pulling her tight against him, and she let him chase away her plaguing thoughts.

It wasn't until much later, when the windows were full of bright morning light, when she lay sprawled across his chest, listening to the sound of his heartbeat under her cheek, that she recalled exactly what he had said.

He had been worried he wouldn't be enough for her. That was what had held him back, kept him from the feelings he obviously had for her. She couldn't help but remember Alice's words, that love could grow over time. Still, uneasiness crept over her.

Because she couldn't help but wonder if there were still someone else who held that kind of power over him.

CHAPTER 15

She started when Ash took her hand into his own, the train rumbling about them, hurtling toward London. His features were tight with worry, and she smiled before leaning into him to kiss him softly on the cheek.

"I'm not scared of the train any longer," she reassured him. "It's only I have some misgivings about returning to London."

After that first near deadly episode, the granite quarry had taken off with alarming speed. Within days the granite salvaged from the hall had been repurposed and sold to fill agricultural orders. Biggins had already received orders for building granite and was orchestrating an order management system to see them fulfilled.

It was clear far too soon that Ash needn't stay in Dartmoor, that he had hired capable men with experience in mining far greater than his, and the demands of the title required him elsewhere.

Only it was far too difficult to leave the relaxed environment of Grant Hall. There were no social obligations as of yet in Dartmoor. The Aylesford estate had been so long neglected Adaline was sure word hadn't spread of their arrival in time to receive any sort of invitation. Their days had been filled with meaningful work and purpose and their nights occupied with each other.

She leaned into her husband then, resting her head on his shoulder as best she could as the train vibrated around them. It still seemed unreal, what had happened between them. She had dreamt of this her whole life, and now that her dreams had somehow became the stuff of her reality, she couldn't trust it. Not yet. It was still too new, and there were still too many things unsaid between them.

"London hasn't always been the happiest place for us," she said after several seconds of his weighty silence filling their cabin.

She felt him relax beneath her cheek, and she knew he felt the same. As the son of a judge and the impoverished daughter of an earl, they had teetered on the very edge of respectable society. It was a tenuous existence at best, and now they were to return to it when they had only begun to explore the new reality of each other.

Could something so delicate survive machinations of the *ton*?

She worried it could not.

He rested his chin atop her head. "I was thinking of much the same actually."

She sat up abruptly and felt his head fall against the seat from her sudden movement. He laughed, rubbing the back of his neck as he straightened.

"You were?" The words came out far more strained than she'd intended. "Ash, why didn't you say something? You never worry over anything."

His expression pinched into a frown. "Hardly. I was very worried the day I almost blew up."

Her shoulders dropped at that. He was right. She would never forget the look on his face when he'd come through the door that day. Truthfully she would never forget her own fear. The worry that had seemed to consume her when she was left to wonder if he were dead or alive, whether or not he'd been injured. She didn't speak those dangerous thoughts. She simply picked up his hand more tightly this time and leaned back against the seat, her shoulder brushing his.

"I suppose if we survived the haunted moor we can survive London, don't you think?"

His breath was warm against her cheek as he said, "Do you know I'm rather disappointed we didn't encounter a single ghost while we were there. Seems rather a waste."

She had hardly heard him jest while they were in Dartmoor. In fact, he'd been more solemn than usual since they had wed, and she wondered if it were the responsibilities of the title that were weighing on him or if it were something else. Namely, some*one* else.

Adaline hadn't forgotten about Lady Valerie. The part of her that had been a wallflower for so many years still worried about the woman. She was after all the object of Ash's love for so many years. Had the distance afforded by the remote hall been the catalyst to Ash seeing Adaline for the first time as the woman she was? Now that they were returning to London would he forget all about her again? Now that Lady Valerie was once more within reach?

She hated to think like that, but it was hard not to. She'd been there that night in the conservatory. She'd seen the rejection on Ash's face, and she hated that another woman meant so much to him to cause him such pain.

Did she mean that much to him? Only time would tell, and they had run out of that.

She smiled now. "I wonder if those footsteps we heard

that first night weren't entirely those of thieves roaming the hall. Haven't you wondered?"

He pulled a grimace, and she laughed, knocking playfully against his shoulder.

"I'm just glad I had you there to protect me," he said, and this only made her laugh harder.

They sat like that in companionable silence as fields gave way to hamlets and villages and then buildings rising along the railroad tracks as they entered London proper.

It seemed impossible that so much time had passed when they finally stepped through the doors of Aylesford House in Mayfair. She paused in the entrance, feeling an odd sense of time repeating itself as she recalled being admitted on her wedding day. Higham had been so kind to her, but she couldn't recall much past that. She had numbed herself against the inevitability of the day, and it seemed somehow unbelievable that she should be filled with such happiness now.

She had left Aylesford House resigned to her fate and returned with a hope she hadn't known she might have.

Now only if things would stay as such.

She watched Ash discard his hat and gloves. The footman came to collect her things next, and Ash disappeared down the corridor, already sorting through the day's post that had been left on the table in the entryway. She felt a pang at his loss, still feeling the memory of his shoulder against hers on the train.

It was all right, she reminded herself. He had tended to business affairs every day in Dartmoor, and it would be much the same here. She knew that. There was no reason to get twisted about by it now.

Her foot was on the first stair when he called out her name from what seemed like his study down the corridor.

She paused, listening, sure she was mistaken, but he called her name again, a note of almost panic in his voice.

She turned and swept down the hallway, picking up her skirts so she could move more swiftly. She wasn't sure what she had been expecting, but when she turned the corner into the study, she froze, her eyes taking in the sight before her.

Ash stood behind his desk, the day's post forgotten in his hands as he considered the stacks of letters on the desk in front of him.

"I thought Higham forwarded any correspondence and papers," she said, stepping carefully into the room.

She scanned the neat piles of letters in front of her much as Ash did. He tossed the few in his hands on top of the other piles, seemingly overwhelmed by the sight of it all.

"He did. These are all recent. Within the past few days."

"How do you know?" She'd reached the desk now and leaned carefully over it, taking in the neat black ink on the letters indicating they were intended for the Marquess of Aylesford.

He picked up a newspaper from the stack on the corner of the desk. "It's from three days ago. Higham knew we were returning and likely didn't forward it as he had earlier posts." He tossed the paper aside and gestured helplessly at the desk. "What on earth do you think this is all about?"

They had received very few invitations prior to their departure for Dartmoor, and even then, Higham would have sorted those out from the post and left them with Mrs. Manning to give to Adaline upon her return. This...this was just...

She picked up a letter and tore it open, no longer able to bear it. Quickly she scanned the first few lines, taking in the meaning of the writer's intent. She tossed the letter aside and picked up another and another. But they all said the same thing.

"Ash," she breathed, but he was preoccupied with his own letters, having dug in for himself when he saw her tearing through them.

"I know," he said, absently sitting in the chair behind the desk, a letter in each hand. "They're all requests for meetings at various clubs." He looked up, his eyes shiny with disbelief. "It seems every titled gentleman in London suddenly wants to have a drink with me."

"They all want to know of your improvements at Grant Hall. About the granite quarry." She looked up from the last letter in her hand. "How do they already know about that?"

She knew Biggins had been swamped with inquiries about granite for building, but how, in just a few short weeks, could news have reached London? And to this extent?

Ash shook his head, tossing the letters he held back onto the pile. "Because every gentleman in London is facing the same thing I am."

Placing her palms on the edge of the desk, she leaned toward him. "Which is?"

"A changing aristocracy." He gestured to the piles. "It's just like the railroad lease I agreed to in Kent. Estates can no longer survive on the rents from tenants, especially as the economies continue to change."

She couldn't stop her smile, unable to form words through her grin.

"What is it?" he finally asked.

"Don't you see? It's exactly as I said weeks ago." She moved around the desk and sat down in his lap, wrapping her arms around his neck. "I knew what you were capable of," she said, eyeing the mound of letters from this perspective, shaking her head slightly in disbelief. "I just never knew it would be this grand."

He tightened his arms around her. "What do you mean?"

"You relied on your instincts," she said, but his face

remained clouded in confusion. "At Grant Hall. I saw your instincts firsthand when you tackled poor Grady Givens that night. I knew you had this in you, but even I had no idea..." She trailed off, unable to put into words how terribly proud she was of him.

"Poor Grady Givens? He was trying to rob me. To say nothing of what he might have done to you."

She waved off his words. "Grady Givens wouldn't hurt a puppy," she said. "Now. What do you plan to do about this? You're certainly in a position to enhance the Aylesford title."

He eyed her suspiciously. "What do you know of enhancing titles?"

"Just as I said months ago now. We can work together to position the Aylesford title for great success in society." She nodded at the pile of letters. "This will only help add prestige to the title." She looked at Ash then, meeting his gaze directly so he understood the weight of her words. "You did that, Ash. You alone did that. You relied on your instincts, and your instincts saw you through what could have been financial ruin for the title. You know that, right?"

He nodded, but she didn't miss the clouds in his eyes that suggested he didn't entirely believe her.

"Even if that is true, I still have another problem to face."

She stilled, her mind instantly picturing that night in the conservatory, which was silly really. He couldn't possibly be thinking of Lady Valerie now. So soon. Again. Still. She was just being insecure.

"What is that?" she finally ventured.

His expression folded into a deep frown. "If I accept all of these invitations, I'm going to get very drunk."

* * *

FOUR DAYS later he wished he wasn't so accurate in his prediction.

He nuzzled his wife's neck as she tried to straighten a string of pearls.

She jerked far enough out of his grasp to finish the task before admonishing him. "Ashfield Riggs, if you think to distract me with your kisses, you are mistaken. Atwood daughters are made of sterner stuff."

He eyed her questioningly. "I would think that of Amelia or Alice, but I have yet to see you prove as much."

Her mouth opened in fake shock. "I beg your pardon." She turned to face him directly, stopping immediately in front of him. He prepared himself for his attentions to be returned but instead she reached up to straighten his cravat. "In this case though, I'm afraid you may be correct. There are times when I think both of my sisters are far stronger."

He stilled her hands with his, forcing her to meet his gaze. "How can you think that? I've seen you face down thieves, and never before have I seen such bravery." He assessed her, running his gaze down the deep navy folds of her gown. "Although I believe your bodice was a great deal looser at the time. Perhaps I should fix—"

He made a half-hearted move to undo the buttons down her back, but she swatted his hands away.

"Ashfield," she said in a scolding voice that oddly had an unexpected effect on him, one he rather liked.

"Ashfield, is it?" He leaned down, bringing his mouth close to her ear. "Do you promise to scold me properly later, my wife?"

She didn't push him away. If anything she leaned into him, her hands moving from his cravat to lay flat against his chest, her face lifting to his.

"Only if you're naughty," she whispered.

He stepped back, sucking in a breath. His desire for

Adaline was still new and startling. What had started as an inconvenient simmer in the early weeks of their marriage had exploded into something raw and easily sparked.

When he thought he might lose her without ever really having her.

That day at the granite quarry when he'd awoken on the ground, his ears ringing, everything had become suddenly so clear he wasn't sure how he could possibly have thought anything differently before then.

He studied her now, his wife, as she peered up at him, a knowing grin on her lips, and wondered how it had come to this. His life. Feelings stirred inside of him, ones he still could not name. He often thought about what Adaline had said when he'd first returned to Grant Hall that day. She had used the word *love*, and it had frightened him, and he hadn't been brave enough to ask her of it since.

Did she love him?

Everything had been so simple before he'd become a marquess. His pursuits had been plain, his goals achievable. But now. Everything was different.

He was standing here in front of his best friend wondering if he loved her. Wondering if she had really told him of her feelings that day in the vestibule of Grant Hall. Feelings she had not mentioned again. He knew that kind of behavior. It was one he was guilty of himself. It was better to keep one's feelings a secret rather than have one's heart broken when they were revealed.

It was all too confusing, and he'd spent the better part of the week attending one meeting after the next. Every night had been much the same, and he longed for the days at Grant Hall when his evenings were spent rubbing his wife's feet while she told him about the moth infestation in the upstairs linen closets.

He stilled as if everything about him had suddenly come

into sharper focus. In his head, he heard his father's voice, the litany of criticisms, and then his stepfathers, the same criticisms with their own personal twists. His pursuit of Lady Valerie Lattimer. The way he had learned to play a room to have everyone laughing. No one would notice he was only the son of a judge if they were laughing.

But it hadn't been that way at Grant Hall. It had never been that way with Adaline.

"Are you all right?"

He realized he'd been silent for too long, lost in the mire of his own thoughts. He roused himself, taking in the crease along his wife's brow. He smoothed it with two fingers, tracing the curve of her brow until his fingers slipped into her hair. She wore it in a braid like always, but she'd added a dark blue ribbon that gave it a refined quality.

"Must we go to—" He blinked, his fingers still toying with the end of her braid. "Where are we going tonight?"

She frowned and tugged her braid from his wandering fingers. "Haven House. It's only a soirée. If you like I can claim a headache after a couple of hours, and we can come home early. But you must speak to Lord Haven about—"

He held up a hand to ward off her instructions. It had been the same every night that week. He must speak to some lord or duke or bishop or something. She ignored his hand and turned him physically in the direction of the door. He didn't miss the smile on her face as he turned though.

"We've been out every night since we returned. Can't we stay in tonight? I should like to hear about linen closets."

She laughed softly. "Not tonight. The season is almost over, and our social obligations will ease considerably then. I promise."

He made a face she couldn't see, but he still felt better making it.

They arrived at Haven House to find the festivities well

underway. It appeared as though the night's soirée was designed to give a platform for the daughter of the house's poetry. Ash was glad he had business matters to attend and immediately began searching out Lord Haven while Adaline wandered off to find Alice.

The guests were crammed in a series of connected drawing rooms, and he filtered through one to the other. Tables had been set up for whist, and a group of gentlemen huddled in one corner with the latest betting sheets, pretending as though they were perusing agricultural manuals. He was relieved when he stumbled into the final drawing room to find the terrace doors open to the night air, another group of gentlemen huddled about the doors, the smoke from their cigars carried away by the night breeze. He spotted Lord Haven among them and headed that way only to be stopped with a hand on his chest.

The gesture was so intimate it froze him in his place. He looked down at the small hand encased in a fine white kid glove. He followed the line of the glove up to a delicate elbow, the ruffle of a gown's sleeve, and then—

"Lady Valerie." He hated how breathless he sounded, how her name tripped from his lips like an oath.

He hated himself, completely and thoroughly in the flash of a moment. How could the mere sight of her stir such a response inside of him? Only an hour before he had held his wife in his arms, his wife whom he very much desired, his wife who he could very well love.

And yet, here he was. Enraptured by this woman who had haunted his dreams for so long.

She was beautiful, her dark hair swept up in curls that framed her face, her soulful eyes shining, drinking him in.

He paused in his study of her face, trepidation creeping along his skin.

333

Lady Valerie had never looked at him like this. Had never surveyed him like he was something...worthy.

"My lord," she cooed.

Cooed?

Something was wrong. Something was very wrong. She shouldn't be speaking to him in such a tone; she shouldn't be—

Oh God, her gloved hand was still on his chest.

His eyes flashed to the other side of the room where the gentleman still clustered by the open doors, but they were paying the rest of the room no heed.

Carefully he eased Lady Valerie's hand from his chest, took a much-needed step away from her.

"I hear you've just returned from another one of your estates." Her eyes *were* shining, but it was unnatural as if it were practiced.

He took another step back, colliding with the doorframe behind him. From this distance, he could take her in properly. The way she held her chin at an unusual angle, but to a casual observer, her neck was elongated, and she would appear elegant. It was only when one really looked did one see how she carefully held herself to appear a different way than she was.

Had he never noticed how short she was?

"Yes," he said, his tone neutral. He had to keep his wits about him. Something was off, and he didn't trust himself around this woman who still had such a stranglehold on his emotions. "My wife and I just returned from Grant Hall in Dartmoor." Did her eyes light at the word *wife*, or was that just his imagination?

"I trust you had a pleasant journey." Had her voice always rung with such false politeness? "I was hoping to have seen you before now, but our social paths have never crossed, I'm afraid. I was hoping to speak with you."

The trepidation that had crawled along his skin burned now with a healthy dose of alarm. Lady Valerie had never been one to shirk his company, but she had never sought him out. He went to answer her when this thought had him stopping. Surely he was mistaken. Surely Lady Valerie had sought him out at some point before. Had he doggedly pursued a woman who had never once shown an interest in him?

He gave himself a mental shake. "Our journey was most pleasant. I'm sorry to say I must speak with—" He had meant to head off any further conversation, his body singing with too many warnings, but then she laid her hand on his arm and leaned far too close.

She peered up at him, her expression intimate and close. "Please, Ash," she whispered. "I must speak with you."

Her voice was stripped of its false politeness, and standing this close to her, he could smell her fragrance, something heavy with lilies. He had never been this close to her. There was the night in the conservatory but even then, he'd kept a respectable distance. The handful of times they had danced, he'd done the same. Always respectable to a degree.

But this.

Had he been thinking clearly, he would have realized his body remained dormant. No matter how his brain registered the sensuality in her gaze, in the nearness of her body, he physically did not respond.

It was his brain that betrayed him.

Lady Valerie wanted him.

This was what he had been seeking his whole life. Just a word from her. A nod from her. A *yes* from her.

A yes from her would finally drown out the sound of his father's voice. He knew it.

Had it been only an hour earlier that he had heard the voices of his father, his stepfathers parading through his mind? Maybe if his emotions hadn't been in such a spiral. Maybe if so much hadn't changed so quickly he would have made a different decision. He would have made the safe decision.

But he wasn't feeling particularly safe then. He was feeling confused and dazzled and overwhelmed, and standing before him was the one simple thing that had stood for his salvation for so many years.

That was why he heard himself saying, "Yes, of course," and looked behind him to ensure no one was watching when he took Lady Valerie's arm, and they slipped from the room.

CHAPTER 16

The only thing that stopped her from bolting after them was Alice's hand on her arm.

"Don't." The single word was spoken with a fierceness Adaline hadn't ever heard from her sister before then.

She shot Alice a glare. "What do you mean?" She looked back to where her husband had slipped away with Lady Valerie Lattimer. "My husband is sneaking off with that... with that..." Even now when she most wished to say something vile, she found she couldn't bring herself to do it.

"That whore," Alice said, the words coming easily and strong.

Adaline looked at her sister again, feeling as if she didn't know her at all. Alice's gaze was unflinching, her features set as she stared in the direction Ash and Lady Valerie had disappeared.

Adaline couldn't stop the sinking feeling in her stomach, the way her world seemed to tumble end over end, but through the torrent, she couldn't help but find an eerie sense of calm.

She'd known this would happen.

She had told Ash as much, had told him of her fears, and yet here he was, bringing them to fruition.

She didn't realize she was moving again until Alice tugged her back once more.

"You can't make a scene here, Adaline. No matter how it hurts." Adaline looked swiftly at her sister then, and she realized when she had thought her sister's face stern before it was actually oddly pragmatic. "You know Ash's position in society is vulnerable. If you give the *ton* any fodder, they will happily push him over the edge. You can't do that."

She was right. She knew her sister was right. Adaline nodded, her tongue suddenly seeming too big for her mouth.

"I'm going to go find Ransom. He'll know what to do."

Adaline nodded again, the motion automatic. Her sister's words registered seconds later, and she turned swiftly, but her sister was already gone.

Ransom? Did she mean the Earl of Knighton? Her sister had used his given name. What did that mean?

For a moment she was utterly distracted from her own torment, her sister's words jarring her from the present.

But only just and not for long. Looking down at her empty hands, Adaline realized no one was stopping her.

Like that night in the conservatory, her heart beat an unnatural tattoo, and she picked up her skirts, heading in the direction she had seen her husband disappear.

It was too easy to follow them, and that made the entire thing even more sickening. How easy it was. How easy her husband had slipped, lured back to the thing he had once so desired.

How could she have believed for even a moment that she had been enough for him?

She shoved the thought aside. She had to keep her wits about her. She had to remain objective. This was for Ash, not for her. She would hurt later. Right now she was tired of everyone hurting the man she loved.

They were behind the third door she pushed open. She didn't bother with stealth this time. There was no point. Not when she intended to speak to Lady Valerie herself.

The scene upon which she intruded was much as she had imagined it. They were in some kind of sitting room. An embroidery hoop stood empty near the hearth, a basket with several skeins of yarn spilling from it rested at its base, and she thought it might have been Lady Haven's sewing room. How domestic.

Lady Valerie stood close to Ash, her hand on his chest, her head tilted up as though ready to receive his kiss.

At Adaline's ungraceful entrance, Lady Valerie turned her head, but she didn't spring away from Ash. Such a move would have been too dramatic even for Lady Valerie.

"Oh." Her voice was breathy and sensual, even now. "Adaline." She didn't bother to address Adaline properly, but it wasn't surprising.

Adaline waited for her to straighten before giving her own greeting. "Parasite." She shot the word across the room with a deftness she didn't realize she had been holding within herself.

Lady Valerie's eyes widened. "I'm sorry."

"No, I am." Picking up her skirts, she threaded her way through the furniture separating them. If she were going to give this woman a dressing down, she would do so properly.

Ash raised a hand then, as if belatedly realizing he was a part of this. "Adaline, nothing happened—"

She cut him off with a raised hand of her own before turning to Lady Valerie. "You're a parasite, but I think you realize that, otherwise you would have selected a husband by now. God knows you've had offers." That night in the conservatory flashed in her mind, but she pushed it away. Not now. She had to protect Ash now. "But you like having the power being a debutante gives you. You string people along, toy with their worth, and flick them away just as carelessly when you've decided you're done playing with them. You're nothing more than a common parasite, and really, I would have expected a better scheme from someone of your—" She paused here to give Lady Valerie the once over she deserved. "Station," she finished.

Lady Valerie's mouth opened without words, her cheeks turning a delicate pink as heat raced up the woman's neck in visible hives. "You, you..." Her words spluttered, and Adaline felt a perverse sense of joy. She had known all along that Lady Valerie Lattimer had no more backbone than an eel, and somehow it was pleasing to see her prediction borne out before her.

"You enjoy these petty games because it's the only delight you can find in your monotonous days." Lady Valerie's eyes flashed, and Adaline knew she had hit the mark. She took a small step forward, closing the distance between them. "Perhaps it isn't that you wish to control how others value themselves but rather you're trying to find your own worth out there somewhere. Is that it, Lady Valerie?"

The flash of recognition melted into something hard and unforgiving, and Adaline knew she had stepped too far. It didn't matter. It was the truth, and she was tired of always hiding the truth, afraid of what might happen if she spoke of it.

Lady Valerie raised a hand and for one moment Adaline wondered if the woman would truly hit her, but then the door to the sewing room bounced against the wall, and they turned to find the newcomers in the door.

"What is going on here?" Ransom Shepard, the Earl of Knighton's voice was big in the small room, but Adaline's gaze caught on Alice tripping through the door behind him, her hand going to the small of the earl's back as if to catch herself in an entirely too familiar fashion.

"Nothing," Adaline said. "Lady Valerie was just leaving so I could have a private word with my husband." She emphasized the last word should the woman forget she was an outsider here.

Ash had not spoken since she had first entered, but she could feel him behind her, could feel the words that were waiting to tumble forth like a tsunami. But not now. Not yet. Not in front of this woman.

Lady Valerie's gaze bounced between Adaline and the earl before her chin went up decisively. "If you'll excuse me, I have better places to be." She left in a cloud of pungent perfume and flouncing skirts.

The earl stepped away from the door just in time to avoid being a casualty of the woman's aggressive flight. He reached out a hand and deftly moved Alice with him, and again a spark of something nudged Adaline's brain, but then the earl spoke, his gaze just to the right of her, and she realized he was speaking to Ash.

"Are you all right?"

She had always thought of Ash as hers. Her friend. The man she loved. And now her husband. But it warmed her to hear the concern in the earl's voice and to think all along Ash had had a friend somewhere else.

"Yes," the word came out in a slight stutter as if Ash had forgotten how to speak or perhaps had meant to say something else.

The earl's gaze narrowed and oddly moved to her, and she realized with a jolt this man was protecting Ash from *her*. She put her hands to her hips, ready to dress him down when Ash put a hand to her shoulder.

"I assure you we're fine. I should like to speak with my

wife though." There was a pause and then more hesitantly. "If you don't mind."

She wondered for a second if Ash were asking this man for permission, but then she noticed Ash's narrowed gaze, and she realized he saw the familiarity between the earl and Alice as well. Had some sort of acquaintance sprung up between them? The wedding had been so long ago now. Surely the earl wouldn't have continued a friendship with a debutante for that long. Not a man with the reputation the earl possessed.

Still the man gave a nod and backed out. He had started to close the door when he saw Alice had not moved. He snatched out a hand and jerked her through the door without ceremony, snapping it shut with a loud click. Grumbling could be heard on the other side, but Adaline would deal with that later.

She turned and for the first time since finding her husband with Lady Valerie, she met his gaze and her heart broke. It was a quiet thing, smaller than she would have expected.

Ash appeared crestfallen, as though he understood he had done something wrong, but she knew he couldn't fathom the depths of his betrayal because he couldn't see them for himself.

She raised her chin. Just as she had accepted this marriage as punishment for neglecting her sister, she would accept this as well.

"Nothing happened, Adaline," Ash said, his voice even and calm, but she was already shaking her head.

"It did happen, Ash. Something terrible happened, and you don't even realize it." Her voice broke, and she closed her eyes. Only a few more seconds. She had to stay strong for just a few seconds more, and then she would put this to rest. For a brief moment, she had glimpsed every single one of her dreams, but she knew it was too good to be true. She didn't deserve this. She didn't deserve him, and now it was all being taken away from her.

She opened her eyes again. "You are still searching for your worth in other people. People you have somehow deemed important enough to bestow it upon you." Her voice cracked again, but this time from disbelief, and she shook her head, turned away from him as if she could breathe again once she put space between them. "Your father and then your stepfathers, they all taught you to be nothing because you were nothing, but they were wrong, Ash. They made you feel small because they were small themselves. And now you can't believe your own worth unless someone tells you it is so, and I can't stand by and watch it any longer." There were tears in her eyes. She could feel them hovering, and she sucked in a breath. She couldn't cry. Not yet.

She watched him, but he stood silent, his jaw taut as if he were absorbing her words rather than listening to them.

"I thought one day you would wake up and realize how foolish you were being. That one day you would magically see what I've seen all along." The tears fell down her cheeks, and she let them come, not having the energy to stop them. "And that day at Grant Hall, I thought it had happened." She laughed, the sound brittle and weak like her dreams. "I thought you had realized how much I love you and that it had pulled you out of this illusion those men built around you. But it wasn't enough." The tears were falling in earnest now. "The moment we returned you went right back to the person you most want to validate you." She sucked in a breath, the sound almost hissing through her teeth because the last thing she had to say was going to hurt her the most. "And that person wasn't me." She closed her eyes, a sob catching in her throat.

Ash did move now. She heard the rustle of fabric and

opened her eyes in time to catch him, raising a hand to stop him. He was trying to hold her, to comfort her, to assure her she had it wrong, but she didn't. She had seen it with her own eyes. The evidence of his delusion.

"It shouldn't be me either, Ash. You." He was close enough now that she dared to place a hand on his chest, look into his deep, unfathomable eyes and feel her heart break again, break for the little boy who had been told he wasn't good enough by the one person who should have loved him unconditionally. "It should be you who approves of you. You're the only one who matters." She shook her head slowly, her mouth open as she forced the last words out. "I don't know how you don't know that. And more than anything, I hate that I can't show you." Again she laughed, the sound wet with her tears. "I thought I could once. I thought if only I told you how much I loved you it would make you see, but I know that's not true now, and I have nothing left to give you."

There it was. It was all out. The whole painful truth, and she watched the last of her hope die away.

She stepped back, and using the palms of her hands, swiped furiously at the tears running down her cheeks. Sucking in another breath, she straightened, rolled back her shoulders. "Now. We need to go out there and present a united front. I shall claim a headache and give our excuses to our hosts, and we can leave. You can choose to come with me or go elsewhere once we're in the carriage. That is up to you. But I promised you a partner in this, and I shall not go back on my promise no matter what it costs me." She moved to the door and held up her arm. "Shall we?"

She waited, and when he gave in without saying a word, that last part of hope that had clung to her died.

* * *

THE DEN WAS quiet at such an early hour a week later, and the few people that were there were ones escaping some unmentionable torment.

He was no exception.

So when he rounded the corner of the library in the private room upstairs, he was surprised to encounter Ransom, his head thrown back, his hands covering his face as he reclined in one of the chairs, his booted feet on the table before him.

"What are you doing here?"

The man did little more than peer through his fingers. "What are you doing here?"

Ash crossed his arms over his chest. "As you were witness to my downfall, I should think you know the answer to that question. And besides, I asked you first. Shouldn't you be sleeping off the effects of your night of debauchery?"

Ransom gave a groan and covered his face with his hands again.

Ash remembered that night in Lord Haven's sewing room. He had thought of little else in the past week, and the scene of the night came to him as though it were still happening. The way Ransom had been so casual with Lady Alice. His behavior had indicated he had more experience with Adaline's little sister than their positions would have suggested.

Ash dropped into the chair beside Ransom's. "I shall withdraw the question if I can secure a favor from you."

Ransom removed one hand from his face to glance worriedly in Ash's direction. "A favor from me? You are the talk of every gentlemen's club in London." He gestured with his chin as if to suggest the perplexity of the situation. "I even heard them talking about you at the boxing club this week. You could ask anyone for a favor and be granted five. Why ask me?"

"Because it's a delicate matter, and I need someone with your experience."

Now Ransom removed both hands and stared openly at his friend. "My experience? Ashfield. Mate. Please tell me you are not thinking of becoming a rake. I don't think you have the constitution for it."

Ash had already opened his mouth to say something else, but this stopped him. "I don't have the constitution for it? Are you mad?" He straightened and tugged on the lapels of his jacket. "I have the constitution of a Viking."

Ransom snorted and dropped his feet to the floor, sitting up and signaling to a passing footman for drinks. "You are made of sterner stuff than most men. I'll give you that. But the thought of disappointing your wife turned you into a ghost, mate." He shook his head. "You wouldn't have the calluses to do what I do."

Ash thought he heard a note of sadness in his friend's voice, but perhaps it was just weariness. The man was up awfully early considering his proclivities.

The footman returned and set a tray with two glasses and decanter on the table where Ransom's boots had only recently vacated. Ransom poured for both of them and then reclined once more in his chair, slightly more upright this time.

"Now then. Tell me what favor I may be able to assist you with."

"I need your help in wooing my wife."

Ransom choked on his drink, snorting into his glass as he sat up, attempting to suck in a breath. "Good God, man. Why would you wish to do that?"

Ash frowned. "Because she was right."

Ransom's eyebrows knitted together in obvious concern. "You're not making sense. Do you require a physician?"

Ash laughed, but it hurt. "No, I'm afraid I don't. Adaline

was right about something, and I don't know how to show her I understand."

Ransom blinked. "Can't you just tell her she is right and be on with it?"

Ash shook his head. "I can't just tell her. She would hardly believe me."

Ransom slouched in his chair. "This is why I avoid romantic attachments entirely." He pressed a hand to his forehead. "You'd better tell me all of it or I will never understand."

Ash sat back in his chair and recited the events that had been reeling on a loop through his mind for more than a week. He left out the other bits though. How quiet the house was. How carefully Adaline moved around him. Always smiling. Always pleasant. As if she had wiped all emotions from her person except the politest ones.

The locked connecting door between their rooms.

He missed her. He ached for her. And she had been right. He had known it the moment he had agreed to follow Lady Valerie, and yet...

How could he simply say she was right? All of those things she had said, the weight of it.

She was right. She had loved him. For *years*. And he—

Oh God, he'd been so stupid. She had been right there. His whole life. And he'd never seen her love.

Ransom was right. Ash was the most revered man in London. Respected by his peers and sought after by the woman he had been infatuated with for so many years.

He told Ransom that part as well. How Lady Valerie had sought him out. How she told him she had made a mistake in not marrying him. How she regretted it.

Her words had fallen like ashes around him, cloying in his mouth and leaving a foul smell in his nostrils. Adaline had been right to call the woman a parasite, and he hated himself even more for not seeing the woman's duplicitous ways.

When he was finished, he waited while Ransom sipped thoughtfully at his drink.

"I still don't see why you can't just tell her she's right. The woman has loved you for years."

It was Ash's turn to nearly choke on his drink. "You know that?"

Ransom cocked an eyebrow. "I don't see how you don't. We both find it odd."

"We?"

Ransom looked quickly away. "Royal we, mate." He flashed a cocky grin as if to distract Ash, but clearly his friend had been speaking with someone on a regular basis that would cause him to use the word *we*.

Later he would question that, but for now, he needed to save his marriage. Hell, he needed to save his friendship with Adaline.

He had told her the truth. She was the one constant in his life and the thought of this distance always standing between them was like thinking he would never breathe air again.

"It's still not enough. If it were, I would have agreed with her on the spot that night, but I had just proven otherwise. She had witnessed it herself. How do I prove to her I'm not that man anymore?"

Ransom's brow furrowed, but he didn't speak. The silence started to grate, and Ash said, "What is it?"

Ransom shook his head. "I think you've got it wrong. You've been this man all along. I just don't think you ever saw it. You've been blinded by those awful men your mother keeps marrying."

His friend's words rocked him, and as he sat there, the conversation of the smattering of other gentlemen in the room buzzing around him, the clinking of glasses, the swish of cards striking green baize, swirled around him as the events of his past fit themselves into a new pattern.

At the center of it Adaline stood, and there she remained even as he filtered through everything he had ever known using a different lens this time. She had been right. Damn the woman. She was turning out to always be right.

That night when he had stopped Grady Givens, Adaline had told him what she had witnessed. How she had believed the drive had been in him all along. And now this from Ransom. The observations of his friends had the power to break through the damaged image he had constructed of himself.

Ransom reached out and put a hand to his shoulder, and as if reading his thoughts, said, "I never really understood what people meant when they said we're our own worst enemy, but I'll be damned if I just didn't figure it out by looking at you." He shook his head and then tossed back the last of his drink, shattering the moment.

The room swirled back together around Ash, and it was as if nothing had happened at all, and yet everything had.

He swallowed. "What do I do, Ransom? How do I show Adaline that I already understood what she told me?" He set down his drink and pushed the palms of his hands against his knees. His skin felt different suddenly. Everything felt different, and he wondered where this lightness had come from. Had it been there all along?

Ransom refilled their glasses. "I'm afraid you're not going to like what I have to say."

Ash accepted his newly filled glass but didn't drink, his gaze riveted on Ransom. "What do you have in mind?"

"What is at the heart of your dear wife's argument?"

"That I measure my own worth by the perception of others."

Ransom cocked an eyebrow. "Are you sure you weren't at Oxford with me?"

Ash only frowned. "You know very well I attended Cambridge."

Ransom nodded. "And so how would you prove that you do not base your worth on the perception of others?" He spoke each word with an exaggerated refinement as if he were a tutor himself.

Ash shook his head. "I don't know."

Now that everything seemed so clear he couldn't recall how he had let himself get so mired in it. Over the past few weeks he had met with any number of gentlemen who had only demonstrated they didn't know anything more about being titled gentlemen than Ash did. They were figuring it out just as much as the next duke, earl, viscount.

It was like being able to see clearly for the first time, but now he couldn't understand how to look back.

"I'm afraid you must humiliate yourself."

The words snatched at Ash's attention, and that long ago night in the conservatory roared back to him. He had thought that night would be his greatest humiliation, but now, sitting here, he understood that was the very best thing to ever happen to him.

"Humiliate myself?"

Ransom nodded. "You must do something extraordinary. Something that catches everyone's attention. All of those people your wife says you look to for validation. They must all be watching as you humiliate yourself."

Ash stared. "I think I'd like to revisit the idea of simply telling her."

Even as he spoke the words, he knew it wasn't possible. He had watched her float about Aylesford House like a specter, impassive to what was happening around her. He could paint a thousand beautiful dreams with his words, and to her, they would all be lies waiting to unravel.

Ransom swirled the liquor in his glass. "I already argued the merits of that case, and the judge struck it down." He waggled his eyebrows. "I have some wonderful ideas for how you can go about humiliating yourself."

Ash set down his glass. "What do you have in mind?"

CHAPTER 17

Sometimes Adaline thought of herself as an amateur artist, and as such, she enjoyed accidental symmetry. That morning as she sat inside the breakfast room, peering through the fluttering curtains of the open terrace doors to the gardens beyond, her sketchbook unopened on the table beside her, her breakfast, uneaten, growing cold at her elbow, she remembered that day in the drawing room when Uncle Herman had come to tell her about Ash's offer of marriage.

Funny how she was just as alone now as she had been then.

It was full summer now, and the breeze that filtered through the curtains was warm and inviting, just the kind of weather that made unspoken promises about what the day might bring. But as she sat there, she felt no promises being made. In fact, she felt nothing. It was the only way she had been able to survive the past several weeks. When she had accepted Ash's proposal, he had still been just her friend, but now...

She was haunted by the memory of them. It had been so

fleeting, but the length of time hadn't mattered. Their passion held a depth that left her scarred, haunted by the memory of his touch, the taste of his kiss. It was little things like the feel of his chest under the palms of her hands, the scrape of his beard against her temple, the sound of his heart beating beneath her ear.

It was the way at breakfast he would groan theatrically as she listed the day's social obligations, and he, in turn, would list the attributes, terrifying or otherwise, of the gentlemen he was scheduled to meet with that day. She even missed the reports from Grant Hall. Biggins wrote regularly of the quarry's progress, and Ash had read the reports to her as they would linger just a little too long over a supper tray as they prepared to go out for the evening.

But all of that was gone now, and in its place was the vision of Lady Valerie, her hand against Ash's chest so intimately as though it *belonged* there.

The sound of wood snapping shook her from her thoughts, and looking down, she frowned at the broken pencil in her hand. Drat. The woman did not deserve such space in her thoughts, and now look what she'd done. She tossed the pencil onto the table by her uneaten breakfast just as she heard the front door down the hall open.

She turned toward the door of the breakfast room, but the light step and swish of skirts soon gave away her visitor, and she brightened for the first time in days. Until that is, she saw the manic look on her sister's face as she swept into the room, a newspaper clutched between her hands.

"What have you done to him?"

Alice was the most unemotional of the three sisters. Always had been. Her mind was too analytical for anything else, but just then, Adaline would have wagered her sister *felt* something.

"What is it?" Adaline asked, sitting up and clutching the edge of the table with both hands.

Alice pushed aside the cups and plates littering the table to make room for the newspaper, slapping it down with far too much force, her finger going to a block of text bordered in thick black lines to make it stand out.

Adaline read quickly while Alice glared, her mouth tight, but the words didn't make any sense. Adaline shook her head.

"This must be some sort of joke or a mistake or something. What…"

But it wasn't. It was inked right there on the page.

NOTICE

Ashfield Riggs, the Marquess of Aylesford, would like to publicly acknowledge the fact that he ardently, completely, thoroughly, and without reason, loves his wife, Adaline Atwood, the Marchioness of Aylesford, beyond all else.

HE HAD NEVER TOLD her he loved her.

But there the word was in newsprint.

Love.

"It's finally happened," Alice murmured now, her finger tapping against the notice. "You've driven Ash mad."

"I've done no such thing." But she couldn't move her eyes away from the notice.

"Then how would you explain this?" Alice prodded.

Adaline shook her head. "I haven't anything to do with—" The words died away, or rather the need for them, as her brain skipped two steps ahead. "Oh God," she breathed, pressing the back of one hand to her mouth. "Oh God, I did this."

Alice straightened and crossed her arms over her chest. "Then you admit your role in the atrocity you've committed against this man."

Adaline reached out involuntarily, grabbing Alice's arm as possibilities tumbled through her mind. "Oh Alice, I think Ash is going to do something stupid."

"What do you mean? The man is constantly doing foolish things. Why should this be any different?"

"Because I finally told him how I feel."

Alice's eyebrows shot up over the rims of her spectacles. "You told him you love him?"

Adaline nodded and then frowned. "How do you know that?"

"Everyone knows that." Alice shook her arm free to grab both of Adaline's hands in her own. "Now I need you to be very clear. You told Ash how you felt first. Is that right?"

Adaline nodded. "Yes, but I don't see how that's relevant—"

"Drat," Alice murmured, her lips pursing in concentration. "I knew he'd win," she muttered.

"Alice?" Adaline had that odd sense of seeing something that wasn't there again.

Alice shook her head. "It doesn't matter. What matters is I fear Ash has some ridiculous plan. There's absolutely no possibility he would stop here."

"How do you know that?" Adaline asked, fear tripping through her.

But her sister didn't need to answer. Adaline already knew because it was Ash. It was *her* Ash, and he had been doing silly, stupid things since she could remember. But that was exactly her point. He did those things to make people laugh so they would forget he was only the son of a judge.

She pulled her hands free and stood to pace away. "This is exactly what I told him. He is only proving my point."

"What point?"

She threw out her hands uselessly. "I told him he bases his worth on the evaluations of others."

"You told him that?" Alice settled a hip against the table as if settling in for a lengthy conversation.

"Of course I told him that. It's the truth." She paced back. "His father was merciless in his degradation of Ash, and Ash accepted it as truth because his father was supposed to love him unconditionally. Only his father didn't. His father was a cruel beast of a man that worked hard to belittle his son and rob him of any kind of confidence he might have." She swung back around. "And now Ash will not listen to anything that might contradict what his father told him, and he goes about seeking confirmation of his worth from anyone he has deemed worthy to give it to him."

"And what did he say?"

"Nothing." The word burst out of her, carrying with it the futility, the loneliness, the hurt she had been carrying since the night of the soirée. "He said nothing, Alice. He only stood there. He—" He'd followed her from the room and performed like a puppet on strings, and she was the puppet master. She collapsed into a chair, placing her bent elbow on the table to rest her head on her fist. "This is all my fault," she said, the fight going out of her voice. "I deserve this."

Alice lowered herself carefully to the chair beside Adaline. "What do you mean, Adaline? Why do you deserve this?"

She moved only her eyes to take in her sister. "I failed

Amelia." She expected tears, but none came. Perhaps she had spent them all.

Alice leaned forward and placed her hands on Adaline's knees. "How did you fail Amelia?"

Her sister's words were carefully spoken as if she were speaking to a frightened animal. Adaline straightened, tucked her braid more firmly over her ear as if to compose herself.

"I should have been there for her. I should have stopped mother from hurting her."

Alice blinked, her eyes wide behind her spectacles. "Whatever are you talking about?"

"You know what our mother was like. She was quick to criticize but slow to give any of us love. I escaped the house to get away from her, and you…"

"Stuck my nose in a book?" Alice supplied.

"Precisely." Adaline rubbed her face with one hand as the tired memory played over and over again in her mind. Of Amelia that day when they'd said goodbye, when she'd left for Kent to marry the Duke of the Greyfair. "But Amelia had neither of those things. She stayed and endured our mother's criticisms, and it—" Finally her voice gave out, and she closed her eyes against the guilt.

"And it made her stronger than either of us."

Adaline's eyes flew open. "What are you talking about?"

Alice leaned back and crossed her arms over her chest. "Do you think either of us would have been brave enough to marry the Ghoul of Greyfair?"

Adaline blinked. "Of course not. But I hardly see how that —" She sucked in her breath as the pieces of her memory reassembled themselves. "Oh God, Alice, you're right." She blinked some more before settling her gaze on Alice. "You're right. I never…saw it like that."

Alice nodded as though their sister's strength were an obvious thing. "I'll admit I always envied her. Her resiliency.

Her strength. I don't have two memories of mother that are worth keeping, and that is too many." She shook her head. "I don't know how Amelia did it, but she deserves all the happiness she has now."

Adaline shook her head at this. "How do you know she's happy?" She bit her lip on the question, feeling too much the accusations she had thrown at Ash. Wasn't she seeking forgiveness through Amelia's happiness?

"She says so in her letters."

"She could be making that up."

Alice snorted a laugh. "Amelia hasn't the time to make things up. It's not like her." Alice leaned forward again. "Adaline, what are you really asking?"

It was as though her sister could read her thoughts, and she looked down, unable to hold her gaze now. "I can't let it go, Alice. Even if Amelia turned out stronger than either of us, it's still my fault."

Alice picked up both of Adaline's hands and squeezed them. "Didn't you just finish telling me that the burden Ash carries, the one he received from his father, is not his fault?"

Adaline stilled, her sister's words once more rearranging her memories. "I suppose I did."

Alice nodded. "You proclaim Ash mustn't seek validation of his worth elsewhere and yet you would sit here and blame yourself. You were a child, Adaline. Just like Ash was. And you expected nothing more than the unconditional love a parent is supposed to give a child. You cannot blame yourself any more than Ash can."

Adaline could only blink as the hopeless thoughts she'd carried around for so long seemed to drain from her mind, and suddenly she understood why it was so difficult for Ash to let it go. It was frightening to release the thing one had built one's entire person on, and it was even scarier to become the person one wished to be, free of the guilt and burdens others had gifted without permission.

"You're right," Adaline said, shaking her head. "But it doesn't make it any easier."

"I didn't think it would, but perhaps it can help you to better understand your husband."

She glanced at the newspaper again, her eyes finding Ash's words.

Love.

Right there in newsprint.

"This must be it, right?" she said then, pulling a hand free to tap at the newsprint. "He just wished for me to see this, right?" She wasn't asking the questions for an answer. She was asking for reassurance because in her mind she pictured poor, vulnerable Ash. The man who relied on everyone else's opinions to tell him how to feel.

But this.

This surely couldn't go further.

* * *

BUT IT DID.

She had accepted an invitation to the Fairfield ball, the last of the season, weeks ago, before everything had fallen apart. That night as she walked into the ballroom, it was hard to imagine that this was where everything had begun for her marriage, and again she was hit with the odd sense of symmetry.

She descended the grand staircase alone, doing all she could to keep her chin up. Ash had not been waiting in the vestibule of Aylesford House when she had come down, dressed to go out, as had been their unspoken custom over the past several weeks. She'd worried at first, but then her mind went to the notice in the newspaper, and trepidation tripped along her neck.

As she placed one careful foot in front of the other, the echoes of her name as the butler announced her ringing through the packed ballroom, following her like a specter, she scanned the crowd, sure her husband would appear at any moment.

But he didn't.

She snatched a glass of champagne from the first footman who passed her with a tray and drank it down in a single gulp. Still Ash didn't appear. She nodded to the appropriate acquaintances, spoke to the matrons she was expected to address, and finally found herself in the familiar corner with the chaperones, the companions, and the wallflowers. Seeing faces she had known for so long lulled her into a false sense of comfort, and soon she lost herself in the buzz of conversation and the pleasant warmth the champagne sent through her.

She was overreacting. Ash wouldn't do anything.

She had settled herself into believing nothing would transpire that night when she heard the first of the whispers.

People were careless in the corners haunted by wall-flowers and spinsters. As though women labeled as such were somehow less cause for concern, and secrets whispered in their proximity were safe. But Adaline was anything but safe from the things she heard whispered.

Ash.

Ash riding through the park and telling anyone who would listen how he loved her.

At first she thought she had misheard. A duchess telling a countess how she had seen it herself. A viscountess whispering to her paid companion, the two conferring on what exactly they had seen, and they both agreed. It was the

Marquess of Aylesford, and he had nothing to say but how much he loved his wife.

She felt her legs weaken, her knees bending, her hand shot out to catch herself against the refreshment table, but her hand met only air. Oh God, she was going to fall right there in the ballroom, faint straight away and then—

Someone caught her. Familiar arms, a familiar chest, a familiar scent.

Her heart contracted, all at once, suddenly so painfully she forgot how to breathe.

"Ash." There were tears in her voice even though she wasn't crying. It was more of a sadness welling up inside of her, a million different sadnesses coming together all at once that filled her, but they weren't the kind she wanted to release. Not yet.

"You really can't be trusted around punch bowls, can you?" He was smiling. At her. His beautiful brown eyes shining in the light of the chandeliers.

"Oh Ash, what are you doing? I saw the notice in the newspapers, and these women, they all say—"

She was cut off by the butler announcing another name, but it was one that didn't make sense. The butler announced...the Marquess of Aylesford. Her gaze flew to the staircase where attendees entered the room under the eyes of all in attendance, but the staircase was empty.

Reflexively she grabbed hold of any part of Ash she could, her mind cartwheeling. "Ash, no." It was all she could get out before he was moving.

Away.

"No, no, no," she hissed, but either he was too strong for her, or some part of her wished to see what he would do because he slipped from her grasp.

He took the stairs two at a time until he was halfway up. He spun about, his arms splayed wide, his face—Oh God, that face. The one she had seen through a thousand heart-breaks and a thousand more laughs. He was smiling, but it was a smile full of warmth and not the kind meant to fool the person seeing it.

"Ladies and gentlemen," he called over the crowd, and it was like a gunshot had split through the air, silencing everyone and everything. There was no clink of a glass, no buzz of a whisper. There wasn't even the soft whine of a violin tuning. Nothing. Everyone was watching Ash. "I just wanted to get everyone's attention this evening. I do beg your pardon for the interruption, but I have a matter of utmost urgency to discuss."

Oh God, no. Alice was right. He'd finally cracked. And it was her fault.

She pushed through the crowd. Propriety forgotten. Manners forgotten. Everything forgotten. She had to get to Ash. She understood now. The pain he carried and how difficult it was to rid himself of it. He mustn't do this. She had to stop him before—

"I want you all to know I very much love my wife."

There it was. She tripped to a stop at the bottom of the staircase. She was too late, but now everyone knew where she was, and the eyes that had been locked on Ash traveled to her, riveted.

Ash was making a fool of himself. And it was her fault.

"I love her so very much, and I've been rather a fool." He laughed at this and scratched the back of his neck as though he were speaking casually to a friend.

Her heart thundered, and her skirts shook where she held them in her trembling hands. But he wasn't done. He dropped his gaze as if he knew exactly where she was.

"I've been a fool because she's loved me all along. Even when I didn't know I could love myself. And now I've wasted all this time. I only hope she'll let me make it up to her." His lips faltered into a smile, and her heart broke with how unsure it was.

Without thinking, she began to climb, her feet carrying her the rest of the way to this man she loved. Her best friend. Her husband.

She stopped on the stair below him, her head bent back to look up at him. "Ash," she whispered. "You don't have to do this. I love you. It's enough. Come down."

But Ash only shook his head. "I'm not doing this for you, Atwood. I'm doing this because these people don't matter, and this is how I prove it to myself."

She studied his face, looking for the telltale signs of whatever game he was playing. The mischievous glint in his eye, the cocky grin. But it wasn't there. This was just Ash, standing in front of her, telling her the truth.

It was then, watching this face she knew better than her own, that the pieces connected, and she breathed for the first time in days.

"You're humiliating yourself." She whispered the words, unable to believe them for herself, but Ash's slow smile confirmed her thoughts.

Ash had always been quick to laugh, but he had never and would never make a fool of himself. Those were two entirely different things, and the man standing before her was something she had never witnessed.

This man cared not a whit for the thoughts of those around him, all these people staring up at him, judging him. Just as his father and stepfathers had done. Ash stood perfectly calm before her, his eyes only on her.

She wondered how this transformation had come to be, but suddenly she didn't care. She reached up and pulled him down, nearly bending him in half as she stood on the stair below him, but it didn't matter. Just then she had to kiss this man.

This man she loved. This man who loved her against all odds.

She kissed him in front of everyone who didn't matter.

* * *

He let her pull him down off the staircase. He had nearly reached the bottom when the roar around him penetrated the haze that had overcome him at the sight of her climbing the stairs. It had felt like a fairy tale, only he was the princess in the tower, and she had come to save him. Everything else had fallen away except for her upturned face, the fall of her familiar braid, the expectant part of her lips.

They were cheering.

He dropped to the ballroom floor beside her, and the crowd surged around them. He was slapped on the back several times, a spin of smiling faces, a chorus of cheers and clapping, and Adaline never let go of his hand. She spun them away from the worst of it, heading around the staircase to a quieter alcove tucked into its curve.

He wasn't sure where she intended to go. His speech had made them the focus of the ball, and the guests trailed after them like a shadow. The slaps on his back turned into handshakes and requests for drinks, a meeting, perhaps just a chat about the work he was doing in Dartmoor.

Everything was there. Respect, admiration, worth. And yet the only thing he wanted was to get his wife alone. Somewhere quiet where they could talk, where he could tell her everything he was feeling, what he had already understood and what he hoped he had proved to her now.

Ransom had been right. He had to humiliate himself if only to prove these people's opinion of him did not dictate his opinion of himself.

But although it seemed to have worked, the plan had other unexpected side effects.

Namely he seemed to be more popular than ever.

He tightened his grip on Adaline's hand as she pulled them away from the crowd. He nodded and shook hands as necessary, murmuring insignificant words of acknowledgment if only to get them through the crowd.

They stumbled into a corridor, and he realized with a jolt where he was.

Had it only been months ago that he had pulled Lady Valerie down this same corridor with the intent of asking her to marry him?

The thought made his stomach churn now, and he tightened his grip on his wife's hand. She seemed to sense his unease because she turned, a soft smile on her lips that had the power to instantly soothe him.

They weren't paying attention, and that was probably why she was able to sneak up on them.

"Lady Aylesford."

He looked up, his entire body stilling at the sight of Lady Valerie standing in the corridor before them, her expression icy, her hands clenched around a fan so tightly Ash feared it might snap in two.

Adaline didn't let go of his hand as she turned to face the other woman.

"Lady Valerie, I trust you are well this evening."

He stood, mesmerized by his wife's quiet resilience. His gaze flicked between the two of them, and he wondered not for the first time how he had been so stupid. How had he not seen Lady Valerie's cold veneer, the way she held herself so carefully as if any sudden movement would shatter the illusion she had created around herself.

"I think you should know something, Lady Aylesford." Lady Valerie's tone gave no room for argument. She had

267

JESSIE CLEVER

clearly intercepted them with the intent of telling Adaline something, and Ash's stomach tightened, his mind racing back over what it could possibly be.

The corridor around him seemed to close in, the air escaping his lungs as everything constricted to a single point.

His proposal.

To Lady Valerie.

Adaline couldn't know. She couldn't know she was his second choice.

Lady Valerie's smile was menacing. "Lord Aylesford asked me to marry him first. You were only his second choice and likely his last hope."

He watched the words as if he could see them travel through the air and hit his wife like a cannonball.

Only they didn't.

She didn't even flinch.

Instead she merely raised her eyebrows. "Is that all?"

Lady Valerie's smile lost its menace, her lips hanging loose in surprise. "Did you hear what I said? Ash asked me to marry him first. I was his first choice."

"I know."

The words were spoken so quietly, with such easy confidence Ash thought he had misheard. But the expression on Lady Valerie's face, that almost made the tension of this moment worth it.

The woman spluttered. "You...know? How? Did he tell you?" She scoffed, taking a step back as if rallying herself for another shot. "Did he tell you how I laughed at him? A mere marquess. Thinking he could have my hand in marriage. What an absolute—"

"I know because I was there. That night in this conservatory actually." She pointed down the corridor. "And as I recall in the encounter you exhibited your true nature, and for that

I shall be forever grateful. It's refreshing to see the truth of someone instead of always playing at charades."

Ash couldn't make sense of what was happening. The world was shifting away from him again only to return in a completely different form.

She knew? She was there? How? Why hadn't she told him?

Once the thought of Adaline knowing about that night might have ended him, but his rejected proposal had lost its sting.

Adaline tilted her head as if thinking considerably. "It's only rather unfortunate and disheartening, wouldn't you say?"

"What is?" Lady Valerie was practically seething now.

"That you should feel the need to be someone you aren't." Adaline reached out a hand then, and Ash watched it like a snake crawling through the grass. She laid it gently on Lady Valerie's clenched hands. "I only hope one day you'll realize you are enough just as you are."

She seemed to shake the other woman's hands and then released her. Tugging on Ash's hand, she led them away. He didn't know what Lady Valerie did then because he could only look at his wife. This incredible, strong creature who had decided he was the one she wanted.

A torrent of emotion so powerful charged through him then he couldn't hold it in any longer. They reached the conservatory in just enough time for him to take the lead, pulling her inside and shutting the door behind them. He wasn't quiet. He wasn't careful. He didn't hold back.

He didn't need to because this was Adaline, and she loved him just for who he was.

He pulled her into his arms, crushing her lips in a kiss that had been building inside of him for weeks. He crushed her to him, wanting to feel every piece of her, every curve and valley. He knew her, knew her body, her mind, and her soul. He knew every piece of her now, and he loved every piece of her.

But it wasn't time to show her again. It was finally time to tell her.

He eased back and cupped her face in his hands as if to physically capture her attention. He wanted her to understand what he said, really understand it, deep in her bones and in the very heart of her.

"I love you, Adaline." He watched her eyes. He needed to see that she understood. That it was so much more than a declaration of love. "I love that you're always there whenever I need you. I love your selflessness. I love your confidence. I love…" Her eyes had grown dark and fathomless, and he forgot for a moment where they were as everything seemed to drop away. "You." He spoke the word with all the confidence he had only recently discovered. Confidence she had shown him the way to finding.

Her eyes searched his face, and he wondered what she saw there. Did she see the truth in his statement? Did she see the weight of his love in his words?

But then her face folded, her eyes turning sad, and he felt the weight of the world crash down around him.

"Oh Ash, I'm so sorry." Her voice was wet with tears, and once again he felt the world spin out around him.

This wasn't what she was supposed to say or do when he declared his love for her. He remembered her rushed words that day at Grant Hall. The words that spoke of her love for him, the ones she'd held in secret for so long. Surely this wasn't the response to seeing that love finally returned.

"Adaline, what is it?" He gathered her close, holding her against his chest as if to comfort her with the sheer presence of his body.

She shook her head, her lips trembling. He'd never seen

her like this. Adaline Atwood was formidable. She did not cower or bend. But this…this…

"I shouldn't have followed you that day. I'm sorry." She placed both of her hands on his chest. "I respect you too much to intrude upon your privacy like that. It was only…"

She was apologizing? It was his turn to shake his head.

"Adaline, no. You mustn't apologize. What happened that night—"

"Is unspeakable." Her expression hardened so quickly, he was momentarily adrift. "That woman is a parasite, and I do not regret saying so. Alice called her far worse, but I shall leave it at that."

He raised an eyebrow. "What did Alice call her?" He couldn't stop his grin, wondering what the more adventurous Atwood sister might have drummed up.

But Adaline was already stammering on. "It was just that…" She paused, licked her lips. He had never seen Adaline so unsure of herself, and for a moment, he grew afraid. "You had only returned from Kent, and I thought you might have seen Amelia, and I just needed to know how she was. That was all. It was just that I let her go." Adaline's voice broke then, and he watched her dissolve in his arms.

It was like watching a dam fail. It was spectacular and awful and completely consuming. He pulled her against him, held her tight to his chest, ran his hand down her back, over and over. She didn't cry; she didn't sob. She only seemed to shake in his arms, as though she were releasing whatever it was that she'd been carrying alone for too long.

"You didn't let her go, Atwood." Her words didn't make sense. Amelia was happily married. He'd seen it for himself. He eased back, cupped his wife's cheek with one hand this time to lift her face to his. "Amelia is well. I assure you. I've seen it for myself."

But Adaline was already shaking her head. "Amelia is

good at pretending. She can convince you of anything you wish to hear. And we sent her to that awful place to marry a complete stranger. I let it happen, Ash. I let her go." She shook her head. "Alice told me it wasn't my fault, but it's not true. I did this."

He put both hands against her cheeks then, stilling her lips with his thumbs. "Adaline, Amelia is happy. I cannot tell you enough. You didn't fail her. Is that what this is? Do you think somehow you let Amelia down because she married a man unknown to you?"

"I know I did," she whispered against his thumbs.

He opened his mouth, ready to pour out assurances once more when he stopped. He knew Adaline. He *knew* her. Wasn't that what all of this had been about?

He released her, taking a step back, a slow grin coming to his lips. He couldn't help running a hand along his jaw, remembering what had happened the last time he'd seen Amelia Atwood and wondering if what he was thinking was wise.

He looked back at his wife, huddled and broken, leaning against the wall in the near dark of the conservatory.

He smiled more fully. "I think it's time to visit another one of the Aylesford estates, Atwood."

CHAPTER 18

*I*t was magnificent.

She pressed a hand to the glass of the carriage window as if she could touch Dinsmore Castle. She'd never seen anything so grand. It wasn't as though the ground was thick with castles in London. And to think it had been built out on that island, so long ago.

When she had first heard the Duke of Greyfair made his home in a castle on an island, she had pictured something cold and remote. But this was nothing like what she had imagined.

As she eyed the causeway they would need to cross in order to reach the castle, she was glad for the good weather.

"It will be a much easier journey once the spur line is put in. The railroad will go directly into the village then. We should be able to get here in a single day."

She leaned back, and Ash's arms were ready for her, enveloping her against his side as the carriage rumbled along the last leg of their journey.

She had been apprehensive at first at the idea of visiting Amelia. Adaline wasn't sure what to expect, didn't know if she would have the strength to see her sister's misery. But Ash had been so convincing. Still, Lady Valerie had fooled him for years.

Even now as the castle grew large before them, she wasn't sure what to expect, and her stomach twisted into knots, apprehension, fear, and worst of all, hope flooding her all at once.

What if Ash were right? What if Amelia was happy? It seemed like too wonderful of a thing to hope for. But then hadn't she found happiness for herself through all of this?

The carriage slowed to a stop, but she found she couldn't move. After so many days spent journeying to the far reaches of Kent, she couldn't get out of the carriage. Ash nudged her.

"I promise you, Atwood." He didn't say what he promised, but by his grin, she could surmise.

He moved first, opening the door and dropping down to the drive. He reached back for her and only seeing his hand held out to her did she move, putting her own in his. The wind caught her as she stepped down, and the air was thick with the scent of the ocean.

Noise.

There was noise all about her, and she didn't know where to look first. A team of men were pulling a cart laden with stone through the castle yard while women carried buckets across their shoulders. A pack of small children raced each other through the yard, their laughter filtering through the ocean breeze. There was so much...life here, and she felt herself tipping, her assumptions falling away as the reality presented itself.

That was when she heard her sister's scream.

Terror struck her, robbing her of breath as she searched frantically for Amelia.

There. She was there. She was—

Running?

Oh God, she was running away. That monster, the Ghoul of Greyfair, was chasing her. It had to be him. Who else could it be? He was yelling at her as he raced after her, kicking up the dirt in the yard in a cloud of fury as he pounded after her poor innocent sister.

No. No, it was all too real. Everything she had feared, it was coming to be right before her eyes.

Her sister was nearer now, her skirts lifted in her hands as she ran. She looked back over her shoulder at her pursuer, and Adaline knew what she saw. She saw the ghoul gaining on her.

Adaline reached out a pathetic hand as if she could do anything to stop it, a cry of outrage lodging in her throat as—

The ghoul caught Amelia, swept her up in his arms even as her sister—

Giggled?

Adaline froze, one hand still outstretched, the other firmly clasped in Ash's grip.

The ghoul spun her sister in a circle before dropping her to her feet, bending her backwards, and—

Kissing her thoroughly.

Right there.

In the middle of the bustling castle yard.

This man was—

She spun around, forcing her eyes to look only at Ash who was grinning devilishly as he continued to stare at the scene behind Adaline. She swatted him.

"Stop looking," she hissed.

Ash laughed. "Isn't this the evidence you came to see?" His expression turned comically ominous. "Oh yes, the Ghoul of Greyfair is devouring your sister in the most heinous—"

She swatted him again. "Stop it." She hissed like some kind of prude.

"Adaline!"

She spun back around at her sister's call to find Amelia standing there, her head turned toward them, but still wrapped in her husband's arms and more interesting, Amelia had her arms tight around her husband.

It was her husband, wasn't it?

Amelia skipped forward, both hands held out in greeting. Her sister was skipping. Amelia was skipping.

Adaline's head swam. What was happening?

Amelia reached her then, concern darkening her brow. "Adaline, what is it? Was it the journey?" Amelia shook her head. "I know it can seem quite lengthy, but once the railroad puts in the spur line it will be a great deal easier."

Adaline reached out, unable to stop herself, and touched her sister's face with two fingers. "You're happy," she whispered, still unable to believe what she was seeing.

Amelia reached up and captured Adaline's hand, squeezing it between her own. "Of course, I'm happy." She glanced at Ash. "Didn't Ash tell you so?"

Adaline could only shake her head, but Amelia seemed to understand. She turned to Ash. "She didn't believe you, did she?"

Was she so terribly predictable?

Amelia made the introductions then, and Adaline formally met the Ghoul of Greyfair. But he was no ghoul. That was immediately obvious. He had kind eyes and a gentle smile, and Adaline loved him immediately. This man who made her sister *giggle*.

"How about a turn about the yard? The fresh air will do you good after your journey." Amelia took her arm as if to lead her away but paused looking back at Ash and Greyfair. "Can you two behave yourselves while I take my sister around the orchard?"

Greyfair shuffled his feet, looking sheepishly at the

ground as Ash grinned idiotically, throwing his arm around Greyfair's shoulders.

"No promises," Ash said.

Adaline frowned as her sister pulled her away. "What was that about?"

"Nothing," Amelia said with a quiet laugh. "Now then. Alice wrote me."

Amelia needn't say more. Alice was not one to mince words nor would she find any subject too delicate for a letter. She remembered her youngest sister's fortitude that night at the soirée and couldn't help but smile.

"I wish she could have joined you. Is Uncle Herman's health truly so poor?" Amelia asked.

Adaline shook her head quickly. "Alice says it's simply the sniffles, but you know what the man is like. She doesn't wish to leave him right now."

Amelia nodded in understanding.

They had reached a grove of trees on the far side of the yard then, and the shade felt good after the direct sun along the drive.

"Now then, what shall I need to do to convince you of my happiness, dear sister?" Amelia said without preamble. "Alice mentioned something about our mother's neglect?"

Adaline suddenly felt squirmy. It was one thing to hold one's thoughts in one's head, but it was another to hear them spoken aloud by someone else.

"I know what it was like. Mother was not always the easiest person to live with, and I thought...well, I'm not sure exactly what I thought. I only knew I had to protect myself from her, and I suppose I assumed you knew to do the same. I never thought..." But she couldn't finish the sentence. It hurt too much to think of how she had abandoned Amelia in that house, alone with their mother.

They had reached the end of a line of trees, and Amelia

stopped. Adaline looked about them. The ground had been freshly turned here, and the air was pungent with the smell of new earth.

"We're adding trees to the orchard," Amelia said. "Mrs. Fairfax—she's the housekeeper—she makes the most splendid apple butter. We're going to try a few new varieties and see what she can develop." She turned and lifted her face to Adaline's, her expression thoughtful. "Have you ever only thought of the future instead of dwelling in the past?"

Adaline stilled. "What do you mean?"

Amelia shrugged. "I think we could spend so much time looking at our past, feeling sorry for the things that happened when we could be looking at our future and wondering at the possibilities."

Adaline wished to speak, but her throat had started to close at Amelia's words. When had her little sister become so wise?

"We were children, Adaline," Amelia said then, echoing Alice's words. "Our parents were supposed to be just that. Our parents. But they weren't, and it's not our fault they weren't. But what is our fault is allowing them to continue to control our future." She shrugged again. "I'm not going to give them that. They don't deserve it." She looked away, across the freshly turned earth. "The only thing we can do now is be there for each other." She took Adaline's hand into her own and squeezed it. Looking back, she smiled, and Adaline saw the little girl Amelia had once been, and her heart constricted. "Will you be there for me in the future, Adaline?"

"Yes," Adaline said, the word nearly falling from her lips, and she squeezed Amelia's hand. "Yes, I will be there."

Amelia smiled and pulled Adaline's arm through her own, turning them back in the direction of the castle yard. "Now then. Tell me what happened when you finally told Ash that you love him."

Adaline laughed. She couldn't help it. Standing in the dappled sunshine, her arm linked with her sister's, she couldn't help the lightness she felt, the laughter that bubbled inside of her, and best of all the hope for the future.

It wasn't until much later that night when they were alone in their room that Adaline told Ash what Amelia had said in the orchard.

"And do you believe her?" Ash asked, settling back against the headboard of their bed, watching her as she finished braiding her hair for the night. She knew such a thing was useless. Ash would only tug her hair free as soon as she reached the bed. Her hair…and other things.

"Yes," she said now. "I think I do." She shook her head and padded over to the bed, climbing in to slip beneath the covers next to her husband. "It's just so hard sometimes to let go of the past."

He touched her chin to lift her face to his. "I think I can help you with that if you're looking for a partner?"

She smiled. "I'm always looking for a partner as long as it's you."

He kissed her softly then, and in her husband's touch, she realized more than anything she felt anticipation. For the future they would make. Together.

But before she could deepen the kiss a noise reached her ears. She stilled, listening, pulling her lips from Ash's. He let her go easily, and she could tell he was listening too, his whole body still against hers.

They had been given a room in the new portion of the castle on the ocean side, far away from the servants and the family rooms. Amelia had told her she wanted her sister to feel comfortable, but she'd winked when she'd said it, and

Adaline could only imagine what kind of ideas her sister's newfound love had sparked.

But that meant they were far from anyone who would have made such a noise.

"Ash," she whispered. "Is that footsteps?"

"I think it was," he whispered back.

Neither of them moved. Even their breathing became shallow, each matching the other in suspense.

The noise came again. A distinct footstep directly overhead.

Their gazes flew to the ceiling.

"Do you know what this means?" Ash said.

"No," she said automatically, her arms tightening around him. "Ash, no."

But he pulled himself free, tumbling to the floor and snatching up his dressing gown as he made for the door. "I'm finally going to find a ghost," he cried as he ran through the open door.

She had no choice but to follow him, her laugh trailing along behind her.

ABOUT THE AUTHOR

Jessie decided to be a writer because there were too many lives she wanted to live to just pick one.

Taking her history degree dangerously, Jessie tells the stories of courageous heroines, the men who dared to love them, and the world that tried to defeat them.

Jessie makes her home in New Hampshire where she lives with her husband and two very opinionated Basset hounds. For more, visit her website at jessieclever.com.

Made in the USA
Monee, IL
29 March 2023